the REFERRAL PROGRAM

the
REFERRAL
PROGRAM

• A Novel •

SHAMARA RAY

STREBOR
BOOKS
INTERNATIONAL

ATRIA

NEW YORK • LONDON • TORONTO • SYDNEY • NEW DELHI

SBI
STREBOR
BOOKS
INTERNATIONAL

ATRIA

An Imprint of Simon & Schuster, Inc.
1230 Avenue of the Americas
New York, NY 10020

First Atria Paperback edition August 2023

STREBOR BOOKS /**ATRIA** PAPERBACK and colophon are trademarks of Simon & Schuster, Inc.

For information about special discounts for bulk purchases, please contact Simon & Schuster Special Sales at 1-866-506-1949 or business@simonandschuster.com.

The Simon & Schuster Speakers Bureau can bring authors to your live event. For more information or to book an event, contact the Simon & Schuster Speakers Bureau at 1-866-248-3049 or visit our website at www.simonspeakers.com.

Interior design by *Yvonne Taylor*

Manufactured in the United States of America

1   3   5   7   9   10   8   6   4   2

Library of Congress Cataloging-in-Publication Data

Names: Ray, Shamara, author.
Title: The referral program : a novel / Shamara Ray.
Description: First Atria Paperback edition. | New York : Atria Paperback, 2023.
Identifiers: LCCN 2023013944 (print) | LCCN 2023013945 (ebook) |
ISBN 9781593096953 (paperback) | ISBN 9781501172588 (ebook)
Subjects: LCSH: Female friendship--Fiction. | Self-realization in women
--Fiction. | LCGFT: Novels.
Classification: LCC PS3618.A9827 R44 2023 (print) |
LCC PS3618.A9827 (ebook) | DDC 813/.6--dc23/eng/20230327

LC record available at https://lccn.loc.gov/2023013944
LC ebook record available at https://lccn.loc.gov/2023013945

ISBN 978-1-5930-9695-3
ISBN 978-1-5011-7258-8 (ebook)

This Book Is Dedicated to
My Sisters

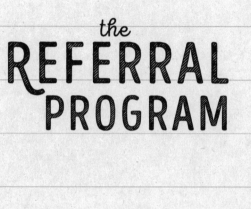

the
REFERRAL
PROGRAM

*D*ylan and Ace were spending the holidays with her family. She had been looking forward to this particular Christmas because she was convinced it was going to be the day he finally proposed. Ace had been hinting for weeks that he was looking for the perfect gift for her, one that would last a lifetime. He had called her father a couple of times and even asked her mother about Dylan's taste in jewelry. Her entire family was coming to dinner—aunts, uncles, cousins . . . She made sure her hair, outfit, and makeup were picture perfect. She talked to her girls nonstop the day before as they tried to calm her nerves.

As Dylan and Ace drove to her parents' house, she talked incessantly, her nerves getting the best of her. She didn't notice how quiet Ace was on the drive over. What did register, just barely, was the constant vibrating of his cell phone. Dylan assumed they were the customary Merry Christmas text messages that people bombarded one another's phones with on the holiday. He parked in the driveway and told her he would be inside in a minute; he needed to return a call. Dylan floated into the house to greet her family.

A half hour passed before Ace finally came in. Dylan met him at the door intending to introduce him to any family members he didn't already know. When she grabbed him by the arm, his body was rigid. She halted and looked up at him. Ace averted his eyes.

"Is everything okay?" Dylan asked.

He nodded. "Yeah. Where are your parents?"

"They're in the kitchen."

Ace pulled away from Dylan and went toward the kitchen, leaving her standing in the living room. She was baffled by his demeanor but brushed it off. She resumed socializing with her family and basking in the holiday spirit. After fifteen minutes or so, just as Dylan was about to go into the kitchen to find out what was keeping Ace, he entered the living room with her dad. Her father patted him on the back and nodded to whatever they were discussing. Ace joined Dylan on the sofa.

"I thought my mom put you to work in the kitchen."

He laughed but it rang hollow.

"What were you guys talking about in there?" she asked.

For the second time, he looked away. "The holidays and the new year."

Dylan's heart skipped a beat. She felt this was the moment. Ace was going to propose. She told herself to be still. They chatted with each other until dinner was served. During dinner they were pulled into other conversations with different family members. Dylan couldn't wait until it was time to open gifts. She knew that was when he would pop the question.

Finally, her family congregated around the tree. Gifts were exchanged, carols were sung, and still she waited. Dylan told herself the special moment would take place during dessert and cordials. She was convinced Ace wanted to present her with a ring after everyone else had opened their gifts. A proposal deserved everyone's attention.

Her family finished dessert and still nothing. Dylan wondered when it would happen. She started to question whether he was waiting for them to be alone. The time passed painfully slow. She was no longer enjoying the festivities. Instead, she was obsessing over the proposal. Dylan was relieved when it finally got late enough for them to bid everyone farewell and head home for the evening.

The car ride to her house was quiet. Ace pulled into the driveway. Dylan reached for the door and paused when she realized the car was idling.

"Aren't you coming in?" she asked, puzzled that Ace hadn't put the car in park and turned off the ignition.

"No, I'm going to head home tonight," he replied sullenly.

"You are?"

"Yeah, I'll be by in the morning."

"Is everything all right?" Dylan felt a pit in her stomach. "What's going on?"

"I'll be by tomorrow."

Dylan reluctantly opened the car door. She hesitated, waiting for Ace to give her a kiss. He stared straight ahead, gripping the steering wheel. She stepped from the car, closed the door, and watched him back out of the driveway.

Dylan went into the house and immediately wanted to call her girls. She refrained because she still wasn't sure what exactly had happened and wasn't in the mood to tell them that she hadn't gotten a ring. Dylan went to bed on Christmas night alone and confused. Ace hadn't called to say he got home safely or to even say goodnight. She spent the night wondering why he hadn't proposed to her. She didn't sleep a wink.

The next morning, Dylan sat at the kitchen table having a cup of coffee. She heard the front door opening. Immediately, she felt nervous. Ace's footsteps approached. Her eyes were fixed on the entryway as he came in.

Dylan pounced. "What's going on, Ace?"

He sat across from her at the table. "I love you, Dylan."

"I know that." She regarded him warily.

"I've been thinking about a lot lately."

"Such as?"

"My future."

"Your future? Not *our* future?"

He continued undeterred. "I've been thinking about my future a lot lately and weighing some things."

"What kind of things?"

"I thought I was ready, Dylan." He faltered. "But, I'm not."

"Ready for what?" Dylan felt her nervousness fading and morphing into a different emotion.

"I wanted to be . . ."

"What aren't you ready for, Ace?" she demanded.

"This is not easy." He stared at his hands.

"Just say it."

"You deserve more than I can give you."

"That's all you got?" she asked, her voice raised. "That I deserve more? Where is this coming from?"

"I've been thinking a lot lately."

"You said that."

"I know. I'm trying to find the right words."

"At this point I'll settle for any words that make sense."

"I realized this is not what I want right now. I'm not ready for marriage and a family. Maybe I'm being selfish, but you should be with someone who wants the same things that you do."

"This is out of left field. I don't even know how to process this."

"I know it seems sudden, and that's one hundred percent my fault—"

"You're damn right."

"But I have been feeling this way for some time."

"Why now?"

"You deserve to know how I feel."

"*Why now?*"

"Because I know what you were expecting."

Dylan scoffed. "You know what I was expecting," she mimicked. "Were you going to ask me to marry you?"

Silence hung over them like a storm cloud. Dylan stared at Ace. He kept his gaze on the table.

"I said, were you going to ask me to marry you?" she repeated.

He nodded. "I was."

"What changed?" Dylan fought back the tears that were threatening to spill over.

"I don't want to do this."

"What does that mean, Ace?"

"I told you that it's me."

"I'm not disputing that. It is you. But I want to know what changed."

"I don't want you to hate me, Dylan. I love you and I want you to always remember that."

"What did you say to my parents in the kitchen yesterday?"

Ace sighed. "I told your parents that they are an example of what marriage should be. I said that seeing their relationship lets me know I'm not there yet."

Dylan shook her head. "Did you tell them that you were ending our relationship?"

"No."

"So, you pulled the wool over my parents' eyes. That may have worked on them, but I want the truth."

"I told you the truth."

Dylan's eyes narrowed. "What changed, Ace?"

"I don't want to hurt you."

"It's too late for that."

"You're incredible. However, I feel you want more than what I can give you. I know that with you, I'll always fall short. You set the bar so high, I'll always leave you wanting. I've felt that way the entire time we've been together. I'm never striving high enough for you, my goals are never big enough for you, and you always think I should be doing more."

"Tell me, Ace, who has been making you feel that you're enough the way that you are? That you don't need to have goals or strive for better? Was it whoever was texting you repeatedly yesterday?"

Ace inhaled. "Don't do this, Dylan."

"You're already doing it. Who is she?"

"This has nothing to do with anyone else. It's what I said. I'm not enough for you. I'm not ready and you deserve what you want—marriage and a family."

"I would respect you more if you were completely honest. Enjoy your life with the woman who has lowered the bar for you. Now, find your way out of my home and out of my life."

Ace left. Dylan didn't move from where she sat for hours. The pang in Dylan's heart was unrelenting. An endless stream of hot tears streaked her face. She was expecting a proposal, not a dismissal. She replayed over and over again the look on Ace's face, his hollow words, his audacity to mention her parents' marriage. *Their* love was genuine, and he showed just how disingenuous he could be.

She thought Ace was her person. She was wrong. As she sat alone at the table, she wondered how she would ever find love again.

ONE

The bouquet coasted over twenty sets of waving hands, banking left toward the sister of the bride. Dylan watched from her table, having refused to join what she considered to be one of the most humiliating traditions for a single woman. Claiming her prize with a one-handed catch, the bride's sister clutched the white rose and calla lily bouquet to her chest. She smiled conspiratorially at her sister and then sauntered over to her table with a token that supposedly meant she'd be the next one taking a trip to the altar.

Dylan collected her purse and wedding favor, bid farewell to the other singles at her table, and attempted to make a discreet exit from the ongoing reception. She glanced over her shoulder as the groom began to explore beneath his new wife's gown to retrieve the garter. The hoots and hollers made Dylan hasten her steps as she left the ballroom. The merriment of the wedding guests echoed down the hallway and ushered her out the door. A warm breeze and the golden rays of the setting sun kissed her face. Dylan heaved a sigh and made a silent vow. That would be the last wedding she attended alone.

The valet patiently waited while she searched for her small blue ticket. As she rifled through her bag, wondering how she could lose anything in such a tiny purse, a gentleman stepped up beside her and smiled. Dylan returned the gesture and continued her search, jostling items from side to side. Sensing his gaze was still upon her, she glanced up. Smile intact, he seemed to be watching her every move. *Nice smile*, she thought, *and he looks good in a suit*. Shoes polished to a shine, nails trimmed and buffed, he was well put together. He was the type of man she wouldn't mind getting to know. In fact, she was prepared to give him her phone number if he asked—*when* he asked, because she knew he would. Dylan asked the attendant to help the gentleman while she located her ticket. He stepped a bit closer to hand his ticket to the valet. The scent of cologne on the breeze wrapped around her. Dylan closed her eyes and inhaled. A little sweet, not quite the scent you would expect on such a dashing figure. It smelled similar to her own fragrance. Her eyes fluttered open. Standing beside Mr. Tall, Dark, and Handsome was an equally attractive companion, linking her arm through his. Dylan felt her cheeks grow warm with embarrassment. While she was in the moment, sniffing the air like a hunting dog, his lady stealthily appeared by his side. It was an effort not to take them in as a pair. Dylan stared straight ahead, not wanting to make eye contact with either of them. She walked a few paces away from the couple and sat on one of the benches next to the valet station. She pulled the wedding program from her purse and there, cradled between the pages, was her ticket.

A sleek, gleaming convertible purred up to the curb. Mr. Tall, Dark, and Handsome handed the valet a tip and walked around to the passenger side to open the door for his companion. Dylan brazenly watched them. The way she placed her hand in his as she slipped into her seat, how he strode around the car like others had a reason to envy him—they were acutely aware of the image they presented.

Dylan felt a tug inside. Unbeknownst to this couple, their interaction catapulted her day from bad to worse, strengthening her resolve that she would never attend another wedding by herself. The valet came over to Dylan and asked if she found her ticket. Wordlessly, she gave it to him, noticing for the first time that the number printed on it, in bold black ink, was one. She looked skyward and shook her head. The message was loud and clear. She was single and had been for a long time. What she planned to do about it was the real question. Dylan pondered that issue as she waited for her car. Unfortunately, the valet pulled up before any answers came to mind. As she slipped him a tip, he asked if he could have her number. Dylan politely declined and chuckled to herself. Right question, wrong guy.

TWO

$\mathcal{D}$ ylan kicked off her heels at the door and left them where they lay. She headed upstairs to her bedroom, unzipping her dress as she meandered down the hall. Dylan paused in front of the floor-length mirror. Adorned in a flowy tangerine-hued ensemble, hair and makeup flawless, she was dispirited no one else was there to appreciate any of it.

She hung the dress in her closet, placing it where she could see it. Dylan intended to wear it again in the near future. It had been purchased specifically for the wedding, but in that moment, she decided it would be a perfect date night outfit. That, of course, would require a date. At the moment, she had zero prospects. It had been five years since Dylan's last serious relationship. She hated to dwell on the past and the reasons why the relationship failed. Failure meant she didn't do something right and that was a hard pill to swallow.

Dylan had been raised to excel in all things. She was aware others might feel that relationships fit into their own category with their own set of rules but, for Dylan, excelling applied to every aspect of her life. Her friends liked to joke that there was a therapist's couch somewhere with her name on it. She'd laugh along with their good-natured humor, all the while disagreeing with their opinions on how to approach the dating game. The hours she spent with Ivy and Brooke discussing life and love were countless. The individual arguments made were endless. Having met in college fifteen years prior, some of the debates were ongoing; others had been put to bed years ago.

Dylan cleansed her face of every trace of makeup and unpinned her hair. Staring in the bathroom mirror, she took a moment to admire her reflection again. Barefaced with loose curls framing her shoulders, she looked much younger than her thirty-four years. She tried not to think about the proverbial biological clock ticking in her ears. It was getting more difficult to ignore, especially with her parents pressuring her to settle down. They couldn't understand what she was waiting for to get serious with someone. She was educated, led her own management consulting firm, and could afford a home in a picturesque community in the suburbs. Unfortunately, that was not enough. According to her parents, in addition to a good education and job, she needed a husband and children—that was the key to truly being successful in life. It didn't help Dylan's case that her younger brother tied the knot before her. Dylan pushed the thought from her mind. She didn't want to think about any of that . . . no pressure . . . no clocks ticking . . . nothing.

Pulling her hair up in a high ponytail, she gave herself a final glance. She knew her worth. The right man would come along. *Come along*. Now there was a dated concept. If she expected to get out of her current dating slump, she would need to take a more proactive approach. Waiting around for so-called "Mr. Right" to knock on her door wouldn't do.

For the second time, Dylan tried to purge the thoughts that kept bombarding her. The harsh reality of sitting alone watching the bride and groom exchange their vows, jump the broom, and have their first dance had been enough torment for one day. She slipped into her favorite cozy romper and a pair of fuzzy socks. Dylan headed straight for the sitting area in her master suite and climbed onto the chaise lounge. She relaxed into the chair and closed her eyes. She missed the time when she had someone special in her life. The first year after the breakup had been tough. She'd had a hard time accepting it was over. There was an abundance of blame to go around and, though it took a while, she finally accepted her share. In retrospect, there were things that could have been done differently. She learned and moved on. A chime from Dylan's phone disrupted her ruminations. She reached for the phone and scanned the text message from Ivy. **Don't forget brunch tomorrow at noon.** She fired off a quick reply. **I'll be there.**

THREE

*T*raffic was impossible. A line of cars, on a single-lane road, moving at a snail's pace. The restaurant was only a few traffic lights up the street, but the congestion and Sunday drivers had turned a quick ride into a drawn-out road trip. Dylan checked the time and calculated that she would only be ten minutes late. No one had called to ask her whereabouts, so she assumed the girls were facing the same challenge. A loud horn blew from behind, startling her.

"What the heck," she stammered, peering into the rearview mirror. She squinted, straining to see the cause of the commotion. The driver behind her was inching closer to her bumper and waving animatedly. Dylan relaxed her grip on the steering wheel as Ivy's broad smile came into focus. She waved back at her friend and redirected her attention on the traffic ahead. That was Ivy. Always full of energy and excited by the smallest things. Dylan glanced in the rearview again. Ivy's head bopped along to whatever tune was likely blasting in her car. She smiled to herself. She loved her friends and the relationship they had cultivated over the years. As their careers had blossomed, life started to get in the way and Dylan had less time to spend with the girls. Their impromptu outings eventually became a thing of the past, and Dylan started feeling like she was all work and no play. That's when she decided something had to change. She suggested to Brooke and Ivy that they meet for a standing brunch date on the second Sunday of every month that couldn't be missed, no excuses allowed. The girls readily agreed and for the past four years this was their time. A time for them to reconnect, decompress, and just enjoy one another's company.

Dylan turned into the parking lot and found a space. Ivy pulled up beside her, exiting the car before Dylan even had a chance to collect her purse. As soon as she stepped from the car, Ivy wrapped her in a big hug.

"I missed you," Ivy said.

Dylan chuckled at her friend's exuberance. "It's good to see you, too, Ivy."

Ivy grasped Dylan's hand as they walked toward the restaurant entrance. "This place has bottomless mimosas, right?"

"I'm not sure. Brooke picked this restaurant."

"I hope they do."

"Rough week?"

"Let's just say there's a drink with my name on it."

Dylan opened the door and nudged Ivy inside. She gave the hostess Brooke's name and they were immediately escorted through to the dining room. Gleaming blond hardwood floors, natural lighting, and white tablecloths brightened the open layout. Nice-looking people were indulging in great-looking food—waffles, omelets, pancakes, baskets of biscuits, steak and eggs. At one table, a group of handsome, well-dressed men were jovially chatting over breakfast. Dylan smiled to herself. This was a place they needed to visit again. Brooke was seated at the center of it all. When she saw them approaching, Brooke tossed her long bob to the side and tapped her watch.

"Traffic was terrible," Dylan offered, bending over to kiss Brooke's cheek.

"Hey, Brooke," Ivy said. She'd immediately sat down and begun perusing the drinks section of the menu. "Have you been here before?"

"It's my first time. One of my clients suggested this place to me." She pointed across the room. "He's at that table over there."

Dylan perked up. "The one with all the strapping men?"

"Yes. He comes here every week with his fraternity brothers. I'm trying to get some client referrals from him."

Dylan playfully grabbed her purse and began to get up from her chair. "Looks like they have room for one more at their table. I'll get some names and numbers for you."

"Girl, stop!" Brooke snatched Dylan's bag from her hand. "Sit down."

They snickered in unison, glancing over at the table.

"They don't look like they need a personal trainer to me. They're in pretty good shape," Dylan replied.

"That doesn't mean they don't have areas to improve upon. I can turn anyone's body into chiseled perfection."

Ivy groaned. "I hope we're not going to talk about work today."

Dylan and Brooke exchanged glances. "I ordered us Bellinis."

"Oh, good." Ivy placed the menu on the table and finally took in her surroundings. "I like the vibe in here."

Music softly played in the background. Quiet conversations contributed to a static buzz energizing the atmosphere. Ivy surveyed the room, her gaze bouncing from table to table. Dylan observed her friend as she people watched. It was apparent something was on Ivy's mind. She would share her thoughts when she was ready.

It was surprising the trio had actually followed through with their monthly gatherings, without fail, for the past four years. All three were guilty of complaining about busy schedules and work obligations, but they weren't allowed to use those reasons for not showing up. Dylan was responsible for planning many of the activities that ensured their close-knit relationship remained intact. It was a role she commandeered in college and had yet to relinquish. She had cajoled her friends into doing everything from karaoke nights to escape rooms, haunted hayrides, peach picking, and even axe throwing.

"What's with you two today?" Brooke asked. "Something is off."

"I can't speak for Ivy, but I had an awful day yesterday."

"Didn't you go to a wedding?"

The server arrived with their cocktails. Dylan waited until the server went through the specials and took their orders before responding to Brooke's question.

"My hairstylist got married."

"Aren't weddings supposed to be happy occasions?"

"I went by myself. I didn't know a single soul."

Ivy raised her glass and drained its contents. "I need another." She turned around in her chair, looking for the server.

"You inhaled that drink. What is going on?" Brooke demanded.

"I'm listening to Dylan's story about yesterday," Ivy said dismissively. When she made eye contact with the server, she pointed to her glass. "Go ahead, Dylan."

"If I'm being honest, I'm tired of being single," Dylan continued. "I'm over thirty with no prospects in sight. Yesterday, I was seated with a bunch of strangers at the notorious singles table. I think that made it worse. These brides throw the singles together like we're supposed to take solace in being seated with each other. I know I don't talk much about my breakup with Ace, but I miss being in a relationship."

Brooke frowned. "It definitely must have been a rough day if you're mentioning Ace."

Dylan slapped the back of her own hand. "Shame on me," she said with dramatic effect. "I don't know what I was thinking. Forget I mentioned him."

"Dylan's allowed to mention her ex if she wants to," Ivy said.

"I never said she couldn't. She usually doesn't, but I've never discouraged her from bringing him up."

"That's not true, Brooke. There have been times when you—"

"Ladies," Dylan interrupted. "Let's not turn this into a debate. We have a lot of other things to catch up on. Ace isn't one of them. I was only saying how difficult it was attending a wedding alone. It didn't help that I made a complete fool of myself when I was leaving."

Ivy and Brooke shared a puzzled look before turning to Dylan and asking at the same time, "What happened?"

"It was nothing serious. I made an assumption, and you know what they say about assuming."

"You basically made an ass of yourself," Brooke said, in her typical direct manner.

Dylan laughed and told the girls about her run-in with Mr. Tall, Dark, and Handsome at valet parking—and his Mrs. Right.

"I would have felt embarrassed, too," Ivy lamented.

"I was watching this couple and feeling like that should be me. Before you say it, I know I have no idea what their lives are like. But the idea of attending a wedding with a handsome man and driving off into the sunset in *our* convertible . . ."

"Please stop," Brooke said, choking back laughter. "Do you hear yourself? Riding off into the sunset? You've been watching way too many romantic movies."

"Have I?"

"It sounds like it to me."

"I think you're missing the point. I'm not trying to romanticize anything. Having someone special at this stage in my life is more a basic necessity than a romantic ideal. Companionship is important. I have so much love to share and want love in return." Dylan leaned forward, studying her friends. They were beautiful, inside and out, successful, funny, compassionate, cared about their community, and loved their families. "Would either of you have thought we'd still be single at this age?"

Ivy shook her head. "Absolutely not. I was sure I'd be married with five kids by now."

"Five whole kids?" Brooke asked, incredulous. There was a glint in her eyes that hinted at a fit of laughter looming dangerously close.

"Yes, five. Maybe more."

Brooke concealed her smile with her napkin. "That's a lot."

"Well, that was then. Now, I'd be happy with one. Heck, I'd be happy if I just had a man." Ivy shrugged. "I'm feeling more and more like I'm destined to be single forever."

"No luck on the apps?" Dylan said, realizing she hadn't asked in a while.

"I deleted them all. I got tired of swiping left, swiping right, accepting dates from men that didn't come close to meeting my criteria and being let down. I was going out with some of the strangest guys just because I was bored and wanted something to do."

Dylan wasn't a fan of dating apps. She applauded those who were willing to take the risk, but she had heard too many horror stories from friends. Misleading profiles and enhanced photos . . . what you see isn't always what you get. Sure, there were folks who'd had positive experiences and were able to make lasting connections. But you had to be willing to sort through a few bad apples, sight unseen, and Dylan wasn't that fond of apples. "At least you gave it your best shot."

"Did I tell you about the guy whose profile said he was a doctor?"

"What's wrong with that?" Brooke said.

"I kept asking what type of medicine he practiced, and he would avoid answering directly. Instead, he would say things like he was a specialist, or he had steady hands. When he picked me up for our date, he was wearing a T-shirt that said Hue Doctor on the front."

"Hugh Doctor? His first name was Hugh, last name Doctor?"

"No." Ivy shook her head. "Hue, as in color. He was a house painter and that's the name of his business . . . Hue Doctor."

Dylan and Brooke erupted in laughter. "So, did you go on the date?"

"Yes, Brooke. I couldn't turn him away. I had already opened the door."

"You could have made up an excuse and closed the door."

"But I was already dressed to go out."

The girls laughed some more. Ivy stared at them, unamused. "I just can't be mean to someone for no reason."

"It's not being mean. It's being real. He was clearly being deceptive. If he would mislead you on something like that, he would probably lie about anything. Who cares that you were dressed already? He could have been a lunatic! You have to be careful on those apps," Brooke said with concern.

"I already said I deleted them. So you can stop worrying . . . and laughing."

Right on time, the server arrived with more Bellinis. A hush fell over the table as they sipped and let the tension ease.

"What about you, Brooke?" Dylan pressed.

"What about me?"

"My question." Dylan watched Brooke intently.

"Did I think I would be single at this age? No. However, I gave up on the fairy tale that my husband is somewhere out there waiting for me a long time ago."

Dylan thought back to the days when they used to sit around and dream up who their husbands would be and what they would do for a living, the homes they'd live in, and the fabulous trips they would take. The plans they had back then were so idealistic. Dylan thought she'd be married by twenty-three, have her first child by twenty-five, and maybe a second one two years later—a boy and then a girl. Her family of four would take a holiday photo every year, to send with their Christmas card, and throw themed birthday parties for the kids.

None of those things had come to fruition, but throwing in the towel wasn't an option either.

"Last night had me thinking about all sorts of stuff, and I'm certain of one thing: I'm not giving up on finding my husband and neither are the two of you."

Brooke leaned back in her chair looking at Dylan expectantly.

"I'm listening," Ivy said.

"So, last week I was having dinner with my parents. As usual, they were going down memory lane, talking about the old days growing up in Brooklyn, the places where they used to hang out with their friends . . . it sounds corny, but I love hearing their old stories. My dad talking about his first job and how it shaped his work ethic made me realize how we have so much in common. The highlight of the evening was them talking about how they met at a party. My mom was there with a date when her girlfriend came over and introduced her to her brother. She had been trying to get them together for a while. I won't bore you with all the details but, by the end of the night, my mom had ditched her date and told her girlfriend that her brother was going to be her husband."

"Scandalous," Brooke chirped.

"It was kind of scandalous but that's not why I brought any of this up. My parents have told a million stories over the years. Something about this one struck a chord. My aunt wanted my parents to meet because she had a hunch that they would be good together. I made a joke that it's a good thing it worked out because my aunt could have been disowned by both of them. They waved off the notion and said a lot of their friends and family met their spouses that way. Back in the day, they were always setting each other up. My aunt met my uncle through a friend. My mother introduced her cousin to the man she ended up marrying. My father set his best friend up with a woman who became his wife."

"That's beautiful, Dylan," Brooke replied with playful sarcasm.

"The point is," Dylan continued, ignoring her friend, "they were onto something back then. How many men do we know individually?"

"I know about—"

"That was rhetorical, Ivy. Among us, we know a heck of a lot of them. Why aren't we setting each other up?" Dylan paused to let the weight of her question sink in. "It makes sense. That's what our parents used to do. There was no internet or online dating or speed dating, none of that. They used to look within their own circles and connect one another. We should be doing that." Dylan could barely contain her enthusiasm. "Why aren't we doing that?"

"It makes sense," Ivy said pensively.

"It makes complete sense. We all have men in our lives that we may not consider dating, but why not introduce them to one another?" The more Dylan spoke, the more she realized this was the answer she was seeking on that bench the evening before. "We'll start a referral program."

"A referral program?" Brooke asked, appearing to need more convincing. "How will that work?"

"I don't know how it's going to work, but I like it already," Ivy said.

"It begins with each one of us taking stock of the men in our lives. Family, friends, and coworkers are a great place to start, but we'll need to dig deeper and think about who else we know."

Ivy nodded. "There has to be some criteria for the men we refer."

"That's a given," Dylan said. "Since we know these men personally, we're only going to refer the good men in our lives."

"Men with jobs, not married, don't live with their mothers, can afford a date . . ." Brooke skeptically ticked off a list of requirements. Never one to relinquish too much control, she wanted to make her prerequisites clear.

"Ladies, the idea is to refer someone we can potentially see our best friend having an enduring relationship with, someone she can marry. I don't want to be single for the rest of my life. If we can help the process along for one another, then that's what we should be doing. I could name at least five guys off the top of my head that fit your criteria, Brooke. In fact, they exceed it."

"I can, too," Ivy said.

"Then why aren't either of you dating them?"

"It's simple," Dylan replied nonchalantly. "They aren't for me. We aren't inclined to be attracted to every good man in our lives. Some are destined to be friends or colleagues and nothing more. You know this."

Brooke exhaled and a smile crept up on her face. "Okay, I'm in."

Dylan matched Brooke's smile, thrilled that Brooke was on board. It was Brooke's nature to push back and resist. She vetted everything fully before making decisions. The Referral Program would require her to step out of the box and act on feeling, rather than fact.

Their breakfast finally arrived and they nibbled at it while continuing to plan.

"When do we start?" Ivy asked Dylan, taking a bite of her toast.

"There's no time like the present. First, let's agree that our ultimate goal is to find our future husbands."

"Agreed," Ivy said.

"Ivy, we know you agree," Brooke added with a laugh. "Especially since you're planning to have fifty kids."

She playfully pounded on the table. "I said five!"

Dylan couldn't suppress her laughter. "Can we hold off on the *five* kids for *five* minutes?"

Ivy straightened up. "Okay, what's next?"

"We also need to make sure the men we're referring are worthy of pursuing serious relationships with."

Brooke nodded. "Great point, Dylan. We shouldn't have to worry about whether these guys are ready for something real."

"Exactly! I don't want a player," Ivy chimed in. "We need to refer men that we wouldn't be ashamed to take home to meet our parents."

"They have to be employed," Brooke declared.

"A J.O.B. is a given," Dylan emphatically concurred.

"Have their own place and transportation," Ivy quickly added.

"And, it should go without saying, they must be eligible. That means no wives, girlfriends, or entanglements."

"Seriously, Brooke?" Ivy chuckled. "Did you really say entanglements?"

Brooke giggled. "Well, entanglements are a thing these days. We have to make sure our referrals aren't involved in any."

Dylan interjected. "Those are all important requirements. Equally important, our referrals cannot be an ex-boyfriend, a person you've dated, or even someone you've had a casual *situation* with in the past."

Ivy and Brooke nodded their agreement.

"What else do we need to take into consideration?" Dylan said.

Without missing a beat, Brooke replied, "I think it's best that we don't tell our referrals about the program."

Ivy's head cocked to the side. "Why not?"

"I just don't think they would fully appreciate the intent of the Referral Program."

"Are you sure that's your only reason? You know we *all* have to fully commit for this to work."

Before Brooke could answer, Dylan spoke up. "I agree with her, Ivy. It could complicate things unnecessarily if our referrals know about the program."

"So, we'll swear to keep the Referral Program to ourselves. We cannot tell the guys."

"I swear," Ivy said. "You don't have to worry about me saying a word."

"Me too."

"We should each come up with a list of six men to start. My list would have three men that I think would be a good fit for Ivy and three for Brooke."

"So, I'll make a list with three guys for you and three for Brooke?"

"Exactly. And Brooke's list will have guys for you and me."

"Ultimately, we'll each have six referrals with the hopes that our husband will be among those men?" Brooke asked with vestiges of her skepticism resurfacing.

"Yes."

"So, I'm expected to go out with six men?"

"Ideally, we won't make it to the end of our lists," Dylan reassured. "If we do, we'll deal with that when the time comes. In the meantime, we'll create our lists and plan to do our first introductions by the end of the week."

"Okay, okay." Brooke raised her glass. "Let's seal the deal."

"To meeting our forever loves."

Ivy, Brooke, and Dylan clinked glasses. It was official. They were embarking on the Referral Program.

FOUR

Brooke sat down at her kitchen table with a pen and pad, all business. That was her approach to pretty much everything in life. She fiddled with the pen in her hand and conceded that needed to change. She was ready to come up with a list of referrals for Dylan and Ivy. She had to get it right. The girls were very clear about their expectations of acceptable men. Brooke wasn't planning to be the one to suggest someone who didn't check all the boxes. She thought about who was available, their personality, career, and looks. That was just a starting point. She reflected on how long she knew the guy, his living arrangement, and whether she had ever seen him exhibit any bad or questionable behavior. Brooke was not under an illusion that this was an exact science, but she put serious thought into all the things that were discussed and mattered most.

Brooke pondered what mattered most to *her* and what she truly wanted in a man. She hoped Ivy and Dylan would refer quality men open to having a real relationship and love in their life. Brooke dropped the pen, suddenly feeling apprehensive about committing to the Referral Program and proactively inviting love into her life. She couldn't recall the last time she had been in that headspace. She hadn't intentionally decided to give up on the fairy tale. It just sort of happened. A string of breakups, constantly redefining what was important, and prioritizing work over everything else had pushed the idea of a husband and family to the back burner. Before Brooke realized it, she'd turned thirty and certain plans had fallen by the wayside. Though she teased Ivy and Dylan from time to time about their mission to find the perfect man, she appreciated their continued reminders to be open to finding love.

There were times when Brooke questioned if she was capable of committing and loving someone unconditionally. "Unconditionally" was a powerful word, she thought. Willing to love completely and without reservation or limitations . . . Putting someone else's interests first . . . That was a tall order she wasn't sure she'd be able to fill. Dylan and Ivy reminded her to try. She was working on that part. Brooke wrote "The Referral Program" at the top of a blank page. She jotted down two names immediately. Tapping her temple with her pen, she thought of who else might be worthy of spending time with her sisters. She laughed to herself. Leave it to Dylan to craft a new scheme and rope her and Ivy into it. She hadn't changed one bit since college. Dylan had a tendency of cajoling them to participate in her frequent whims. Thanks to Dylan, Brooke had attended more events, volunteered countless hours, and visited too many places to recall.

Brooke added four more names to the list. When she was done, she held out the list and admired it. She was pleased with what she came up with—six quality guys she could not imagine her friends wouldn't find appealing. Brooke felt a twinge of enthusiasm. She wondered if she really could meet her husband through the Referral Program. Knowing Ivy and Dylan, they were probably all in and convinced the program would be a success. Brooke wanted to have that kind of blind faith, too. But her struggle with the concept of unconditionality prevented it. She promised herself she'd work on that, too. If Brooke did find her husband through the program, it would definitely help if she could love him unconditionally.

Brooke made her way out to her garden. The vines were heavy with red and green peppers, tomatoes, cucumbers, and eggplant. She had neglected it the past couple of weeks and there was plenty to pick. She grabbed a pair of garden shears and draped a harvest basket over her forearm. Gardening was one of the pleasures Brooke usually made time for during her busy week. She planted a garden every spring, as soon as the cold weather departed. She looked forward to working the soil, breaking it up and fertilizing it in preparation for the vegetables. She loved the feel of the cool, nutrient-rich soil running through her fingers. Down on her hands and knees, Brooke found that planting seeds made her feel grounded and connected to the earth. Watching the garden spring to life with subtle changes at first, a simple sprout, and then rapid growth with twisting vines and large leaves, reminded her of the importance of renewal in your life. The importance of starting fresh and flourishing. She would enjoy a bounty of healthy, organic vegetables until early fall.

Brooke delicately cradled a bright red plum tomato and snipped it from the vine. There was an abundance of ripened tomato plants in the garden. She barely had to move any leaves to search for which ones were ready. As she placed them in the basket, she thought about making a pot of sauce. There was nothing like growing your own food and knowing exactly where it came from. Eating healthy was a priority. Brooke allowed herself the occasional indulgence, especially during the monthly brunches with her girls, but she worked out every day and believed in taking care of the mind, body, and soul. She was lean, but not hard, and still had curves in all the right places. Her favorite motto for clients looking to tone up: Squats are your friend.

She plucked a green pepper and noticed a ladybug perched on it. She gently brushed it away, watching it take flight. *That's good luck*, she thought, harkening back to her childhood.

"Hey, neighbor," a voice called over the fence.

Brooke turned around and waved with shears in hand. "Hi, Daveed."

"It's about time you tended to that garden."

Brooke placed her basket on the ground and put a hand on her hip. "Since when are you so concerned with my garden?"

"Since you haven't brought over any fresh veggies in a few weeks."

Brooke laughed. She and Daveed had been neighbors for the past three years. When he first moved to the neighborhood, she welcomed him with a basket of produce from her garden. He had just relocated from Boston and was starting a new job in the attorney general's office. They chatted for over an hour about the neighborhood and Brooke's recommendations on everything from restaurants to dry cleaners.

He was right. She would typically leave a small basket on his side of the fence any time she picked vegetables. Usually the next day, the basket would be back on her side of the fence with a bottle of wine inside. They had their own little barter system. "You know," she said, "instead of leaning on the fence making comments, you can hop over here and do some picking."

"Oh, no. I'll leave that to you," he said, flashing a smile.

"I figured you'd say that."

"Do you have any yellow or green squash today?"

Brooke looked over her shoulder. "There's some yellow."

"If you have any extra, I'd love some of that."

"What are you making with it?"

"The last time I roasted it with rosemary, sea salt, and olive oil."

"You should try it with balsamic and honey."

"Maybe I will."

"I have quite a few over here so you can roast it both ways."

"You're too good to me."

"I know."

"I have a new wine for you to try. It's a Shiraz."

"Do you have plans this evening?" Brooke asked.

"Not a single one."

"Why don't you bring the wine over and I'll get your veggies together. I want to run something by you."

"I hope it's not about me picking the vegetables in the future," he said with a laugh.

"I wouldn't trust you in my garden."

"Thank goodness. I'll see you in about an hour."

Brooke hurriedly harvested the garden. As soon as she finished, she went inside the house and grabbed her notepad. She crossed off the name at the bottom of her referral list and added Daveed to the top.

FIVE

*I*vy tried not to bring her work home, but it was nearly impossible. She saved the report she had been updating and closed her laptop. Although social work was rewarding, and Ivy felt she was making a difference in the lives of the families she assisted, it came with many challenges. At times, it took a toll on her emotionally. She had to learn over the years when to disconnect in order to get the job done. The problem was she started to disconnect in other areas of her life as well.

Ivy's last relationship ended when her boyfriend told her that he didn't think they were compatible. After two years together, he decided she wasn't the woman for him. Ivy should have known they were headed in different directions. No matter how much she accommodated his wants and needs, it was never enough. He commented that neither of them would die if they didn't end up together. She should have known then that it was time to let go, but she chose to dig in deeper and fight for love. She refused to acknowledge that love was already on the ropes and the fight had been called.

Countless hours of tears and introspection later, she couldn't place all the blame on her job. The roots were deeper than that. Ivy conceded that she had done all the right things to a fault on the surface but, in actuality, had held back emotionally in her relationship.

The Referral Program was a fresh start. If Dylan and Brooke were going to be recommending good men in their lives, she couldn't be the friend with emotional baggage. Ivy was open and ready to prove she had worked out her issues. She loved that Dylan always had an idea brewing. Some of them were a bit out there—even Dylan could admit that—but all were created in the right spirit. Her dear friend wanted to see them excel, achieve, and ultimately be happy. Ivy wondered who they had in mind for her to date. She trusted Brooke and Dylan. They knew her likes and dislikes. They also knew she didn't have a type. Ivy hoped that would make it easier for them to find men for her list. She was eager to start.

Ivy stepped out onto her balcony and took in the scenery from the twenty-fifth floor—clear blue skies, green treetops lightly swaying in the breeze, and people strolling along the sidewalk on a late Sunday afternoon. The view overlooking the park sealed the deal when she was searching for a condo. The three-bedroom, two-bathroom unit was two thousand square feet of luxury and comfort. A daddy's girl from the moment she was born, Ivy had been gifted the condo from her father. He was the CEO and founder of one of the largest tech companies on the East Coast and always made sure she was taken care of.

Ivy had created a balance between growing up affluent and a career where she improved the well-being of others. Her parents had hoped she'd choose a different career, but Ivy chose her own path. She appreciated the advantages her parents afforded her, but was keenly aware of her purpose and responsibility to others. If there was one specific attribute she wanted Dylan and Brooke to identify in their referrals, it was a man that cared about and gave back to the community.

Ivy heard the phone ringing inside and rushed to grab it. "Carter?"

"Ivy," a deep voice said, "how are you?"

She plopped down on the living room sofa. "I'm good. Thanks for calling me back."

"When my favorite volunteer needs something, I'm on it." Carter ran a nonprofit organization that prepared high school students for college. He had helped thousands of kids with their study skills, exam preparation, college applications, and scholarship assistance.

"There is something I want to talk to you about," Ivy said.

"Is everything all right? We haven't seen you in weeks and the kids have been asking about you."

"Yes, I'm fine. My work schedule has been crazy. I promise to get there within the next few weeks," she assured him.

"No pressure. I understand. So, what's up?"

"This is purely a social call."

"Really? I'm surprised."

"You do know we can talk about something other than higher education?"

Carter laughed. "We can talk about whatever you like."

"Do you mind if I ask you a personal question?"

"Not at all," he replied.

"Are you seeing anyone?" As far as Ivy knew Carter was single, but she had to verify.

"Well, no." He hesitated. "No, I'm not."

"That's great," she said with a smile that could be heard through the phone.

"Why is that?"

"I have a friend that I'd like to introduce you to, if you'd be interested in meeting someone, of course."

"You want me to meet your friend? Like for a date?"

"Yes."

"I was not expecting this when I received your message."

"I can imagine."

"You've managed to catch me off guard, which is rare."

"This isn't the type of thing you leave on someone's voice mail." Ivy was starting to second-guess considering Carter.

"Can you tell me something about this friend you want me to meet?"

She relaxed her grip on the phone and settled into the couch. "Absolutely. I can tell you plenty."

SIX

Dylan was sitting behind the desk in her office reviewing the quarterly profits for one of her clients. A quick rap on the door drew her attention away from the computer screen. Her assistant approached with a guest in tow.

Dylan was up and greeting him before her assistant said a word. "Vincent, I told you that you didn't need to stop by."

"And I told you that I had a meeting in the area this morning."

Dylan hugged Vincent and smiled. "I appreciate you coming in." She turned to her assistant. "Thanks, Callie. Could you close the door on your way out?"

"Let me know if you need anything," Callie said before exiting.

"Have a seat, Vincent." Dylan motioned to one of the chairs in front of her desk. She sat down next to him, smoothing her skirt. "I was going to stop by your office this afternoon."

"Well, I saved you a trip."

Dylan gave the man beside her a once-over. He wore a charcoal gray suit and a slate-blue tie. Every time she saw Vincent he was impeccably dressed. Vincent had been Dylan's accountant ever since she started her firm. He knew her finances inside and out and, over the years, they had developed a friendship.

"You're looking well."

Vincent playfully straightened his cuff links. "Life is good. Business is good. I can't complain."

"How's the love life?"

"That's a different story," he said, shifting in his seat. "My love life could use some work."

"An attractive man like yourself?"

"Hard to believe, right?"

Dylan tried not to fire off a barrage of questions. A more subtle approach was necessary in the moment. "I won't lie. I was expecting you to say something different."

"What? That I have more women than I can handle?"

"Something like that."

"Why would you think that about me?"

"I can state the obvious. You're handsome, successful, and a nice guy. Women are attracted to all the above."

Vincent smiled. "Thanks for the compliment. You must be looking for a discount on my fee."

Dylan laughed. "How could I forget to mention your sense of humor? I'm not looking for a discount. I was explaining why I'd think you'd have a few ladies in your life."

"I can tell you one thing about me. I'm not the type of guy that juggles a lot of ladies. That's never been my style."

"Not even when you were younger?"

"Sure, when I was young, I had my moments. I think most people, both men and women, have. But, at some point, you have to grow and mature. I haven't played the field since I was in my midtwenties."

"You make it sound like that was a long time ago."

"It was long enough. That's not the life I choose to live."

"So, you're open to having a meaningful relationship?"

"Dylan, I meet a lot of women and, occasionally, I date. Unfortunately, what I've discovered is there are too many people focusing on the wrong things in life. I know what I want, and I haven't found it."

Dylan nodded. She completely understood what Vincent was saying and appreciated his candor. It also gave her reassurance that he would be perfect for the Referral Program. "I think I can help."

Vincent's brow furrowed. "How do you plan on doing that?"

"I have someone I want you to meet. A friend of mine."

Vincent's expression brightened immediately. "I was wondering where this conversation was going."

"I mean, if you're interested . . ."

"Of course I'm interested. You know what they say, birds of a feather . . ."

"I'm not familiar with that saying," Dylan said, laughing.

"If she's anything like you—" He abruptly stopped himself. "Take it as the compliment it's intended to be. If you want me to meet one of your friends, how can I say no?"

"I was hoping you wouldn't."

SEVEN

$\mathcal{D}$ylan hurried home after work to get on a call with Ivy and Brooke. They were planning to share the names of the first guy each of them would meet. She poured herself a glass of merlot and anxiously waited for eight o'clock. Dylan moved from the kitchen to the family room and back to the kitchen again. She poured herself a refill. She couldn't believe she had butterflies fluttering in her stomach. She wanted the Referral Program to work.

The phone rang. Dylan quickly tapped the screen to join the Group FaceTime. Brooke and Ivy were both on. They exchanged pleasantries about their workday while Dylan attempted to contain how eager she was to move on to the purpose of their call.

Brooke spoke up first. "I'll admit when we left brunch the other day, I still had my reservations. I want you both to know that I'm committed and going into this with an open mind."

"That's all any of us can do. We all want the same thing. It's up to us to make sure it happens," Dylan said.

"All right, let's get started!" Ivy said, bursting with excitement. "I'll go first."

"Wait," Dylan interjected. "We need to go over a few more parameters."

"Typical." Brooke shook her head.

"I'm just saying we have to acknowledge a few things first."

"Such as?" Ivy asked.

"Such as, we need to keep in mind that we have personal relationships with these men. So, remember that we're an extension of one another. What we do reflects on each other. I don't want to ruin any of your relationships, and I definitely don't want any of mine ruined."

"We're aware of that, Dylan. I'm not—and I'm sure Ivy isn't—going to do anything that would cause a rift with any of our referrals. What else do we need to be mindful about?"

"If it doesn't work out with one referral, you must move on to the next one on your list. The idea is to stay in the game. There's no bailing on the program unless you've found *the one*."

"That's fine with me," Ivy said.

"And last, but not least, we must remember that we have one another's best interests at heart. I won't hold you accountable if your referrals don't work out and I hope you won't hold me accountable if yours don't pan out either. Agreed?"

"Agreed," Ivy replied.

"Me too," Brooke said.

"Can we start now?" Ivy said impatiently.

"Yes, I'll go first, since I'm the mastermind of this amazing plan." Dylan beamed at her girls.

"There she goes . . ." Ivy said, smiling.

"Yup, here I go!"

"No, there you *went*!" Brooke added.

The three friends erupted with laughter.

Ivy shushed them. "Okay, okay. Why don't we run through our referrals? I have created the ultimate list of *the most* eligible, personable, and creative men. But, Dylan, as the *mastermind* you can go first."

"I knew you'd see things my way."

Ivy rolled her eyes. "Hurry up before I change my mind."

"All right. We won't go into specifics about each guy until you have to move on to your next referral."

"Makes sense," Brooke replied.

"Ivy, Brooke has your first referral but, as a preview, I have three guys for you that are the cream of the crop. Linc is a Realtor and has been a commuting buddy of mine for years. He tells the best stories and has a zest for life that's downright infectious. Xavier is the owner of a few car dealerships and is about his business. Justin is the CFO at a hedge fund, super attentive, and a great listener."

Ivy's eyelids fluttered dramatically. "Wooo, they sound promising."

"Only the best for you, Toots." Dylan winked. "Now, Brooke, I took care of you, too. You'll be thanking me for the men I have lined up for you. Paul is an MD and gives the hottest TV doctor a run for their money. Blair is a detective with a heart of gold. He's a deacon at my church."

"When's the last time *you* went to church?" Brooke joked.

"Hush or I won't tell you about my first referral for you. And believe me, he's a winner."

"I'm listening."

"Vincent is smart, successful, thoughtful, and good-looking. He's my accountant. I've known him for many years, and he's now at a place in his life where he's ready for something real."

"I'll be the judge of that."

"Open mind . . . remember?" Dylan said.

"Of course," Brooke responded. "I guess I'll go next. Dylan, you aren't starting with any of my guys but let me give you a little taste of what's to come."

"A taste? Thank goodness I haven't had dinner yet."

"Now who's the comedienne? Dylan the diva, I have put a lot of thought into who would be a good fit for you. Bachelor number one is Reed. He's a pharmacist and used to be a client of mine. He has a great sense of humor. Bachelor number two is Barrett—a family friend and smart as a whip. He's an attorney. Bachelor number three can light up your life, literally. His name is Ambrose and he's an electrician."

Dylan laughed. "I see what you did there, cute."

"He's that, too. On to Ms. Ivy. I wanted to select guys that I thought would match your energy. One of the guys, Banks, is a college football coach with the spirit and physique of a warrior. Chad is also on your list, and he is a sweet soul. Thoughtful and easygoing. He's a mechanic and can *tune you up*. I meant, give your car a tune-up."

Ivy's eyebrows raised. "You're so bad."

"You love it! You'll also love your first referral, my next-door neighbor, Daveed. He's a cybersecurity expert who works for the attorney general's office. He's a techie, a wine enthusiast, and loves to cook. And, since you're culinarily challenged and relish a nice glass of wine, Daveed is a solid referral for you."

"I do love my wine." Ivy giggled with her friends. "Okay, it's my turn, finally! Brooke, I wish you were going out with my referral first, but you'll get to them soon enough."

"Not if I fall head over heels for Vincent."

"Time will tell. Until then, let me tell you a bit about who I chose for you. Eli likes to build things, including relationships. He's a construction worker and owns his own business. Noah can keep a pretty little smile on your face. He's a dentist with a beautiful smile of his own. Sebastian is by far the best of the best. He's a psychologist, motivational speaker, and *my cousin*. What else needs to be said? Actually, I think you met him, Dylan?"

"Sebastian?" Dylan tilted her head. "I don't think so."

Dylan thought back to the one cousin she had met of Ivy's and she was sure his name wasn't Sebastian. Her face grew warm from the memory. Ivy stirred her from her thoughts.

"Either way," Ivy continued, "all three are wonderful men. I suppose that leaves my referrals for Dylan. Numero uno is Malcolm, an engineer who works in the automotive industry. He loves classic cars."

"Maybe he'll be the one to drive Dylan into the sunset in his fancy cars," Brooke teased.

Dylan shook her head. "Maybe."

"Ladies, can I continue please?"

"We're sorry. Go ahead."

"*We?*" Dylan whispered.

"Next is my artist friend, Brian. A talented creative, he has an art gallery in Williamsburg. He's one deep brother. Last, but not least, your first referral is Carter. There's so much I can say about him. He is one of the most genuine people I know. He founded a nonprofit organization that is responsible for advancing the education of our youth. He's attentive, caring, giving, and an amazing conversationalist. Like you, he's a planner and full of ideas. I can only imagine what the two of you could come up with together."

"The wheels are in motion and all I can say is I want all of them!" Dylan wished they were together in person instead of on FaceTime. She would give Brooke and Ivy the biggest hug.

"We're really doing this," Brooke added.

"Did everyone tell their referrals to reach out by this weekend?" Dylan asked.

"I provided your contact information," Ivy said.

"I guess that means we're all set! Let's check in on Sunday evening."

Dylan ended the call and squealed with delight. The men sounded great. She had an indescribable feeling inside and the smile on her face wouldn't go away. The Referral Program was really happening, and she couldn't be more ecstatic.

EIGHT

*T*he gym was bustling when Brooke walked through the door. She stopped in on her way home for a brief meeting with her partner, Michael. She greeted the staff as she headed to her office in the back and found Michael was on the phone. He held up a finger and mouthed that he'd be off in a minute.

Brooke was initially hesitant to invest and become a co-owner in the business. She wondered if owning a local gym made sense when fitness chains were abundant. She considered whether the investment would be a profitable endeavor or a financial drain. Brooke consulted with her financial advisor, family, friends, and even her pastor for good measure. She went over the books, projections, membership, and marketing strategy before deciding that it was a promising opportunity.

She unlocked her office door, flipped on the light, and placed her purse on the desk. She headed directly to her certifications hanging on the wall and straightened one that was crooked. For the past few weeks, every time she came in, the frame was askew. They recently added new cardio classes and the studio was on the other side of her office wall. She figured it was the vibrating bass of the music being played. The last thing Brooke wanted to do was clean up broken glass if the frame happened to fall from the wall. She made a mental note to have maintenance secure it.

Brooke turned on her computer and logged in to the scheduling system. Her only client booked for Saturday morning had canceled and she didn't accept personal training appointments on Sundays. Her weekend was officially wide open.

She looked up from her screen and saw Michael leaning against the doorframe, arms crossed in front of his chest. His biceps strained against the fabric of his short-sleeved shirt. "It looks like you've bulked up some," Brooke commented.

"I switched up my routine."

"Don't get too big. Right now, you look good."

"I want to add a little more mass." Michael came into the office and sat on the edge of Brooke's desk. "Then I'm done."

"As much as I enjoy talking about your fitness goals," she teased, "let's start this meeting so I can get home."

"Sorry, I was trying to wrap up that call before you got here. I wanted to talk to you about hiring a few people. I think we need another trainer, an aerobics instructor, and a front desk attendant for evenings."

"You know what my first question will be."

"Can we afford it?" he said, imitating Brooke's tone and mannerisms.

"Exactly. Can we?"

"I wouldn't suggest it if we couldn't. Our membership has increased by thirty percent over the last thirteen months, and we really do need the help."

"If we hire three new employees, at one time, we need to make sure we're bringing in people who have a devoted following and clients that will come with them," Brooke said.

"We can check the social media of whomever we consider and create a marketing campaign, targeting their followers, announcing they're new to our gym, and offering a special, limited time discount."

"All good ideas. I'd like to run the numbers before I make a decision. Let's discuss on Monday."

"Sounds like a plan."

Brooke grabbed her purse. "Now, I'm getting out of here."

"Thanks for coming in tonight. I know you have a lot going on."

"More than you know."

o o o

BROOKE GOT HOME five minutes before her phone rang. Dylan texted earlier in the day to let her know that Vincent would be calling at eight o'clock. She had just enough time to kick off her shoes, grab a bottle of water, and quickly scan her mail.

She picked up on the third ring. "This is Brooke."

"Brooke, this is Vincent. Dylan's friend . . ."

"Hi, Vincent," she replied with a smooth, honeyed tone to match his.

"Is now still a good time to chat?"

"Yes, I was expecting your call." Brooke's pulse sped up, a case of nerves threatening to take over. Brooke took a deep breath. There was no turning back now.

"Apparently, Dylan thought it would be a good idea for us to meet. I'm flattered she would introduce me to a friend."

"She told me a bit about you."

"I'd like a chance to fill in the blanks."

"Why not start with what you'd like me to know."

Brooke stood in front of the wall of windows overlooking her backyard. Landscaping lights illuminated the pathway, patio, and garden. She gazed out into the yard and listened to Vincent's voice, its timbre and tone, his inflection and enunciation.

"Let's see. I'm thirty-six years young. I was born and raised in Maryland, and I'm the oldest of three children. I earned my bachelor's and master's degrees from Georgetown. I currently work for one of the Big Four accounting firms and lately I've been considering striking out on my own. And although I've never been married, I was engaged once . . . a very long time ago."

Brooke came away from the window and took a seat in the living room. "If you don't mind my asking, what happened?"

"She decided she wasn't interested in taking the journey with me. Building and growing together wasn't as appealing as instant gratification. She left me for an athlete."

Brooke regretted asking. "Sorry for prying."

"I don't mind. It's been eight years. I got over it a long time ago."

"Well, we have something in common."

"You were engaged, too?"

"No," Brooke swiftly replied. "I'm also one of three children."

"The oldest?"

"Middle child."

"Oh, the Jan Brady," he joked.

Brooke laughed. "I'm nothing like Jan Brady."

"So, you don't have middle child syndrome?"

"Is that a real thing?"

"Spoken like a true middle child."

"All right," she said, still laughing. "I know all about middle child syndrome. I, however, don't have and never had any issues stemming from being the middle child."

"I guess I'll have to take your word for it . . . for now. What else should I know about you?"

"Let's see. I'm a physical therapist and personal trainer."

"Dylan did mention that you're a fitness buff."

"Is that what she said?"

"Her exact words."

"Well, I wouldn't call myself a fitness buff. Obviously, I think physical fitness is important, but I think spiritual and emotional health is just as important."

"What do you recommend for spiritual and emotional well-being?"

"I think it depends on the person and what they have going on in their lives."

"What do you do for yourself, or is that too personal?"

"Not at all." Brooke put her feet up on the ottoman in front of her. "For one thing, I love gardening. I go out in the yard and plant and pick vegetables and it helps me unwind. It's just me working the earth, alone with my thoughts. It gives me a sense of inner peace."

"That's sort of how I feel about kayaking. Sometimes I'll take a trip Upstate and spend the entire day by myself on the water."

"Kayaking, huh?"

"Have you ever tried it?"

"I can't say that I have."

"Would you?" he asked.

"Perhaps . . ."

"Not one for adventure. Noted," he said, as if writing it down.

Brooke found herself laughing again. "That's not true. I like adventure."

"Don't worry. I understand. You're a fitness buff that sticks to the basics. Well, maybe you can relate more to this. I also try to run a few times a week."

"Another thing we have in common. I'm actually thinking of running the New York City Marathon this year."

"How many miles is that?" he asked.

"Twenty-six."

"That's definitely out of my league. I'll stick to my paltry few miles a week."

Brooke laughed. She was enjoying the easygoing flow of the conversation. "It takes training, but I could get you ready for a marathon. It's what I do."

"How about I politely decline," he replied with a chuckle.

"If you change your mind . . ."

"I have your number." Vincent cleared his throat. "And I hope you don't mind if I use it again."

"That depends on the reason why you're calling," Brooke said coyly.

"I'd call to invite you to dinner on Saturday night, but I suppose I can do that right now."

"I suppose you could."

"Brooke, would you like to join me for dinner this Saturday?"

"Yes, Vincent, I think I would."

NINE

Perched on a park bench, with an open book in her lap, Ivy watched a man in the distance glance at his wrist yet again. She checked her own watch. It was 2:57 p.m. Out of all the people bustling through the park, she kept her eyes on him. He had arrived at 2:45 p.m. but didn't venture much farther than the entrance. The first time she saw him look at his watch, she knew it had to be Daveed. And now, as he came toward her with a measured gait, she was sure of it. They'd made plans to meet at 3 p.m. and he was timing it down to the second.

Ivy looked down, feigning interest in her book. She looked up when she heard his voice for the first time.

"You must be Ivy." He extended his hand. "I'm Daveed."

Ivy peered up into a pair of light brown eyes. Her hand moved in slow motion to grasp his. "Nice to meet you, Daveed." She patted the bench next to her. "Please, sit."

They silently gave each other the once-over. Daveed smiled first. "It is so nice to meet you. Brooke described you perfectly."

"Did she tell you to look for the lady with the big, natural hair?"

"Not quite. But she did say you have a beautiful smile, and I can see for myself your beautiful curls."

Ivy tried her best not to blush, failing miserably. "Thank you."

He motioned to her lap. "What are you reading?"

She looked at the book, noticing it was upside down. She quickly closed it and turned the cover toward him so he could see. "The latest by Ta-Nehisi Coates."

He took the book from her hands and read the back cover. "Sounds interesting. Lately, I don't have much time to read for pleasure. Unfortunately, I've been bogged down mostly with technical books and manuals for work."

"I would imagine as a cyber expert you have to stay abreast of quite a lot, considering how much cyberattacks have increased over the years."

"Cybercrime is ever-changing, and we can't be caught asleep at the wheel. However, on this gorgeous summer day, I'm sure the last thing you want to do is talk about my work."

The truth of the matter was Ivy was enjoying hearing Daveed talk. They had only texted during the week. When he sent an initial text message, she didn't mind. It took some of the pressure off meeting someone new. Though she anticipated they would have a phone call prior to meeting face-to-face, it didn't happen that way. They texted back and forth, neither of them ever calling. Now she was sitting next to him on a park bench, trying to refrain from staring into his hypnotic eyes, watching his mouth as he spoke and the way his smile played across his lips like a sunrise on the horizon. His voice wasn't too deep or too high, it was somewhere in the middle. As he spoke, she determined she liked the sound of it.

"Tell me, Daveed, if you weren't here with me, what would you be doing today?" She wanted him to say he was glad to be with her and there was no other place he could imagine being in that moment. But Ivy knew she was being foolish. This was only their first meeting and the whole purpose of the Referral Program was to be discerning in finding the right man, not rushing to judgment after five minutes on a park bench.

"I might be grilling in my backyard or watching the game with a

few of my buddies. Maybe taking a ride out to the beach a little later
in the evening to watch the sunset."

"How about a rainy day? Love 'em or hate 'em?"

He thought about it for a moment. "It depends."

"On?"

"Whether or not I'm in a relationship."

Ivy tilted her head slightly. "Go on."

"When I'm in a relationship, I love staying inside and cuddling,
watching movies, drinking wine . . . you get the idea."

"And when you're not?"

"I don't love them so much. They have a different effect on me.
I tend to brood a little."

"Oh, I see. You're a brooder."

Daveed smiled. "Honestly, I can be."

"I'll have to keep that in mind."

"I know that's not a selling point, but I'm into full disclosure."

"That's something I'm still working on. Sharing, I mean."

Daveed nodded, making a mental note that Ivy shared something
that wasn't necessarily a positive characteristic. He appreciated that.
He'd been on too many first dates where he met the representative, the façade. He had a feeling he was meeting the real Ivy. Daveed wanted to know more, but he was also being cautious. He didn't
want to bombard her with too many questions at once. He was an
analytical guy, always looking for answers. He did his best to rein in
his inquisitive nature and take a more conversational approach. He
typically gravitated toward communicating via email and text at work
and struggled with not letting it bleed over into his personal life. In
that moment, he realized that he had missed an opportunity. "I could
have called you to coordinate our date."

"Okay . . . where did that come from?" she asked, with a puzzled
look on her face.

"You mentioned you're working on sharing. It made me think of what I need to improve on. Picking up the phone more . . . It would have been nice to speak with you and hear your voice."

"I did tell Brooke I didn't know what type of guy she was introducing me to."

Daveed's eyes opened wide. "Aw, man—"

"I'm kidding." Ivy threw her head back and laughed. "I didn't say anything to Brooke."

Relief washed over Daveed's face. "Thank goodness."

"Texting you helped me convince myself that I could actually go through with this program."

"Program?"

Ivy startled. "I meant date. To show up here . . ." she stuttered. "I meant to say texting made it feel more casual and not like we were meeting for the first time on a blind date."

Ivy was cursing at herself inside and knew Dylan and Brooke would do worse if they knew she almost spilled the beans about the Referral Program. They all swore that they wouldn't reveal any information about it to any of the men. And here she was on her very first date and she'd already slipped up. She hoped Daveed would let her reference to a program go in one ear and right out the other.

"As long as you don't hold it against me," he said.

"Believe me, you're fine."

"Ivy, I like your energy."

"You just met me. How could you possibly know that?"

"Your energy radiates from you. I'm sure I'm not the first person to tell you that."

"No, I've heard it before. Never on a first date."

"You're saying I should have kept that to myself?"

Ivy laughed. "Maybe until the end of the date or our next one."

Daveed raised his eyebrows. "So, there's going to be a next one?"

"Definitely. If you call me . . ."

TEN

*D*ylan snatched up her briefcase and rushed out of her office. She shouted goodnight to Callie as she ran past her assistant's desk. The elevator to the parking garage was taking its sweet time arriving on the sixth floor. She'd planned to leave the office an hour earlier but received a pressing call from a client who had experienced a significant increase in expenses and needed to be talked off the ledge. That impromptu counseling session cost her time she didn't have to get to the Schomburg Center in Harlem. She was meeting Carter for a lecture and then dinner.

She was doing it. Her first date on the Referral Program. Butterflies fluttered in her stomach. She willed the red stoplights to turn green so she could make it uptown on time. Dylan hated being late and for a first date, that was even worse. She contemplated calling Ivy to let her know she was about to meet her referral but reconsidered, thinking that might make her more nervous. There was no turning back now.

She was twenty minutes late, fretting as she bustled up the street. She saw him as she approached, standing in front, waiting for her. "Carter, I am so sorry," she said, hurrying up to him. "A client called, the traffic was insane, and I couldn't find parking. I usually take the Long Island Rail Road into the city, but I drove today. You didn't have to wait for me. You're missing the lecture."

"Wow, that was some greeting. First things first—it's all right. Catch your breath." Carter extended his hand. "Dylan, it's a pleasure to meet you."

51

"Likewise." Dylan grabbed Carter's hand and squeezed. "Shall we go in? I've made you miss enough of the lecture."

Carter opened the door and led Dylan inside.

∘ ∘ ∘

THEY SAT ACROSS from one another in a quiet restaurant at a cozy table in the corner. Carter frequented the place and raved about the French and African cuisine. Dylan took in her surroundings. There were a few couples and one group of five dining together. Everyone seemed engaged in interesting conversations. The group laughed and sipped cocktails, clinking glasses with one another. Dylan wondered whether they were celebrating a special occasion or just toasting to a poignant discussion point. Carter cleared his throat.

"I'm sorry, did you say something?"

"I asked if you enjoyed the lecture."

Dylan blushed with embarrassment. She was so preoccupied with the other table that she didn't hear what her own dinner companion had said. "I did," she finally replied. "He really laid out a strategic plan for ensuring our communities continue to grow and the obligation of Black business owners to give back."

"I thought his message was on point. The delivery needed some work."

"I suppose there were a few times when he did come off as a little preachy. I think he was trying to navigate between educating and motivating the audience."

"I bet he was raised a preacher's kid. The fire and brimstone were bubbling beneath the surface the entire lecture."

Dylan laughed. "You're probably right. Thank you for inviting me. I truly did enjoy it."

"Well, now we can do all the talking. A lecture isn't the ideal forum to get to know someone. Probably not the best first date choice."

"Isn't that why we're having dinner now? So we can pick each other's brains and divulge our deepest, darkest thoughts?"

"Ivy warned me about your wit."

"Oh, did she? That takes a bit of the fun out of it. I wanted you to wonder if I was serious or not."

"Oh, we can get deep if you want. Let me see what I can tell you . . ."

"No, no." She waved her hands in protest. "We can keep it light."

"Agreed."

They chuckled together, clinging for a moment to the levity in the air.

Dylan picked up the drink menu. "So, what cocktails do you recommend?"

"Do you prefer something sweet or strong?"

"Always sweet."

"You can't go wrong with one of the martinis. If you like, I can order one I think you'd enjoy."

"Sure, why not."

Dylan closed the menu and gazed at Carter. Smooth cocoa skin, a strong jaw, and beautiful dark eyebrows. She smiled.

"Now I am wondering what you're thinking," he said with a smile.

She shook her head. "We're keeping it light. No deep thoughts."

He nodded. "Okay. Tell me, what's the last movie you saw?"

"I haven't been to the movies in a while."

"I guess it doesn't have to be a movie. It can be a TV series, documentary, whatever."

"I recently watched a horror series centered around a virus in the rain that infects the population around the world."

"Horror. I didn't expect that."

"What about you?"

"I just watched a documentary on the Exonerated Five."

"I expected that," Dylan quipped.

"I'm not all social action and documentaries. I enjoy a good horror movie every now and then."

"Really? What else are you watching?"

"A series on prison reform."

"I figured as much."

Ivy told Dylan enough about Carter for her to know that he was the textbook definition of woke. That was one of the things that made her interested to meet him. She did want to pick his brain but not at that moment. She wanted to find out what else there was to him. What gave him pleasure in life? What did he do for entertainment? Was he buttoned up or easygoing? She didn't expect to uncover all of that on the first date, but she surely wanted to find out some of what made him tick.

"Okay," he continued, "a few weeks ago I binged the last season of *The Office*."

Dylan feigned surprise. "Is that so?"

"I used to watch regularly when it was still on the air but didn't see the last season. It's a great show."

"I've never watched."

This time Carter was surprised, and he wasn't pretending. "How is it possible that you've never watched one of the greatest shows on television?"

"Isn't that a bit of a stretch?"

"No, I'm serious. The show is hilarious. It's funny but it's smart."

"I guess I missed the boat."

"It's not too late. It's on streaming."

"I don't know. I'm not going to be able to watch all those seasons."

"Give it a try. A few episodes at least. Maybe we can watch it together."

"You've already watched."

"The show is *that* good. You can watch episodes again and again."

Dylan shrugged. "I don't know . . ."

"I see you need convincing. We can start with one episode and if you don't like it, I won't mention it again."

"Okay, I can agree to that."

The waiter interrupted their banter. Carter placed the drink order and included a couple of appetizers. The gesture didn't go unnoticed by Dylan. She liked that he took the lead. However, she quickly scanned the appetizer list to make sure what he ordered was something she would even eat. She didn't want any escargot to show up on the table. Regardless of what they were called, they were still fancy snails in her book.

Carter placed his menu on the table. "I was a little thrown when Ivy asked if I would like to meet a friend."

Dylan looked down at her menu. "Why is that?"

"Well, we've known each other for years and never really discussed our dating lives. I didn't imagine she would even think of me for one of her friends."

She maintained her air of preoccupation with the dinner offerings. "I suppose when a whim hits Ivy, she runs with it."

"I'm glad she did." Carter gazed across the table at Dylan. "Do you see anything you like?"

Dylan finally looked up now that he had moved away from the subject of being set up. She focused on that skin and those eyebrows again. "Yes, I see a couple of things that I like very much."

"Everything here is delicious. You can't go wrong."

"I hope you're right."

ELEVEN

$\mathcal{I}$ vy refilled her friends' margarita glasses. They were in their paja-mas lounging in her living room. Music played softly in the back-ground while the television, tuned to CNN, was on mute. Brooke was perched on the floor with her legs in lotus position, glass in hand. Dylan was on the loveseat with one leg thrown over the armrest.

It had been a week since their first dates. They were eager to get together to discuss how the first week of the program had gone. Ivy suggested a sleepover at her place. It had been a long time since they'd had a girls' night in and even longer since they'd had a slumber party. They ordered in Thai food—Brooke had vetoed pizza insisting there were too many carbs—and Ivy made a big batch of margaritas. Dylan threatened that if anyone—meaning Brooke—had a problem with the margaritas, they were going to get locked out on the balcony. Brooke had put her hands up in surrender and was already on her third drink now.

"These are perfect," Dylan mused. "The right balance of tart and tequila."

"Definitely tequila," reveled Brooke with a giggle.

"Drink up, ladies, there's plenty more." Ivy placed the pitcher on the coffee table and settled back down on the couch.

"So . . . how were your first dates?"

"How was yours?" Ivy said, mimicking Dylan's curiosity.

Dylan smiled. "Carter was a really nice guy. We had a good time together."

Ivy squealed. "I knew you would like him!"

"I thought the evening was off to a bit of a shaky start because I was late getting to the lecture—"

"You two went to a lecture for your first date?" Brooke asked, wrinkling her nose.

"If you let me finish . . . that was the *first* part of the date. We went to dinner afterward."

"That's my boy," Ivy chimed in.

"Okay, Ivy. You don't have to be the cheerleader on the sideline." Dylan chuckled. "As I was saying, initially, I was a little nervous because I showed up late and didn't want to make a bad first impression. Especially since we all agreed to be mindful of the relationships that we have with these guys. So, when I finally arrived and I saw how chill and understanding he was about my tardiness, it helped me to relax. We went to dinner, had very nice conversation, a couple of drinks, and we even shared dessert."

"Who cares about dessert. Did you share anything else?" Brooke asked.

"Like what?"

"Don't be coy. Did you kiss? Go back to his place?"

"Go back to his place? What kind of question is that?" Dylan replied.

"You know Dylan better than that. She did not go back to Carter's house," Ivy said with a laugh. "However, I did invite Daveed back to mine."

Brooke and Dylan couldn't keep the surprise off their faces. "Do tell . . ."

"The man is gorgeous. We spent hours chatting in the park. After a while, he suggested we go to a wine bar that he loves."

"He does love his wine," Brooke commented.

"I noticed. He was extremely knowledgeable about wine varietals, regions, pairings, and such. We ordered a charcuterie and cheese board and talked and laughed . . ." Ivy had stars in her eyes as she reminisced on her evening.

Brooke prodded her along. "And, then you both ended up here, how?"

"We held hands as we walked back to my place. Daveed is such a gentleman that he insisted on seeing me to my door and I invited him in."

Dylan and Brooke waited in suspense. "And . . . ?"

"And he said no because it was getting late."

Dylan rolled her eyes. "Oh, brother."

"But we shared the sweetest kiss, and I can't wait to see him again."

"Suppose he agreed to come in, what were you planning to do?"

"I wasn't *planning* to do anything, Brooke. I just didn't want the evening to end."

"Sounds like a good first date to me," Dylan said.

"It was."

"I wish I could say the same, ladies, but unfortunately—"

Dylan started shaking her head. "Oh no."

"There just wasn't a love connection," Brooke continued.

"It was only a first date. There isn't supposed to be a love connection. You're supposed to be taking it slow and exploring the possibilities."

Immediately Dylan started to wonder what could have happened. She knew her friend and how closed off she could be. She also knew Vincent was a good catch and she hoped that Brooke had given him a fair chance.

"Let me start by saying that Vincent is a really nice guy."

"*But,*" Dylan added impatiently.

"But, it just didn't feel right." Brooke took a sip from her glass. "We made dinner plans and he wanted to surprise me with where we were going. I figured it would be some trendy spot in the city, which was fine with me. Well, I was completely wrong. He wanted to dine at some restaurant that he said had the most beautiful view of the sunset. He picked me up at four in the afternoon, which I thought was a bit early for dinner in the city, but I didn't say anything. Well, once we got on the road, he told me that the restaurant was in the Hudson Valley region—a three-hour drive."

Ivy giggled. "I guess that gave you plenty of time to chat with one another."

Brooke gave Ivy a pointed look. "Three hours? That's a road trip."

"Were you being open-minded or did you shut down after you heard how far you had to drive to get there?" Dylan said.

"I hadn't shut down . . . yet. He went on and on about the sunset and how the restaurant was on the water and the food was absolutely amazing. So, I tried to be positive. Now, I want you to know I was dressed to the nines in a tight black dress, four-inch heels, and wearing just enough perfume to massage his senses. When I opened my front door, I thought he looked a little underdressed, a tad casual, but I told myself maybe his attire just wasn't as dressy as mine."

"Vincent is usually a great dresser," Dylan said. "I can't imagine him showing up any ol' kind of way."

"I didn't say he looked like a bum. I'm just saying that his attire compared to my outfit . . . Well, there was just no comparison. So, here I am on an unplanned road trip, in a tight dress and high heels—"

"You're repeating—"

"Okay, let me finish."

Dylan quieted down and let Brooke talk. It was her story to tell, and she didn't want to take anything she was saying about Vincent personally.

"Our conversation on the drive was all right. We talked a lot about our work. We talked about you for a while, Dylan. We talked about past relationships." Brooke sighed for effect. "The past relationship conversation went on for too long. He got into a lot of specifics about why his past situations didn't work. If you ask me, I think he was the cause of the breakups."

Dylan held her tongue. As much as she wanted to chime in to ask whether Brooke was nitpicking, she didn't. She wasn't on the date with them and until she spoke to Vincent, if she dared to bring it up, she would take Brooke at her word.

"Are you sure you weren't being too critical of him?" Ivy asked.

Dylan wanted to hug Ivy for asking the question. She waited eagerly for the response.

"Absolutely not. Don't get me wrong. He's a nice guy. All I'm saying is that he's not for me. We get to the restaurant and he's right about the scenery. It was beautiful. However, we walk inside and everyone in there looks like they're either on a camping, hunting, or fishing trip."

Ivy burst out in a fit of laughter and it egged Brooke on.

"I mean they're wearing coonskin hats, waders—you know, the pants fishermen wear to stand in the water—and plaid shirts."

Dylan couldn't hold back. "You're exaggerating."

Brooke held her hand up in dramatic fashion and crossed her heart. "I promise you I'm not. The entire time we were dining I'm thinking why on earth didn't he tell me I was overdressed? He could have told me as soon as I answered the door."

"How was the food?"

"Lots of fresh fish on the menu."

Brooke and Ivy shared a hearty laugh. Dylan sipped her drink silently. She was annoyed. She wanted Brooke to like Vincent and wasn't keen on the idea that she had set her friend up on a bad date.

Brooke noticed Dylan wasn't appreciating the humor of her story. "It's okay, Dylan. We knew that not every date would be a success. That's why we have a *list* of referrals. I'm ready to move on to the next man on my list."

Dylan nodded. "Well how did your road trip end?"

Brooke smiled at her friend. "On the ride home, we listened to some music and I nodded off."

"Oh goodness," Dylan lamented.

"Even though my date with Vincent wasn't the best, the concept of what we're doing, and the fact that I have more options, is encouraging."

Ivy raised her glass. "Cheers to that."

TWELVE

*D*ylan sat at her desk watching the clock. It wasn't quite nine in the morning, and she was doing her best to wait until the top of the hour to make her call. She fought the urge over the weekend, but it was first thing Monday morning, and she was losing the battle. She had to know what happened.

She pressed the speaker button and dialed. Vincent answered on the first ring. Dylan started talking immediately. "Was it a terrible idea for me to set you up on a blind date?"

A warm laugh emanated from the speaker. "Not at all. I thoroughly enjoyed meeting Brooke. She's an engaging woman. I get the sense she wasn't as taken with me."

Dylan searched for the right words. "You know I think the world of you."

He laughed again. "And I appreciate that. Listen, I have to run into a meeting. Let's do lunch soon."

"I'll be in touch."

"Again, thanks for thinking of me."

Dylan tapped the speaker button to end the call. She could have pried to hear Vincent's side of the story but decided to let sleeping dogs lie. Vincent seemed fine and their relationship was intact. She came to the realization that if his unsuccessful date with Brooke would have impacted their friendship, then they didn't have much of a friendship to begin with.

She wanted Brooke to have a successful first date like she and

Ivy had. Brooke was the most skeptical of the three. Dylan didn't want her to become discouraged with the process or to abandon it altogether. She dialed Ivy on the phone.

"Good morning, my sister," Ivy sang.

"You're in an awfully good mood this morning."

"I guess I am. I have plans with Daveed this evening and I'm looking forward to seeing him."

"Wow, that's good news."

"Yes, it is. What about you? Have you spoken to Carter?"

"We texted back and forth over the weekend, but we haven't made any plans yet."

"Don't let your usual busy routine get in the way of the program."

"I know, I won't."

"Make sure."

"You have my word," Dylan promised. "In fact, that's why I'm calling. I want to make sure we keep Brooke involved in the Referral Program. We need to get her connected with the next guy on her list. It'll be your referral this time."

"No worries. I've already reached out to my cousin, Sebastian. He's a great guy and I'm not just saying that because he's family."

"Okay, as long as we have a plan. Did you tell Brooke that Sebastian will be in touch?"

"I'm going to call her as soon as we hang up."

"Perfect. I'll talk to you later and enjoy your date tonight."

"Thanks, and you reach out to Carter."

"I will."

Dylan hung up and reclined in her chair. She knew she should take her own advice. She sent Carter a text asking if he was free for lunch. He texted back immediately with apologies that he was booked but invited her to come over in the evening to watch *The Office*. Dylan typed **No, thank you** then deleted it. She retyped **Sure, what time?** and stared at her phone for a moment, then hit send.

They texted back and forth for a few minutes, finalizing their plans. Dylan reminded herself that the Referral Program was supposed to get her out of her comfort zone. It was time to do things differently and try new approaches. That's what she intended to do . . . later. She had a busy day ahead and plenty of work waiting for her attention. She'd immerse herself in the program later on.

THIRTEEN

$\mathcal{B}$rooke did a double take. She shifted her sunhat back from her eyes so she could see clearly over the fence. She placed her basket of vegetables down and put a hand on her hip.

"Ivy? Is that you?" she called out.

Ivy waved and strolled over to the fence, beaming. "Hey, girl."

"Hey, girl? You're next door and didn't even call to tell me?"

Ivy swatted at Brooke trying to get her to lower her voice. "I didn't think you were home. You're usually at the gym at this time. Plus, I didn't want Daveed to think I couldn't come see him without being joined at your hip."

Brooke shook her head. "You sound crazy. He knows we're friends. *I* introduced you."

"Of course he does. But, *he* invited me to come over for dinner. I don't want him to think you two are a package deal."

"What does that even mean?"

"Meaning if I come to see him, I don't want him thinking that I'll be at your house spending time, or you'll be coming to his house to see me."

"You are creating quite a scenario in your head right now."

Ivy lowered her voice. "Don't worry about what I'm doing. Focus on your progress in the program. Did my cousin call you?"

"Yes, he called me," she said, intentionally raising her voice.

"Shhhhh!" Ivy said, swatting at Brooke again.

Brooke started to laugh. "He's not even out here and has no idea what we're talking about."

"I want to keep it that way. So, get back over there and pick your vegetables, Farmer John." Ivy started walking away from the fence.

"You have some nerve," Brooke shouted through giggles.

"Love you," Ivy called back.

Daveed came out of the house and waved to Brooke. "Don't forget to leave me some goodies."

She almost retorted with something about Ivy and her goodies but decided against it. "You just make sure you have my wine."

"I always do," he said with a smile.

Daveed and Ivy wandered inside his house, leaving Brooke scratching her head. This felt weird. Ivy was next door and didn't bother to let her know. Even if she was at the gym, she could have told her that she would be in her neck of the woods. There's no way Daveed would mind if either of them wanted to say hello to each other. Brooke picked up her basket and returned to her garden. As she plucked tomato after tomato, she couldn't shake the strange feeling of seeing her friend next door. All Ivy had to do was call, or even text for that matter, to let her know what was up. Brooke couldn't imagine being in Ivy's neighborhood without telling her.

Brooke gathered the rest of the vegetables that were ready to be harvested. She almost didn't leave Daveed anything, but knew that would be a petty move to spite Ivy for her behavior. She left his favorites on his side of the fence, as she always did, and then headed inside. She dialed Dylan to tell her about Ivy but got her voice mail. She didn't bother to leave a message.

FOURTEEN

$\mathcal{D}$ylan watched Carter having the time of his life out of her peripheral vision. He hadn't stopped laughing since he started the episode of *The Office*. She was mildly entertained, but he was over the moon about the show. He kept pausing the episode to explain who the characters were and give background on their quirky personalities. Dylan started to feel like she was in her own episode and was ready to do her own on-camera confessional about the date.

After the first episode, Carter asked if she wanted to watch the next one. When she said no, he looked surprised. "Don't tell me you didn't think that was hilarious."

"Okay, I won't tell you."

"Seriously?"

"Seriously."

"Your funny bone must be broken."

"And you must have more than one."

"Well, there's that wit Ivy told me about, so I know you have a sense of humor."

"It's not that it wasn't funny. I just don't think it's my type of funny," she said, attempting to let him know that she didn't hate his show.

"Fine. What's your type of funny? I'll put it on."

"You don't have to do that. We could just talk . . ."

"Nope. Tell me something you find funny, and we'll watch that."

67

"It's really not that deep," Dylan said with a chuckle.

"Oh, it is to me. You've insulted my show and now you have to give me a chance to reciprocate." Carter rolled up his sleeves intimating that he was ready for a challenge. He went to the main menu on the streaming service. "It's on now. Pick something."

They both laughed as he continued to prod Dylan.

"Fine. Put on season two of *Martin*. The episode when he goes to court to fight a traffic ticket."

"*Martin?*"

"Yes, *Martin*."

"I'm already disqualifying you from this challenge for suggesting a thirty-year-old show."

"A thirty-year-old *classic* show."

Carter shook his head. "You're right. Maybe we should just talk."

Dylan snickered. "Agreed."

"Can I refresh your wine?" he asked, motioning to Dylan's almost empty glass.

"I'm good, thanks."

He topped off his glass and then poured the remaining last drops into Dylan's. Puzzlement washed over her face.

"There was only a drop left and my glass was full," he said, responding to her wordless expression.

That was an overstep, Dylan thought to herself. At that moment something Brooke said popped into her head. She said something about Vincent *just didn't feel right*. She pushed the thought away.

Carter turned off the television and turned on his electric fireplace. Dylan was always curious about them. She didn't know anyone who actually had one, until now. "Setting the mood for some intense conversation?" she quipped.

"It's not quite the real thing, but the ambiance it sets is close."

"And what vibe are you going for right now?"

"One that fosters meaningful discussion."

Dylan wondered if she would've been better off watching *The Office*. "The floor is yours."

"Tell me, Ms. Dylan, what are you looking for in a man?"

It's going to be one of *those* talks, she thought. "My instinct wants to respond to your question with a question."

"What question is that?" he replied.

"Why do I have to be *looking for* a man?"

"The independent woman's retort."

"True."

"I'm going to ask that you not follow your instinct and answer the question I asked."

Dylan took a sip of her wine, letting his question hang in the air. "I guess in a way, we're all looking for someone either consciously or subconsciously."

Carter pivoted on the sofa to face Dylan. "Please, go on."

"Of course, this is my opinion. Essentially, depending on your age or stage in life you seek different things. A relationship or a partner has varying levels of importance at different times in your life. You might be young and in love, committed to someone with passionate fervor, or young and living your best single life. You might be middle-aged and single, wanting to be loved or in denial about it because you haven't connected with the right person. And, though you're saying you are fine with being single, your soul is aching for a mate. You also might be middle-aged and scarred from past hurts and bad relationships and want nothing to do with love. Or just maybe, somewhere deep down inside, your subconscious is crying out for someone to love the hurt away. Maybe you're in your senior years and have been with the same person for decades and on a good day, you appreciate the years you've put in together. On a bad day, that same person makes you want to pull your hair out at the roots, and you feel you can't go on another day with them. Maybe you speculate what it would be like to be with someone new after all those years."

"Where do you fall on the conscious or subconscious spectrum?"

"Until recently, I wavered between the two. Sometimes I told myself I didn't need anyone and if there was someone out there for me, then they would find me."

"And other times, what did you tell yourself?" he asked solemnly.

"That love wasn't going to come knocking on my door."

"Subconsciously, you're always looking?"

"Looking . . . or maybe wanting is more accurate," Dylan said pensively. "You want that special someone whether you're actively looking or not. Whether you're acknowledging it or not."

"So regardless of what stage you're at and the level of importance you place on it, the heart always has its way."

Dylan shrugged. "Or tries to."

"This is what you truly believe?"

"These are my thoughts today, in this moment. Tomorrow I might think something completely different."

"Your ideology shifts that frequently?"

"Beliefs are supposed to change, evolve. Don't yours?"

Carter shook his head. "Not when it comes to matters of the heart."

"What do you believe?"

"I believe you know whether you want to be with someone, or in a relationship, or married. At a bare minimum, I believe you know whether you're looking for someone to date."

"It's just that black-and-white, huh?" Dylan asked facetiously.

"For me it is. I don't fool myself or try to convince myself that I don't want or need someone in my life. Whether I have someone or not, I'm cognizant of what I want."

"I guess you're just woke in every aspect of your life."

Carter frowned. "You make that sound like a negative. A Black man who knows what he wants is a detriment these days?"

"That's not what I meant, Carter."

"Not having the same ideology doesn't make either of us wrong."

"No, it doesn't. However, you insinuated that I'm fooling myself if I think I don't need a man."

"I stand by that. Every woman needs a man, and every man needs a woman."

Dylan resisted pointing out the obvious flaw in his argument— entire demographics that don't classify as heterosexual. Instead, she looked at her watch and opted for a more conclusive and neutral response. "This has indeed been an engaging discussion, but it's getting late. I have to be in the office early tomorrow. Thanks for the wine, television, and eye-opening conversation."

Carter seemed surprised by the abrupt end to their evening. "I'm sorry you have to go so soon."

"Yes, it's getting late," she repeated. "Early day tomorrow . . ."

Carter walked Dylan to the door. He replayed what transpired in his head and wondered if he came on too strong. He leaned in close and she gave him her cheek to kiss. Feeling at a loss for words he kept it simple. "I had a nice time."

Dylan looked over her shoulder as she left his apartment. "Thanks, again. Take care."

In that moment, as she walked to her car, there was one thing she knew definitively. That did not feel right.

FIFTEEN

$\mathcal{B}$rooke decided to take control of her first date with Sebastian. After the road trip debacle with Vincent, she was not going to let Seb settle on the location for their first meeting. She was fully aware that she was dealing with Ivy's family and was making a conscious effort to go into this date with an open mind. However, she wasn't interested in another dinner date. She opted for something a lot more hands-on.

Sebastian was standing out front as she approached the art studio. Ivy didn't lie. Her cousin was Brooke's type and a sight to behold. Over six feet, chiseled in all the right places, an inviting smile that bordered on mischievous and a burnt caramel complexion that looked like he spent a few weeks on the islands. She couldn't stop herself from smiling when she extended her hand.

He pulled her into a warm hug. "Hey, Brooke."

"Hey," she replied, matching his familiarity.

When he pulled away, she almost asked for another hug. They stood on the sidewalk sizing each other up as others walked past them and into the art studio.

"Ivy described you perfectly," he said.

"She's been one of my best friends for a long time."

"She told me. I'm surprised we haven't met until now."

"I know," she said, taking him in again from head to toe.

He flashed a smile and motioned toward the door. "Shall we?"

Brooke snapped out of her reverie and nodded. Seb held open

the door and she walked inside. She had signed them up for a paint and sip class. When she told Sebastian what she had in mind, he told her he wasn't familiar with the paint and sip experience. She explained that it was basically a painting lesson with alcoholic beverages. He thought it sounded fun and was looking forward to the class.

There were two empty seats near the back. Brooke didn't mind because she intended to chat throughout the lesson. She didn't want to encroach on anyone else's experience with her and Sebastian's chatter. As the instructor's assistant distributed the paint supplies, Brooke took the opportunity to find out a bit more about Sebastian.

"A lot of the paint and sip classes serve only wine. When I called to book this class, the assistant told me they have a full bar available. What's your poison?"

"I'm a Black and soda kind of man."

"Scotch." *A manly drink for a manly man*, she thought.

He nodded. "You look like you enjoy a nice merlot."

"I do enjoy a nice red, but I also like a good tequila."

"Tequila," he said, eyebrows raised. "Okay."

Brooke chuckled. "In moderation, of course."

"Of course," he echoed.

"I have to tell you, I've been extremely curious ever since Ivy told me you're a motivational speaker. What types of speeches do you give and to whom?"

"I help all kinds of people with all kinds of challenges in their lives. My speeches vary, but the basic tenet is being your best self. The motivational speeches are only one part of what I do. I have my PhD in psychology and my own practice."

Brooke's stomach fluttered. Helping people to be their best selves was at the core of what she did every single day. She willed her butterflies to be still. She wasn't even an hour into her date and there was still much to learn before she'd allow the butterflies to take flight.

"I'm a physical therapist and personal trainer and can relate to helping people with their wellness."

"People are increasingly in need of assistance with their mental and physical health. It's great that you're in the trenches doing the work."

"Thank you for that. I'm pretty assertive when it comes to my career and personal life. I've spent most of my post-college life helping people with injuries regain their strength and mobility. Two years ago, an opportunity to become a partner in a local gym became available and I added entrepreneur to my résumé."

"It sounds like you do a lot."

"It's not easy juggling two careers, but I make it work. I enjoy helping people improve their health and transform their bodies."

"How much time does that leave for a personal life, in particular, dating? I'm asking for a friend."

Brooke smiled. "As I said, I make it work."

She made time for occasional dalliances, but not much more. Brunch with Dylan and Ivy was the only social obligation on Brooke's calendar from month to month.

"Keep up the good work transforming lives and bodies."

"I'd be remiss if I didn't acknowledge that you apparently have some sort of routine yourself," she said, taking him in again.

"Oh, definitely. Four times a week."

"It shows."

"If you don't mind my saying, I couldn't help notice that you're in great shape."

Brooke smiled. "I don't mind and thanks."

A server interrupted their chatter to take their drink orders. Brooke was surprised Sebastian ordered a club soda, no alcohol. She was going to inquire why but decided not to pry. If he wanted to share, then he would. Brooke ordered a glass of Malbec and prepared to segue into her next line of questions.

Sebastian beat her to it. "Is this your first painting lesson? I mean am I sitting beside the next Picasso?"

"Hardly," she replied with a giggle. "I've been to one other paint and sip, and I tossed the end product in the back of a closet."

"That bad?"

"Worse."

Sebastian's laugh gave Brooke goose bumps. It emanated from him like it originated down deep in his soul. "I should probably tell you that in undergrad, I minored in art."

Brooke shook her head. "It figures."

A broad smile spread across his face. "I'm kidding. You shouldn't expect much out of me. I'm not artistic."

Brooke giggled. "Just have fun with it."

The instructor took his place in the front of the room and unveiled the piece the class would be painting. It was a golden sunset reflecting off the rolling waves of the ocean.

Sebastian pointed at the canvas. "We're supposed to paint that?" He threw his hands up in mock defeat. "I just hope you don't judge me by my finished product."

"I won't judge."

"You must be a church girl."

"I was raised in the church but weren't we all?"

"Back in the day it was more common. My grandmother had me in church every Sunday and on Wednesdays for Bible school. She wanted to keep me out of trouble." Seb dipped his brush in the paint and imitated the instructor, stroking the canvas with a touch of golden yellow. "My parents never went to church. I think my grandmother saw her second chance to get it right with me."

"What's your church home?"

"I'm almost ashamed to say that I don't have one. I haven't been to church in years. I do watch online occasionally," he said, with a wink.

"Don't be ashamed. I know it's no excuse, but my work hours are so crazy that on Sundays I'm at home relaxing. I attend church only once in a while these days. God knows my heart."

"Amen, Sister Brooke."

Brooke chuckled at Sebastian's levity. She was trying to be in the moment and not get absorbed by her inner thoughts, but she was enjoying herself. It was a completely different experience to the one she had with Vincent. She scolded herself for even thinking of Vincent and comparing him to Seb. She had the rest of the date to get through. Anything could happen, good or bad. She glanced over at Sebastian intently working on his painting. She liked what she saw.

"I think the instructor said to mix the orange and yellow for that section of the sky," she told him when she saw him going for too much orange.

"Good catch, thanks." Sebastian blended the colors on his palette. "I couldn't help noticing that besides the instructor, I'm the only male in this class. Is that coincidence or by design?"

"I don't know why, but it seems that the paint and sips appeal primarily to women."

"The events might need a bit of rebranding. They can start with the name."

"What's wrong with paint and sip?"

"How many men do you know that say they're sipping on wine?"

Brooke thought about it for a moment. "I guess that's true."

"Men taste, guzzle, or even down our drinks. I bet the interest would be higher if the events were called draft and draft. Draft as in beer and draft as in drawing."

"That's awful."

"Wow, you're harsh. How about sketch and taste?"

Brooke made a face that said she wasn't convinced. "That's a *little* better."

"All right. I've got it. Paint and party. That says it all."

"It says something," Brooke said, with a laugh.

Sebastian gazed at Brooke for a moment while she painted. He wondered why his cousin hadn't introduced them sooner. Brooke was intelligent, beautiful, knew how to joke, and devoted herself to helping others. He wanted to know more about the intriguing lady sitting beside him. He noticed, from the moment he walked in, some of the other women in the class were checking him out. He didn't care. Brooke had his unwavering attention. He hadn't always been that type of man. In his younger days, he would've been looking right back, trying to figure out if there was a way to get a few numbers. He was only on a first date, after all. But with age, and a past peppered with relationship drama, come maturity and discernment, and he had both in abundance. Sebastian was enjoying Brooke's company and didn't want the date to end too soon.

"So, Brooke, do you have anything else on the agenda for us after the class?"

Brooke hadn't planned anything other than the class. She wasn't expecting to be so taken with Sebastian. Her mind launched into overdrive, but she was coming up with nothing. "I was going to ask you if there was anything you wanted to do," she replied.

"There's a new vegan restaurant a few blocks from here. Would you like to have dinner with me?"

Brooke felt herself holding back a smile. "I would love to have dinner with you."

SIXTEEN

*I*vy was sprawled across her bed like a teenage girl. She was on the phone with Dylan and just connected Brooke to the call. They had agreed to check in midweek with their progress on the Referral Program. Ivy wanted to call earlier in the week but decided to wait so she'd have plenty of details to share with her girls.

Brooke was still at work and trying to clear her office in order to chat in private. It never failed. Anytime they had something pertinent to discuss, her partner wanted to hang around, droning on about something they had already covered extensively during a previous discussion. She finally shooed him out and was ready to debrief with Ivy and Dylan.

Ivy excitedly took the lead. "I trust everyone is having a good week."

"It's all right," Dylan said.

"Yup, all good," Brooke added.

"And I'm having a great time getting to know Daveed."

"You couldn't wait to get that out."

"Don't rain on my parade, Brooke."

"I'm not," Brooke rebutted.

"He has been . . . just . . . wonderful. We talk on the phone multiple times a day. Which in the beginning I was a little worried about because he prefers to text. But he calls throughout the day. We chat at night before bed. We've been on a few dates. He's been to my apartment. I've been to his house twice—"

78

"Twice?" Brooke asked incredulously.

"Yes, and both times he cooked for me."

"You mean to tell me that not once, but twice, you found yourself next door to me and didn't take the time to let me know you were in the neighborhood? Literally next door?"

"Remember the first time I saw you I explained that I didn't want to make it an issue. The last thing I want is for Daveed to think that you're involved in our situation just because we're friends."

"That's ridiculous, Ivy. If you were at my house, would you let Daveed know that you're next door?"

"That's different."

"Explain to me how."

Dylan butted in before the conversation went completely in the wrong direction. "Ladies, we're all going to need to adjust. We're used to communicating and doing things a certain way. Considering our individual relationships with these guys, we have to change it up. I can understand Ivy not wanting to make it seem as if she can't spend time with Daveed without coming to see you, Brooke. You have to cut her some slack. She's navigating this new situation and you know what our ultimate goal is."

"That doesn't mean Ivy can't send a text message or call before she even gets to Daveed's house."

"I know, but try not to take it personally if she doesn't."

"Fine," Brooke mumbled.

"How was your date with my cousin?" Ivy asked Brooke.

"I guess it's my turn to be evasive."

"Are you really going to be that petty?" Ivy asked.

"I couldn't even if I tried," Brooke giggled. "It was too good not to talk about."

Ivy squealed with delight. "I knew it! Sebastian is perfect for you."

"We've only gone on one date, but it had two parts. We went to a paint and sip and then had dinner at a new spot *he* suggested."

"No coonskin hats this time?" Dylan teased.

"Not one in sight. Ivy, Sebastian is a charming guy. And I don't always use 'charming' as a compliment. There are too many slicksters out there feigning charm. Sebastian was a real charmer. We talked and laughed for hours. We basically closed down the restaurant. He has such a positive outlook on life. I'm sure he can motivate anyone to do anything."

"And what did he motivate you to do after you left the restaurant?"

"Dylan, get your mind out of the gutter. It was a perfect first date. We chatted about our upbringings, goals, the challenges of running our own businesses, and fitness . . . I was telling him that I'm considering running the New York City Marathon and he said he might want to start training for it, too."

"I'm so glad to hear that. Dylan and I were a little worried after your date with Vincent. We thought you might bail on the program."

"Any objections I had were before we started. I'm committed to the program now."

Ivy sighed with relief. She knew her friend well. It took prodding to get her to do something she wasn't sure about and if it didn't go her way, forget it. She would never look back. Sebastian was a decent man. He was raised right and tried his best to live right. She crossed her fingers that Brooke would give him a chance. Sometimes the slightest thing would turn her off from someone. She hoped that Brooke saw enough in Seb to make exploring the possibilities with him worth the effort. Ivy wanted to see them both happy.

"I'm committed, too, but, Ivy, it's not going to work with Carter."

Ivy sprang up on the bed. "No! Why not?"

"To borrow a line from Brooke . . . it just didn't feel right."

"Did he do something?"

"I wanted to like him, but we didn't click. I got the sense that there was no middle ground with him. It was either one extreme or the other."

"Can you give an example?" Brooke asked.

"Well, he was super woke—which is fine, of course. Yet, he didn't have an intrinsic understanding that there are nuances when it comes to matters of the heart. He seemed like he could be extremely judgmental if you weren't operating on the same frequency as him."

"On to the next," Brooke chirped.

"My next guy is your referral, Brooke."

"I know, and I think this will be a good match for you. I've known Barrett since kindergarten. We lived around the corner from each other and literally grew up together. We went to the same schools from kindergarten until the twelfth grade. His family was like an extension of my own and vice versa."

"I'll do my best to behave for your childhood friend," Dylan said giggling. "Remind me what he does for a living?"

"He's the attorney."

"Oh, right."

"A divorce attorney."

"I'm looking for a husband and he specializes in divorces. That's depressing."

"There's something else you should know, but I don't want you to hold it against him."

"You're starting off with a caveat? What is it?"

"He's also a divorcé."

"Seriously, Brooke, a divorcé? You know how I feel about that," Dylan griped.

"I do but hear me out. He was only married for a little over a year, a very long time ago. He doesn't have any children and, as far as I can tell, no residual baggage. He's not anti-marriage or anything resembling that. He's a good guy, Dylan. You know I wouldn't refer him if he wasn't."

Dylan sighed. "Okay. I guess I'll be giving the divorcé a try."

"His name is Barrett and he's not defined by his divorce."

"That's fair," Ivy offered. "Dylan, remember we have to be open."

"Yeah, yeah. I know. I already said I'd be on my best behavior."

"That's all we can ask. Right, Brooke?"

"Right, Ivy."

SEVENTEEN

*I*vy snuggled closer to Daveed. They were watching a movie at her place and deciding whether they wanted to order in or go out for dinner. In a short time, they had fallen into a routine. Daily text messages, long evening phone calls, and time spent together a few times a week. They enjoyed walks in the park, eating at sidewalk cafés, outdoor concerts, reading excerpts from some of Ivy's favorite books, and loafing on the couch together. Ivy was getting Daveed back into the habit of reading books other than his technology manuals. He was ensuring that she was a bit more tech savvy and alert regarding cyber risks. Ivy was basking in the newness of it all and relishing the level of comfort they had with one another.

She was grateful for the Referral Program. It opened her up to an entirely different way of approaching the dating game. She wanted her friend's referral to be the one for her like it might have been in the old days. Every night she prayed that she wouldn't have to go back to the list. She wanted her first referral to be her only referral. Brooke and Dylan didn't hit it off with their first referrals. They went back to the list and started again. Ivy realized that having a list of referrals made it a little easier not to languish in a situation that wasn't a right fit. Both of her girls decided it didn't feel right and moved on immediately. There was no going back and forth or dating for months before ending the situation. Ivy knew firsthand that it wasn't uncommon to stay with the wrong person for too long, just because you didn't have anyone else. Ivy remembered the days when she would date someone out of boredom because she didn't have anything else to do or wanted some masculine company. Dylan had done the same. They both brushed it off as if it were nothing. Brooke was different. She would rather stay home alone before she went out with someone who didn't meet her standards. Ivy admired that about her. She always wanted to get to the place where her own company was enough. Ivy thought maybe she wasn't cut from that cloth. She enjoyed being in the company of a man, even at times when she knew he wasn't the right one. She peered up at Daveed from the crook of his arm and prayed he was the right one. It was still early, and Ivy knew better than to rush it, but she said the prayer anyway. *Let this be the one.*

Daveed looked down at Ivy. "What are you smiling about?"

Ivy hadn't realized that he was watching her. She was almost inclined to tell a half-truth, but she was working on sharing and being more transparent. "This."

"Care to elaborate?"

"I was smiling at this moment—sitting on the couch—watching a movie with you. It reminded me of my parents, before the divorce, when they still liked each other."

"When did they get divorced?"

"My freshman year of college and it challenged everything I knew about relationships, love, and marriage."

"In what way?"

"I had watched my mother take care of our family, putting everyone else above herself, especially my father. Sure, there were things I wasn't privy to but, on the outside looking in, my mother catered to us. She gave one hundred percent to making sure we had everything we needed."

"It's tough for children to truly know what goes on in their parents' marriage."

"I know that now, but when my parents split, it was difficult to adjust to their new dynamic. I still had a wonderful relationship with both my mother and father, but they were separate and no longer shared."

"How did it affect you, especially being in college?"

"It took some years for me to process. Only after a breakup of my own did I realize that I had been detached on some level in all my previous relationships."

"That's understandable after seeing your mother give her all and it not be enough."

"I carried their stuff with me into my relationships."

Ivy had mirrored the doting and borderline smothering she'd witnessed growing up. She provided an ear if her ex wanted to vent and a comforting shoulder when he needed support. What she didn't do was acknowledge that he was ready and willing to do the same for her. She didn't use his broad shoulders to help bear the weight she was carrying. She didn't use him as a sounding board to resolve any issues. She prodded him to be open with her but didn't do the same in return. Through her introspection Ivy understood she wasn't enough and too much at the same time. She swore she would do everything in her power to not repeat her past behavior.

"Are you still toting their stuff around?"

"I don't believe so. I've had time to work through it."

Daveed moved Ivy's hair back and kissed her on the forehead. "Thank you for sharing that with me."

"I'm trying to do better."

"Did you decide if you want to go out to eat?"

"We have been inside all day. Maybe we should get some fresh air."

"If that's what you want."

"Is that what you want?" Ivy purred, not moving an inch.

"I want whatever you want." He placed another kiss on her forehead.

Ivy craned her neck and puckered her lips. Daveed leaned down, his mouth softly touching hers. She playfully kissed and nibbled his lips. Her right hand cradled his face, holding him close to her.

Daveed pulled away. "Let's order in."

Ivy giggled as she got up from the couch. "I'll grab some menus from the kitchen. Do you have a taste for anything?"

"Is that a trick question?"

Ivy stopped and looked over her shoulder. "It was a direct question. Do you have a direct answer?"

"I do but I'm trying to behave myself since we agreed to take things slow."

"We sure did," Ivy said, whimsically. "Maybe we need to get out of this apartment for a while before we start misbehavin'."

"I wouldn't mind a little misbehavin'."

Ivy returned to the couch and grabbed Daveed by the hand, pulling him up to stand in front of her. He wrapped his arms around her waist and began to place kisses on her face and neck.

"As amazing as that feels . . ." Ivy moaned. "As hypnotic as those light brown eyes of yours are . . . we are definitely going out to eat."

Daveed's arms dropped to his sides. "You win."

Ivy gave him a quick peck on the lips. "I always do."

◦   ◦   ◦

DAVEED GRABBED IVY'S hand as they exited her building's lobby and walked into the warmth of the late afternoon sun. He squeezed her hand. "I'm glad we came out. It's a beautiful day."

They headed toward the corner to cross the street. Tourists obliviously meandered on the sidewalk, blocking the paths of those trying to get to their destinations with purpose. Ivy wasn't in a hurry and, for once, did not mind the tourists. It didn't matter that she was on a busy city street. Strolling hand in hand with Daveed was like walking along the shore or promenading through the park. He gave her a sense of comfort and ease, a feeling of contentment. Ivy wanted this feeling to last.

On their third date, Ivy and Daveed decided to take sex off the table—for now. They acknowledged the power of sex to cloud judgment and hinder the process of truly getting to know someone. For now, they wanted to explore one another's values, beliefs, dreams, purpose, goals, and much more. They wanted to learn about each other on a spiritual level before taking things to a sexual one. Daveed and Ivy were honest with each other. They both had past experiences where they'd had sex too soon, with a person they barely knew. It wasn't something either was interested in at this stage in their lives. Though the attraction between them was palpable, they were waiting.

Daveed pointed down the block. "There's a street fair going on. I guess that explains the number of tourists today. We can cut through the park to avoid the congestion."

They walked in the direction of the park entrance. "A picnic would've been nice today. It's not too hot, there's a breeze, and it looks like the park is pretty empty because of the fair."

"If you weren't holding me hostage in the apartment, we could have done that."

"Nobody was holding you against your will." Ivy swatted Daveed's arm. "Let's not forget I had to force you to leave to get some food."

Daveed wrapped his arm around Ivy's shoulders, pulling her in close. "I know, babe."

Babe. That was the first time Daveed had called Ivy that. She beamed from the inside out. She could feel what was happening between them. A connection. It felt like the beginnings of something real.

"Did you decide whether you want sushi or barbecue?" she asked.

"I told you earlier. I want whatever you want."

EIGHTEEN

Dylan entered the Brooklyn Bowl expecting it to be relatively empty. She could not have been more wrong. As she walked through the crowd toward the lanes, she noticed a band setting up onstage. She hadn't bothered to check the website in advance to see if there was a show booked for the evening. She crossed her fingers that whoever it was, they would provide a nice background soundtrack while bowling.

Barrett had texted Dylan when she was five minutes away to let her know he had already arrived and secured a lane. She spotted him immediately by the canary yellow shirt he told her he would be wearing. *Not bad*, she thought. Dylan loved a man with a low cut Caesar and a goatee. Barrett looked like he had just paid his barber a visit. Though he was wearing jeans and a button-up, somehow Dylan could envision him in the courtroom donning an expensive, tailored suit.

She tucked one side of her hair behind her ear and approached him with her most dazzling smile. "Barrett?"

"Dylan, you made it." He reached out to shake her hand. Barrett had a firm grip and an intense gaze. He quickly studied her, taking care not to linger on any one area for too long. "I see you have your own ball, too."

"My own ball and shoes."

"You didn't tell me I would be bowling with a professional tonight," he chuckled.

"I'm not that good. Trust me. I just hate wearing the rented shoes."

"That makes me feel better. I'm warning you in advance that I'm a little rusty. I haven't bowled in about five years."

"I haven't been in about two, so this should be good."

Dylan and Barrett sat down while she changed into her bowling shoes.

"Did you have trouble finding a parking space?" he asked.

"I found a space a couple of blocks down. Did you have trouble?"

"No, I had my driver bring me."

Dylan silently acknowledged that he had his own driver. "I guess that explains why you beat me here. You didn't have to circle the block multiple times."

He laughed. "I arrived only a short time before you."

"I was surprised to see it's so packed."

"The attendant at the front desk told me there's a Prince tribute band tonight."

"Are you serious?"

"That's what he told me. Is that a good or a bad thing?"

"We'll see. It depends on the band. I happen to *love* Prince, so they better come correct."

"Oh, you're a real Prince fan."

"Die-hard. My first concert ever was a Prince concert. When the Welcome 2 America tour came to New York, I was at all four shows at Madison Square Garden."

"I regret never seeing him live in concert. Such a devastating loss . . ."

Dylan nodded. "There's no one like him. We'll see what this band can do. I don't want to have to boo them off the stage." She laughed but was only partially kidding.

Barrett seized on the moment. "I'm just hoping you won't boo me once you see my bowling skills. I got us set up on the screen. We can start when you're ready."

Dylan unpacked her glittering purple ball from her bowling bag and carried it over to the ball rack. She turned back toward Barrett. "Do I get a practice roll?"

"Absolutely," he said, with a dramatic motion toward the lane.

Dylan stepped forward, standing behind the foul line. She focused on the arrows down the lane, aligning her position. She released the ball, sending it sailing over the center arrow and the one to the right of it. The pins toppled over slowly with only two left standing. She spun around and clapped her hands. "Not bad after two years."

"Looks like I'm in trouble."

"Don't worry. I'll go easy on you."

Dylan's ball made its way back to the return. She repeated the process and managed to knock down one of the two pins.

Barrett smiled. "I thought you were going to pick up a spare."

Dylan walked back to their seats. "Now let's see what you're working with."

Barrett stood up and rubbed his hands together. "Remember, be kind." He picked up his ball, stepped over to the lane, and got into a stance. He stood still and silent for what seemed like a minute. In one swift motion, he extended his arm and sent the ball down the lane in a powerfully smooth release. The pins crackled as the ball made contact. All ten pins fell with force. Barrett pumped his fist. "Striiiike!"

"Someone has been bluffing," Dylan accused. "Are you sure it's been five years since you've bowled?" She put her hand up for a high five as Barrett returned to their seats.

"Honestly. It's been that long. I guess when you've got it, you got it."

Dylan felt her competitive spirit rising. "Okay," she said standing up. "I was going to go easy on you. Now, I'm taking the gloves off."

They bowled the next frames like they were old nemeses, neither giving an inch. Barrett was leading in the score by twenty points. Dylan was convinced she could catch up. As she got her second strike of the night, that unmistakable chord from one of Prince's most famous tunes blared out of the speakers. She looked toward the stage. The band was assembled and the crowd was already starting to go crazy.

She did a peppy two-step to the music on her way down from the lane. As Barrett made his way up, he joined her with a two-step of his own. Dylan couldn't hold back her giggles. They looked like two teenagers at a high school dance. He grabbed her hand, spinning her around and back again. "They don't sound too bad," he shouted over the music.

"They're all right."

"Just all right? You're a tough critic."

"When it comes to Prince's music, yes," she said.

Barrett freed Dylan's hand and started to play air guitar along with the song.

Dylan stood watching him, amused. "Guitar solos and dancing aren't going to stop me from beating you in this game."

"Did you check the score? I'm leading," he retorted.

"For now."

He pretended to toss his imaginary guitar to the side. "You're right. Let me get back to winning this game."

"Don't be so sure. I can easily overtake you."

Barrett made a face that said he wasn't concerned. "How about a friendly bet?" he asked.

"It depends on what we're betting."

"Okay. If I win the game, we abandon bowling and go over to the performance area to watch the rest of the concert."

"And, if you lose?"

"You get to decide what we do after bowling."

Dylan raised her eyebrows at the presumption. "After?"

When they made arrangements for the date, there was no discussion about doing anything after bowling. She wasn't offended, but she did wonder what he had in mind. One thing was clear, Barrett wanted to prolong the time they were spending together.

"Did I say something wrong?"

"How about this? If I win, we don't go to the concert area. Instead, we can sit here and chat, where we can hear the music, and get to know each other better."

Barrett nodded. "That's fair."

"I expected more of a debate out of a hotshot attorney."

"I reserve that behavior for the courtroom."

Barrett grabbed his ball so they could resume the game. The ball went flying into the gutter.

Dylan laughed and couldn't resist heckling him. "That's not how you win a bet."

His next ball followed the path of the first in the frame. Dylan cocked her head to the side and watched him as he returned to their seats. She gave him a suspicious look as she went to bowl her next frame. Seven pins fell and she picked up the spare. Barrett threw his ball with minimal effort, knocking down two pins. He looked at Dylan mischievously.

"I guess I lost my mojo," he said, with a shrug.

"Oh, knock it off. If you're just going to let me win, we can end the game now." She patted the seat next to her. "Come sit down and let's chat."

"Was I that obvious?" he asked, as he eased down on the leather seating.

"Clearly."

He chuckled. "Yeah, I figured but throwing the game was a win-win for me."

"As an attorney, I would imagine winning is a big deal to you."

"Doesn't everyone like to win?"

"I think people weigh it differently."

"Do you agree that most people hate to lose?"

"I don't know about *most* people, but do *you* hate losing?" she asked.

"I'm not accustomed to it."

"No one wins all the time."

"I do my best to put myself in a position to win."

"Yet, you just threw our game."

"I did. In order to position myself for this very moment—sitting next to a beautiful woman, having an engaging conversation."

Dylan blushed. "I was looking forward to beating you fair and square."

"So, I'm not the only one who likes to win."

"Oh, I can be extremely competitive."

"I'll keep that in mind."

"So, as a divorce attorney, how do you gauge the win?"

"What do you mean?"

"I mean is the win clear-cut when dealing with divorce? Is anyone truly a winner? There's a marriage ending, assets to divide, maybe custody issues . . ."

"I see," he said. "My job is to represent my client and ensure they come out in the best position possible. When I do that, it's a win. It's that simple."

"Seems more complicated than that."

"I skipped the intricacies in favor of a concise rationalization. Divorce isn't easy, but I make the process bearable and the outcome advantageous for my clients."

"Aside from your work, what are your personal feelings about divorce?"

"I think it's a necessary evil."

Dylan saw an opening and took it. She asked a question to which she already knew the answer. "Have you ever been married?"

Barrett hesitated, clearing his throat before responding. "Yes, I have."

"How long did it last?"

"Thirteen months."

"How long have you been divorced?"

"About twelve years. We were both in law school at the time. We were young, idealistic, and not prepared to function within the confines of a marriage. Add in the pressures of law school and it was a recipe for disaster."

"I can only imagine."

"What about you? Have you ever been married?"

Dylan hated being asked the marriage question by single men. However, she had opened that can of worms when she decided to question Barrett on something she already knew. So, it was only right that she respond in kind. She did her best to strike a balance of nonchalance and aspiration. It was tough to convey that it was no big deal that you aren't married but something you definitely want in your future. "I haven't but it's on my to-do list right along with seeing the Nazca Lines in the Peruvian desert."

Barrett didn't miss a beat. "You're intelligent and beautiful. I have to wonder why no one has snatched you up."

In most situations, that comment would have annoyed Dylan. It always felt as if the man asking was implying and trying to uncover what could be wrong with her. Given Barrett's openness with his past and the fact that he was an attorney and programmed to question, she wasn't offended.

"I think it has more to do with not finding the right person or maybe it was me not making time to find the right person. I focused more on my career and family and friends and didn't necessarily place finding a husband at the top of my list."

"I did hear you place it alongside of travel a few moments ago. You'll have to tell me more about those Nazca Lines a bit later." He chuckled.

Dylan appreciated his approach, laid-back but engaged. "I wouldn't rank marriage the same as travel. My point was that it's on the list. Where it's located on the list has changed over the years."

"I can relate. I turned thirty-five last month and I'm reevaluating my priorities—again. For so long, I have made my career the pinnacle of what success means for me. One day I looked around and thought about what else I've accomplished. I'm an only child and if I have to hear my mother tell me one more time that she wants grandchildren, I'm going to relocate to . . . what did you say . . . the Peruvian desert?"

Dylan laughed. "Yes."

"Yeah, well, I'm going to relocate to the Peruvian desert."

They shared a lighthearted moment. Dylan could completely relate to everything Barrett was saying. She, too, had focused on her career, spending most of her time building her company and making sure it was successful. Though there was a time Dylan thought she and her ex, Ace, would end up married, that wasn't their fate.

"Don't do that. I've only just met you," she said.

Barrett looked at Dylan intently. "I'll stay . . . for you."

He's smooth, Dylan thought. She decided to steer the discussion in another direction. "So, do you like to travel?"

"My passport has a few stamps in it."

"Where have you been most recently?"

"Italy, Paris, Argentina, Greece, and Bonaire."

"That's a lot of travel."

"I work hard and, lately, I've been taking time to *relax* even harder."

"I need to take a cue from you. I don't travel enough. The last real vacation I took was two years ago. I went to Cuba with a few friends."

"I do a lot of traveling on my own. It's not always easy to find traveling companions. And, not many people have the flexibility to travel as frequently as I do."

Dylan was beginning to wonder who this person was that Brooke had set her up with. Smart, successful, handsome, and worldly—he was checking all the boxes. Why hadn't she thought of the Referral Program years ago? There were quality men in their lives, men that they could have been exposed to and potentially been establishing a rapport with over the years. Dylan felt an overwhelming sense that she and her friends were on the right path. This first date with Barrett was confirmation that the agreement to give the process a chance was the beginning of something transformative. She was open and receptive to everything the program had to offer.

"I always said I would travel the world when I retire," Dylan commented.

"Don't wait. There are no guarantees in life. If you can afford to take the time, you should do it while you can. Tomorrow isn't promised."

"Maybe I'll join your travel club of one."

"You'd be more than welcome."

"Just like that, huh? You don't even know me."

"I'll get to know you as we travel the world together."

"You're into taking risks."

"What makes you think that?"

"I don't know too many people willing to travel the world with someone they just met."

"Did Brooke mention that we've been friends since we were five years old?"

Dylan nodded.

"There are a lot of years and there is a lot of trust in our relationship. She's the closest thing that I have to a sister. If she tells me that you're an amazing woman and someone that I should get to know, I have no reason to doubt that."

Barrett's level of surety made Dylan want to call her travel agent. She could see herself taking a trip with Barrett, trying something new. The sense of adventure was alluring. Getting to know someone while exploring foreign and exotic lands . . . Seeing how they would react to the world and the different cultures within it . . . The idea of it all was appealing to her.

"I'll have to thank Brooke for the glowing assessment."

"She didn't rave about me?" he asked, jokingly. "You're taking too long to respond, so I guess not."

"You came highly recommended," she replied. If he only knew. He made the referral list. That in itself was a glowing review.

He looked at Dylan with dubious eyes. "I'll have to call Brooke. I don't believe she shared my many positive attributes. Did she tell you I can make waffles and sing?"

Dylan cackled. "You are hilarious."

"I just thought you should know that," he said with a smile.

"Maybe you can sit in on a song with that dreadful band."

"Oh, now they're dreadful?"

"I've been listening while we've been talking. If you ask me, they aren't doing Prince justice."

"But dreadful?"

"Okay, maybe not dreadful . . . more like awful."

"That's the same thing."

"Fine. They're dread-awful."

Barrett convulsed with amusement. "Do you want to get out of here?" he asked. "We can go to a lounge or my place to have a drink."

"You live in Brooklyn, right?"

"I have a place in Fort Greene and one in Hudson Yards."

"I wouldn't mind having a drink at your place. However, I don't want to drive to Manhattan since we're already in Brooklyn."

"Of course, we can stay local. Can I ride with you, or should I call my driver?"

"Don't be silly. We can ride together."

NINETEEN

Sebastian stretched his calves. Brooke had invited him to take a spin class at her gym. She didn't warn him beforehand that it was an advanced class. After an hour of hard-core cardio, his tank top was drenched. Sebastian was in shape, but the workout was extreme. He'd underestimated the level of intensity and was certain he would feel the effects the following day.

Brooke was on the spin bike next to him and throughout the class she made it look effortless. Toned but not muscular, her body was fitness goals for women and men alike. After the class, she got Sebastian settled at the juice bar in the gym and then excused herself to handle a bit of business. As co-owner, there was no such thing as dipping in to take a class without doing some work.

Sebastian ordered a beet, apple, and strawberry juice and watched the activity in the gym while he sipped. Considering it wasn't a national chain, he was impressed by the size and layout, number of machines, and the number of members working out. It seemed to him that Brooke had a successful venture on her hands. He admired entrepreneurship and especially with a focus on well-being.

He noticed two women at the end of the bar peering at him. One raised her cup of fresh juice in a discreet salute when she saw him looking in their direction. He reciprocated the gesture. Brooke stepped up beside him as he was lowering his cup. "I see you have a couple of admirers flirting with you," she said.

"Is that what that was?" he asked in jest.

"I know those two members well and, believe me, they were sizing you up since you came through the door."

"So, you're running a real meat market," Sebastian said with a grin.

"I don't encourage the behavior, but it sort of comes with the territory. You have people here working on getting in shape or maintaining it, and others appreciating it. We ensure the members are respectful of one another and don't make anyone feel uncomfortable, though. Did the ladies make you uncomfortable?" Brooke fought to keep the smile off her face.

Sebastian playfully clutched the front of his tank and tugged it up toward his neck. "I'll be all right."

"Go easy on him, ladies," Brooke called out toward the end of the bar. "It's his first time here." The ladies laughed together. They knew Brooke was kidding. Sebastian actually seemed a little bashful. Brooke squeezed his shoulder. "C'mon, let's get out of here. I'm going to make you a hearty omelet with vegetables from my garden."

∘ ∘ ∘

BROOKE PLACED A plate in front of Sebastian, seated at the table on the patio in her backyard. She sat across from him with her omelet.

"This looks amazing," he said, scanning his breakfast consisting of an omelet, roasted red potatoes, wheat toast, and sliced strawberries on the side.

"I hope you enjoy it. The tomatoes, peppers, and spinach in the omelet came from my garden."

Sebastian sampled a little of everything. "It tastes even better than it looks. Thank you for this wonderful meal."

"You're welcome."

"I don't know the last time anyone has cooked for me."

"Now that's surprising."

"I'm almost scared to ask why you would think that."

"We're not going to pretend that you have trouble in the women department."

"I knew you would say something like that, but it goes deeper."

"Please, enlighten me."

"Let me start by saying this is *my* opinion based on *my* experiences. It may not be a popular one, but I own it."

"Okay, you've issued your disclaimer . . ."

Sebastian laughed, shaking his head at the same time. "I can admit that I haven't had any challenges when it comes to dating. But it's not a matter of finding someone to date. Finding the right person is a different story. What I have noticed over the years is that people have abandoned traditional roles. They don't believe we should have specific roles within relationships. I see that look you're giving me."

"I'm not giving any look. I'm listening to what you're saying."

"Please don't think I'm some sort of caveman, because I'm not. I happen to think couples should be able to have expectations for their partners. I'm taking out the garbage, doing the yardwork, taking the cars to the mechanic, fixing things around the house, grabbing items you can't reach on the high shelf in the cabinets."

That made Brooke smile. "What if she's taller than you?"

"Then I can take that off my list of *manly* responsibilities." He chuckled. "But you know what I mean. I've had women look at me like you just did when I asked them if they knew how to cook. In my book, that's not an inappropriate question. I cook, too. In fact, I'm a great cook. I don't expect anyone to be chained to the stove. A meal every now and then isn't too much to ask, especially since I do my share of the cooking. Honestly, she can expect me to do all the things a man *should* do for his woman."

"So, basically, what you're saying is I racked up a few cool points for making you an omelet?" she asked lightheartedly.

"You get way more than a few for using food from your own garden."

"I aim to please."

"You can make me a veggie omelet any day." He ate another forkful of his food. "We're joking around, but I want you to know I would never give out points to anyone. However, I do appreciate it and you have made a unique impression on me. I want to get to know much more about you."

Brooke sobered up. She was busy trying to make jokes and Sebastian wanted to have a real conversation. If there was one thing she learned over the years, it was to take your openings when you can. If Seb wanted to get real, then she'd get real. "I have to agree with you that relationship dynamics change. Societal norms change. I've dealt with similar situations. Some men see an independent, single woman and think that I don't need a man that I can rely on and feel secure around. I want to know that he has my back, and I can lean on his strong shoulders when needed. So, I can relate to you wanting a woman who can care for her man. I want a man who will care for me in the same way. I hate taking out garbage."

Sebastian gazed at Brooke. "I'll take your garbage out for you and whatever else you need me to do."

He made "whatever else" sound so enticing. Brooke told herself to be still. She had only known him a couple of weeks. It takes time to get past the words and to see the actions. She intended to find out more about Sebastian by the way he acted, his character. "Let me ask you a question," she said. "If a woman meets *all* of your standards except for cooking, is that a dealbreaker?"

"Yes."

Surprise registered on Brooke's face. "You would pass on a good woman just because she doesn't cook?"

"Absolutely. In the beginning it might not bother me, but give it some time and it becomes an issue. If you're not getting what you want in a relationship, those are the things that fester and become the catalyst for arguments. I don't like feeling that my needs are being overlooked and I don't like to argue. You said you hate taking out the garbage. Could you be with a man who wouldn't do that for you?"

"If he checked all of my boxes except for that one?"

"Everything else about him is on point."

Brooke thought about it. "That's tough. It's not easy finding someone that meets all your needs."

"It sounds like you'd be willing to take the garbage out."

"When you say it like that . . . I can see how it would become a problem down the road. Either I would have to accept it or, like you said, it would be an issue that causes problems in the relationship."

"It all has to do with whether we're willing to settle." Sebastian put his fork down. "I've done enough settling over the years. And, hopefully, the woman I'm with isn't settling when it comes to me. Can you imagine the amount of grief you'll get when your partner isn't happy because they decided to tolerate you?"

"You make a good point."

Brooke had said many times in the past that she wasn't settling anymore. She had been there, done that. Now Sebastian had her questioning whether she was still willing to settle if the issue was small enough. Was she willing to let a good man slip through her fingers over putting the garbage out? She wasn't sure. Listening to Sebastian she felt as if she should have been able to say resoundingly that if her partner isn't taking out the garbage, then it's a deal-breaker. If she hated doing something, and wanted her man to take care of it, she wondered why on earth she'd be with someone who wouldn't.

Brooke knew what men thought of her. She had been accused of being emotionless, uncaring, lacking feeling, hard—bordering on cold. Nothing could be further from the truth. It took time for Brooke to let her guard down. She didn't let just anyone get too close. Some men didn't recognize that she was trying to protect her heart. They assumed that she didn't need a man and didn't know how to treat one. Brooke could admit she wasn't the best at stroking the male ego, but that was because she preferred men who didn't require a constant ego boost. Dylan and Ivy had been telling her for years that there's a balance between managing the male ego and demanding respect within the relationship. Brooke didn't have a problem catering to her man, as long as it was reciprocal.

Sebastian interrupted Brooke's thoughts. "I prefer to go into a situation knowing exactly what a woman is looking for in a man. Tell me . . . what are you looking for?"

"You expect me to start rattling off a list?"

"We're having a conversation. I'd like to know your thoughts."

"Are you analyzing me, doctor?"

"I'm not wearing my psychologist hat. I'm enjoying brunch with a beautiful woman, hoping I possess the qualities she's seeking in a man."

Brooke smiled. "I bet you always know what to say."

"Not all the time," he joked. "I make sure I'm prepared for my motivational speeches, but that's about it."

"Somehow I doubt that."

"You don't have to answer the question if it makes you uncomfortable."

Brooke reminded herself that she was trying to do things differently with the Referral Program. She needed to let down her guard. Now was a perfect time to start. Brooke sighed. "I haven't verbalized what I'm looking for in a long time. Maybe because a part of me started to think he may not be out there."

"He might be sitting in front of you right now. What is it you want in a man?"

"A true partner. An honest man, someone I can trust. A man who radiates strength. Understands the importance of compassion and forgiveness. I'm looking for a man who isn't afraid to express himself and show emotion. A lover who will never stop trying to woo me. A provider and a protector. I want a man who I love talking to and we're never at a loss for conversation . . ." Brooke trailed off.

"That's quite a list."

"Well, you asked."

"And I'm glad I did."

"Why is that?"

"Because I can be all of that and more. I'm exactly what you're looking for in a man."

Brooke took in the specimen across the table. She peered into his eyes, searching for any indication that he wasn't being sincere. "I suppose only time will tell," she said.

"Listen, Brooke. We're just getting to know each other. I think we need to go into this with open hearts and open minds."

"Am I giving the impression that I'm not being open?"

"I just find that saying things like *time will tell* means you're expecting me to show you something that contradicts what I'm saying."

Brooke reminded herself for the second time that afternoon that she needed to give this a chance. "Okay, I receive that." She leaned in, placing her elbows on the table. "It's my turn to ask you a question."

"Shoot."

"Are you actively dating?"

"No, I'm not."

"Are you looking to be in a relationship?"

"Yes, I am," he said, without flinching.

"Are you going to woo me?" she teased.

"Without a doubt."

"And how do you plan to do that?"

"I've learned it's not just the grand gestures, but also the small ones." Sebastian stood up. "I'm going to start with these dishes." He started clearing the dishes from the table.

"You don't have to do that."

"I really appreciated breakfast. The least I can do is the dishes."

Brooke watched him clear the table thinking it was a sweet gesture. "I'll tell you what. We can do the dishes together."

"Sounds good to me. Can you open the door?"

Brooke opened the door and they went inside. Sebastian stacked the dishes near the sink and turned on the water. Brooke nudged him to the side. "I'll wash, you dry," she said, handing him a dish towel.

"You're not going to make this easy, are you?"

"Trust me. I will absolutely let you woo me. However, cleaning my kitchen is an entirely different story."

"I get it. You're territorial about your kitchen."

"I guess I am."

Sebastian grinned. "I'll make note of that."

"I know why you're smiling."

"Am I smiling?"

"Oh, stop it. I know this fits right into your views on relationships."

"Maybe it does, but I'm willing to do whatever you ask of me."

"Right now, all I need you to do is dry the dishes. We'll see what else you can do to try to woo me."

TWENTY

*P*hase College was bustling. Ivy greeted student after student as she made her way through the prep center. The kids loved her, and she loved them. Carter had created something special and was making a difference in the lives of so many teens. When Ivy first started volunteering with the Phase College program, she helped the kids with college applications and financial aid forms. She would show up every two weeks and stay a couple of hours. As the months passed, and she got to know the students better, she found herself at the center a few times a week staying hours on end, helping the kids with any and everything. She ran study sessions and helped out with the exam prep classes. Contributing to the future success of the students gave Ivy a sense of purpose.

Carter was in his office when Ivy arrived. She knocked, waiting for him to acknowledge her presence. He looked up, waving for her to come inside.

"Hey, stranger," he said, coming around his desk to give Ivy a hug. "Long time, no see."

"I know," she conceded. "I've been missing in action."

"I figured you must be busy with work."

"Something like that," she mumbled. Ivy didn't intend to tell Carter that she had been preoccupied with her social life. The time she was spending with Daveed had replaced a lot of the time she would normally spend at the center. "But I'm here today to help out however I can."

"We're happy whenever you can make time for us."

Something about the way Carter said that struck a nerve with Ivy. She hadn't made time for the students and needed to do better. "I've missed the kids. You know if you're ever in a bind or short staffed you can call me."

"I was going to call you a few weeks ago."

"Really? Why didn't you? Seriously, Carter, anytime you need help—"

"Well, it wasn't about the center."

"What was it about?"

Carter looked down at his desk and shifted in his chair. He cleared his throat before looking up at Ivy. "I wanted to talk to you about Dylan."

"Oh, I see." Ivy had hoped he wouldn't but knew there was a chance he might bring up her friend.

"I don't want to put you in an uncomfortable position, but I have to ask what went wrong. I'm sure she confided in you. I mean, I felt like we had a good first date and had some great conversation. I thought there was natural chemistry between us. The next date seemed to be going fine and then it was like she just shut down on me."

Ivy's mind raced as she tried to figure out how to respond to Carter's question. "She didn't say much."

"What *did* she say? One moment we were having a discussion and the next she was rushing from my apartment."

"You didn't speak with her after that date?"

"We texted a few times, but they were all initiated by me. The last text I received from Dylan she declined my invitation for dinner and said she hoped we could be friends. I replayed the discussion we had at my place. We joked about our favorite television shows. We also talked about knowing whether you want to be in a relationship. I said people should know that at a bare minimum. She didn't necessarily agree. I wasn't sure what exactly set her off, but she called me 'woke' and it wasn't in a complimentary way."

"I really can't say what went wrong, Carter. One thing about Dylan is that she doesn't think there's a one-size-fits-all approach when it comes to relationships."

"I'm a good man, Ivy."

"Of course you are. I wouldn't have introduced you to my friend if I thought otherwise."

"I'll admit it sort of bothered me when she said I was 'woke' as if there was something wrong with it." He shook his head. "How many women say they want a good Black man?"

"We all do at some point or another."

"Exactly."

"Dylan never said anything that conflicts with you being a great guy."

"Maybe it's not fair of me to ask you these questions."

"Carter, I consider us friends. You can ask me anything."

"Be honest with me. Do you think I did something wrong? After Dylan expressed that she only wanted to be friends, I questioned whether it's me. I haven't been involved with anyone seriously in a while. Maybe it's something I'm doing?"

Ivy hated that Carter was doubting himself and that she had played a role in causing that doubt. The girls had agreed to take care when dealing with the referrals. She was certain Dylan hadn't treated Carter unfairly nor was disrespectful in any way. She also knew that it was a possibility their referrals would ask questions about why things didn't pan out.

"I don't think you did anything wrong. I think you were being yourself and that's why I wanted you to meet my friend. Unfortunately, you two might not have been a good fit. I don't think it's anything more than that."

"But if you have all these women looking for a good man and one shows up, why not give him a chance? I'll tell you why. I don't think women truly know what they want these days."

"Now I'm going to disagree with you there."

"Ivy, a lot of women are out here focusing on the wrong things. They're discounting men based on the type of car they drive or the clothes they wear. Hardworking men get overlooked if they don't have the right kind of job or can't buy lavish gifts. I know women complain about the number of quality men out there, but we have some of the same concerns."

"That doesn't mean women don't know what they want. Even the ones you described know what they want. They're just prioritizing what's important to them."

"Yeah, overlooking and underestimating men like me."

"Dating is challenging for men *and* women. Believe me, there are plenty of women out there, with their heads on straight, focusing on the right things. Plenty of women would see you as a catch."

"Dylan didn't and I'm self-employed, I have a nice place, I'm connected to my community, I come from a wonderful family. What else could she want?"

"Compatibility."

Carter sighed. "You're right. I was probably too opinionated about my views. I'm so used to lecturing to these kids about how and what they need to do . . ."

"She thought you were a really nice guy. She didn't have anything negative to say about you. Knowing Dylan the way I do, if your views didn't align with hers, she would definitely feel you're better off as friends."

"I appreciate your candor. I'm sorry it didn't work out."

"Me too."

"If Dylan ever mentions to you that she's had a change of heart, please let me know. I would still like to take her out."

"You know I will," she said, standing to exit the office. "I'll catch up with you later. I'm going to see if I can help out with applications and essays."

Ivy left Carter's office and made her way through the center, reflecting on their conversation. She knew that Dylan had already moved on to Brooke's referral, but she had hoped it would've worked out with Carter. He truly was a good catch; apparently, just not for Dylan.

It spoke volumes that he was still interested in her friend. Dylan handled Carter in a way that did not impact Ivy's relationship with him. That was all she could ask for since they didn't have a love connection.

There were no guarantees in the Referral Program. And, after her conversation with Carter, Ivy was keenly aware of the potential risks.

TWENTY-ONE

*B*arrett held the car door open as Dylan slipped into the backseat. He walked around to the other side of the luxury sedan and slid in next to her. The driver idled in front of the restaurant as Barrett quietly conferred with Dylan on what she wanted to do next. He had picked her up from the office earlier in the evening and they went to dine at a new restaurant in the Meatpacking District. He ordered an expensive bottle of wine and they indulged in an eight-course tasting menu. Dylan was learning that Barrett enjoyed the finer things in life and she didn't mind enjoying them with him.

"Joe, we're going to Hudson Yards," Barrett told his driver.

"You got it," Joe replied. He pulled away from the curb and merged into the Friday night traffic.

Taxis darted in, out, and across the lanes as horns blared and pedestrians bustled along the sidewalks. Joe navigated the frenetic rush effortlessly. It took skill to drive on the aggressive New York City streets.

"Joe, can you turn on some smooth jazz?" Barrett asked.

The mellow sounds of piano keys and a saxophone filled the car. *Barrett was as smooth as the music playing*, Dylan thought. "That sounds nice," she said.

"Did you enjoy dinner?"

"It was absolutely divine."

"That's what I love to hear."

"Are you trying to spoil me?" Dylan cocked her head to the

side and waited for Barrett to respond. There was a playful smile on her lips.

"Would you like me to?" Barrett grabbed her hand and cradled it between his own.

Dylan tried to read the expression on his face. She wasn't quite sure how to answer. She wanted Barrett to know that she was interested in getting to know him, not necessarily what he could or would do for her. On the other hand, she didn't want to downplay that a woman likes for a man to treat her like she's special. She searched for the words that would let him know she was far from a gold digger but receptive to a little spoiling.

"Just keep doing what you're doing."

He released her hand and brushed a lock of hair over her shoulder with the rest. "You make me want to spoil you."

Dylan felt her cheeks grow warm. "I haven't done anything."

"I beg to differ."

Dylan didn't reply. She wasn't sure if Barrett noticed her reaction to his words, but she was terrible at concealing her emotions. She turned her head toward the window to recover.

Barrett continued, "It's been a while since I've wanted to spend any real time with someone."

"Why is that?" Dylan asked, redirecting her attention to Barrett.

"That's a good question. The simplest explanation is that I haven't prioritized it."

"You've grown accustomed to being a bachelor?"

"It's not so much being a bachelor. It's more about settling into a routine, acknowledging that's what you've done and not doing anything to change it. I was in that space."

"And you're not anymore?"

"I'm working on realigning my priorities."

"I seem to remember you mentioned that on the night we met."

The car pulled up to the front of an apartment building. Joe and

Barrett exited simultaneously. They spoke for a moment before Barrett came around to open Dylan's door. She stepped from the car and gazed up at the tower. Panels of glass and windows rose high into the night sky. He took her by the hand and escorted her inside. The lobby shone with gleaming marble and granite floors. Elaborate orbs were suspended from the ceiling. Barrett exchanged pleasantries with the lobby attendant as they strolled by his desk toward the elevators. As they stood waiting, he looked over at Dylan and nodded.

"What are you nodding about?" she said.

"Nothing."

She was about to ask a follow-up question when the elevator doors opened. Barrett playfully nudged her inside and pressed the button for the fortieth floor. They rode up in silence. Again, he gazed at her, only breaking eye contact once they reached his floor. Barrett led her down the corridor. Dylan noted the beautiful art hanging on the walls and floral arrangements in oversize decorative vases. He stopped in front of the door at the end of the hallway, punched in a code on a keypad, and the door lock released. He ushered her into the apartment.

The first thing Dylan took in was the lights of the city skyline glittering through the floor-to-ceiling windows. "What a view . . ."

"Come on in and have a seat," he said, heading into the living room.

Barrett turned on a floor lamp and it filled the room with a warm glow. He took a remote from built-in shelving on the wall, fiddled with a couple of buttons, and then music began to pipe through unseen speakers.

"Do you mind if I take off my shoes?"

"Make yourself comfortable."

Dylan slipped out of her heels and placed them beside the sofa. "This is a beautiful place. The development of Hudson Yards has been unbelievable."

"Thanks. I'm still settling in."

"How long have you been here?"

"I moved in about a year ago."

"And you're still not settled?" she asked.

"I spend most nights in Brooklyn. I purchased this condo because the building was a new construction and a good investment, but I intend to start staying here more." He went over to the bar. "Would you like a cocktail?"

"I'll have a glass of wine."

Barrett uncorked a bottle of chardonnay. He joined Dylan on the sofa and handed her a glass. Classic R&B slow jams played softly in the background.

"*Salud*," he said, tapping his glass with hers.

Dylan took a sip. "This is nice . . . buttery."

"It's one of my favorites. I came across it on a trip to Napa."

"You really do travel everywhere, don't you?"

"I try to. It's good for the soul. I've learned a lot about myself while exploring the globe."

"What's one thing you've learned?"

Barrett contemplated what he should share with Dylan in that moment. "I learned to lead with kindness."

"Is that something you've struggled with in the past?"

He reclined on the couch and crossed his legs. "It was something I needed to be more cognizant of when interacting with others. We meet someone and they get introduced to our representative. We're programmed to present the person we want the world to see. With me, they might have met the aggressive attorney. I started to realize a common thread when traveling and meeting people from different cultures and walks of life. Overwhelmingly, I'm greeted with kindness wherever I go in the world. It's one of the reasons I love to travel. The more I became aware of the common thread, the more I knew I needed to contribute to the collective fabric. I resolved that no matter where I was, or who I met, I, too, would lead with kindness. That's a stark contrast to what I confront here in New York City on a daily basis, but I wanted to carry that sense of peace that I feel when I'm on my excursions. I wanted that kindness to stay with and emanate from me."

"That's an admirable takeaway from your globetrotting," Dylan said, with a smile.

"It's one of many. How about you? I know you told me you haven't been anywhere in some time. Where would you like to go, other than Peru?"

"With the amount of time I spend working, I'd be satisfied doing nothing but lounging on a hot beach with a cool drink."

"Island life . . ."

"Yes indeed. There's nothing like it."

"What's your favorite island?"

"I have by no means traveled as extensively as you. I've only been to the Bahamas, Aruba, Barbados, and Puerto Rico. Not enough to name a favorite, but I loved something about all those destinations. I'm craving the feel of hot sand between my toes." Dylan wiggled her perfectly pedicured feet.

Barrett looked down the length of her body sitting beside him on the sofa. Dylan's sleeveless black dress stopped mid-thigh, revealing her bare, toned legs. "We'll have to see what we can do to get your pretty little feet back into some hot sand."

"Oh, you are a smooth one," Dylan said, finally verbalizing what she had been thinking the entire evening.

"I hope that's not a bad thing."

"On the contrary. I find it very sexy." Dylan took a lingering sip from her glass while watching him over the rim.

Barrett nodded. "I'm finding *you* extremely sexy."

"Are you?" she teased. "Tell me why."

He took a drink of his chardonnay. "You're effortlessly sexy—the best kind of sexy."

"You spoil women and flatter, too?"

"I'm stating the obvious. It's not flattery."

"What do you consider sexy?" Dylan pivoted on the couch so she could fully face Barrett.

"What do I consider sexy," he repeated, mulling over the question. "It's the way a woman carries herself. The way she wears her hair, how she dresses. Her level of self-confidence. Her sexiness has nothing to do with beauty . . . though you *are* beautiful."

"Thank you."

"It's in your voice . . . your gaze . . . your graceful movements. It's your smile, your laugh. The way your perfume accentuates your allure . . . That's what I consider sexy."

Dylan wanted to fan herself, but she refrained. She didn't realize Barrett would make it about her specifically, but she welcomed it. His words made her feel sexy, attractive, alluring, and a host of other emotions she hadn't felt in quite some time. "I think a man complimenting a woman is sexy," she responded.

"What else do you think makes a man sexy?"

"A man who knows what he wants. A man who treats a woman like a lady. One who makes me feel comfortable, at ease, and like I can be myself. A man who challenges me mentally, supports me emotionally, and grows with me spiritually. He's stylish. Self-assured. Masculine without being boorish. A man with a magnetizing gaze, like yours. And, of course, he has to smell good." She added that last part with a little wink.

"I smell good," he joked. "In fact, I'm wearing new cologne just for you."

"Are you? I can't smell it."

"Maybe I should come a little closer . . ."

"Well, maybe you should," she replied coyly.

Barrett placed his wineglass on the coffee table and closed the space between them on the sofa. "How about now?"

She shook her head. "Nothing."

He leaned in, getting close enough for his cheek to brush Dylan's. He hovered, whispering in her ear, "You are so sexy."

Dylan tilted her head and Barrett placed a trail of delicate kisses along her jawline. Instinctively, she turned her face toward his. Their eyes met, reading one another. The music faded into the background as Dylan fixated on Barrett's approaching lips. He kissed her—one soft kiss. He moved back enough for them to gaze into each other's eyes and glimpse the spark.

He placed a firm hand on her back and guided her closer, as their lips connected again. Barrett took Dylan on a slow and steady exploration, becoming acclimated with the feel of her lips on his. Barrett's tender, gentle kisses were met with lingering expectancy. He fanned the spark, caressing her lips with his own, giving equal attention to the top, bottom, and corners of her mouth. Where he kissed, she mirrored on him.

Dylan wrapped her arm around Barrett's back and he pulled her into a deep kiss, his tongue easing into her mouth. The taste of apple notes from the wine mingled with their kiss. She led him on a journey . . . tasting, exploring, savoring the sensations. Their bodies inched closer, hands moving slowly to new destinations. Dylan felt her way up Barrett's back, tracing fingers up his spine toward his broad shoulders.

Barrett encircled her waist, drawing her in as he reclined on the couch. Dylan lay alongside him. He ran his fingers through her hair, grasping the nape of her neck. She tilted her head back and he seized the opportunity to lightly graze a trail from her earlobe to her shoulder and back up to her beguiling lips.

D'Angelo crooned in the background, providing a sultry soundtrack to their intimate interlude. Dylan stroked Barrett's biceps, feeling the muscles through his shirt. His hands unhurriedly embarked on a downward path from her neck, brushing the side of her breast, gently squeezing her waist before setting upon her hips with splayed fingers. His powerful hands massaged with a rhythmic intensity that made Dylan think of other rhythmic motions. A quiet moan escaped her throat. Barrett pulled away from their kiss and looked at her. The spark had ignited—she saw the fire in his eyes. He didn't make a move. He waited on her with that magnetic gaze. Dylan drew him to her, his chest pressing against her breasts. He moaned. One of his legs covered hers. She felt him growing against her thigh. This time, she led the exploration, nibbling his lips before luring him in for a breathtakingly deep kiss. Their tongues spoke to each other, fed off one another.

Barrett stroked the curve of Dylan's derriere, as if he was memorizing the feel of it in his hand. He cupped her ass and pulled her into him, letting Dylan feel his hardness.

She pulled away with a sharp intake of breath. "Whew," she said, gently nudging Barrett back. Her eyes traveled from his chest down to the imprint of the erection straining against his pants. She bit her bottom lip. "You are dangerous."

"You did that," he whispered.

"*We* did that." Dylan had yet to lift her gaze. As enticing as it looked, she knew she needed to pump the brakes. Slowly, she sat up and started to straighten her dress.

Barrett stayed exactly where he was on the sofa. Dylan couldn't stop glancing at all he had to offer.

He chuckled. "I'm flattered."

"You aren't making this easy," she said in a singsong manner. "Laying there looking all sexy."

"Smelling good . . ."

They laughed together.

"Yes, you smell good," she conceded.

Barrett sat up next to Dylan. He turned her face toward his and began to attentively finger comb her hair back into place. "Would you like another glass of wine?"

"It's getting late, and I still need to get back to Long Island."

"You don't have to worry about that. I'll have Joe drive you home or you can stay, if you like." Barrett laughed. "I see that look on your face. I meant you can stay in the guest room."

Dylan shook her head and smiled. "I'll take that refill and we'll see what happens next."

TWENTY-TWO

*I*vy rang the doorbell for a second time. She moved her umbrella to the left to ward off the blowing rain. She waited a few more seconds, then turned to head back down the walkway. She heard the door open.

"Ivy is that you?" Brooke asked.

"Surprise!"

"Girl, come in out of that rain. What are you doing here?"

Ivy shook the water from her umbrella and stepped into Brooke's foyer. "I happened to be in the neighborhood."

Brooke rolled her eyes. "Clearly you're going next door to Daveed's. What's the matter, he isn't home?"

"Stop it. Yes, I am going next door and he *is* home. I wanted to come say hello to you first."

"That is surprising. Come in. I'm making sauce with the tomatoes from my garden."

Ivy followed Brooke to the kitchen. "When I grow up, I want to be just like you with my own garden and homemade sauces," she teased.

Brooke laughed. "I'm one of a kind."

"So I heard," Ivy said in a knowing tone.

"What does that mean?"

"I spoke to my cousin last night," she said, taking a seat at the kitchen island.

Brooke had an array of tomatoes along with garlic, basil, and a host of other herbs Ivy couldn't readily identify spread across the counter. A cutting board with diced onions and green peppers sat next to them.

"I just got off the phone with him a few minutes ago," Brooke said.

"How are things going?"

"Sebastian is a really nice guy."

Ivy stared blankly at Brooke. "That's all you got?"

"What?"

"Don't play with me, Brooke."

Brooke chuckled. "We're getting to know each other."

"And all you have to say is he's a nice guy?"

"I'm saying . . . I know this is the Referral Program and we report back on our progress, but Sebastian is your cousin."

"So!"

"So, I don't want you to be too involved . . . Does that make sense?"

"Not one bit."

"I just think *if* things go awry, you might be a bit more invested in this one."

"I promise you, I won't."

Brooke twisted her lips. "Somehow, I don't believe that."

Ivy crossed her heart. "I'll be cool."

She sighed. "Oh, all right."

Ivy giggled and clapped her hands. "Let me ask again. How are things going?"

Brooke stopped chopping her vegetables. "Girl, as much as I give Dylan flack for her schemes, this one might be the best."

"Hey, I'm the one who introduced you to my cousin."

"I know, I know." Brooke was hesitant to discuss her thoughts on Sebastian. There were feelings brewing that she wasn't sure if she was ready to own. She liked him. Plain and simple, she liked Sebastian. He was a good guy *and* she liked him. "So far, so good, Ivy. I'm enjoying getting to know Sebastian."

Ivy grinned. "I knew you would."

"He's a good man."

"He thinks you're a good woman."

"Wait. I don't know if I want you to tell me what he said."

"Are you sure?" Ivy asked, eyebrows raised.

"Okay, go ahead," Brooke said with a laugh.

"He didn't say too much, but he said one thing that stood out."

"What did he say?" she replied impatiently.

"He said 'you might have introduced me to my future wife.'"

"Oh, he was probably just saying that."

"No, Brooke. I know my cousin and he was serious."

"Like I said, I'm enjoying getting to know him." Brooke smiled to herself and continued cutting her ingredients. "How's Daveed?"

Ivy dramatically put her hands over her heart and heaved a sigh. "I like him. A lot."

"I can tell. Are you sure it isn't more than just like?"

"Maybe it is, but you see how easy it was for me to say that? I like Daveed!"

Brooke chuckled. "Okay, take it easy."

"I would love to sit here telling you about him, but I'm going next door to be with him."

"I'm not holding you. You're the one that rang my doorbell . . . uninvited."

"I'll let myself out."

"Have a good time, but be cool."

The friends shared a laugh and a hug and Ivy departed. Daveed was expecting her, and she didn't want to keep him waiting.

o o o

DAVEED GREETED IVY at the door, enfolding her in his arms. Her face rested on his chest. She could feel his heartbeat. He grasped her shoulders, moving her back enough to get a good look at her. He grabbed her hand and turned her in a circle. "That's a beautiful dress. I'm sorry the weather didn't cooperate for our picnic today."

"I was bummed, too."

"No worries. All is not lost."

Ivy looked at Daveed with questioning eyes. "It's not?"

"Nope."

She knew they couldn't be going anywhere because he was barefoot and wearing a pair of loose-fitting lounge pants and a white T-shirt.

He led her through the house. The windows were open. The breeze carried the scent of rain, grass, and blossoms throughout the rooms. Ivy loved Daveed's home. It was the right amount of masculine with touches of feminine flair—dark colors and leather, with fluffy pillows and throws on the couch. African artwork hung on the walls with images of women and children. Dried flowers mixed with rustic, earthy stones on the coffee table.

Daveed guided her into the family room. Ivy squeezed his hand. A blanket was spread out on the floor in the center of the room. A picnic basket sat on the corner of the blanket along with a champagne bucket and two flutes.

"This is sweet." She turned and kissed him on the lips. "You are so thoughtful."

"I know it's not what we planned, but I thought we could improvise."

"It's perfect."

Daveed walked over to the blanket. Ivy removed her sandals. He sat and held out his hand as she eased down to the floor. "The champagne is chilled. I have an assortment of cheeses, crackers, and fruit.

I know you enjoy a bit of St-Germain in your champagne. I can get you some of that, if you like."

"No, the champagne is fine."

"I even have a book of poetry."

Ivy couldn't keep the surprise off her face. "Wow."

"Don't act so shocked. You know I take my reading seriously these days." He uncorked the champagne and filled the flutes.

She raised her glass. "Rainy-day picnics and poetry."

"All to make you happy, babe."

Ivy liked the sound of that. She appreciated the thought behind it even more. When Daveed said they would spend the day at home since it was raining, she expected an afternoon of Netflix and chill. "You succeeded."

"Was there a lot of traffic on your way here?"

"No, it was fine. I stopped at Brooke's for a few minutes."

"How was she? I didn't see her this past week."

"In her element—making tomato sauce."

"I better slide over there tomorrow to barter for some. I have a nice bottle of merlot for her."

"She does love her wine, but if you really want to get on her good side, bring her a good tequila."

Daveed raised his brows. "Really now? She's never mentioned that."

"I'm not surprised." Ivy knew her friend well, but she was not an open book. She was more like a locked journal. "Just don't tell her that I told you."

He put his hand out for a fist bump. "We make a good team."

Ivy tapped his fist. "We better sign up for the next Olympics."

He gazed at her. "Why are you so damn cute?"

"It just comes naturally," Ivy said with a chuckle.

"You know, Ivy, you're like a lodestone."

"I don't know what you mean."

"Just like a natural magnet, there's something in your spirit that draws me to you. It's hard to explain. It's like I can feel your energy as soon as I'm near you. It's like the feeling you get when the sun warms your face. I want to bask in you."

Ivy felt a tingle down her spine. She wanted an instant replay of what Daveed had just said to her. "I'm just being me."

"That's why I'm so drawn to you. I know this is who you are. No airs. No façades. Your beauty is authentic, inside and out. That's what men want in a woman."

"Not all men. Some are more than happy with an enhanced illusion."

"*This* man knows what he wants and you're no illusion." Daveed reached over and grabbed the book of poetry. "I want to share something with you. I read this last night and it made me think of you."

"Okay." Ivy curled her legs to the side and got comfortable.

"In a fleeting moment your world can change. An unplanned shift, momentous in scope. The passing of time, slowing. The passing of hours, speeding. The minutes, suspended. The seconds, occurring. Unexpected encounters redefine perspective. First impressions tilt the axis in a different direction. Seasons of drought and solitude transform into a season of abundance and togetherness. In a fleeting moment, the world changed. It shifted. Time was of the essence. Perspective evolved. Impressions redirected. I was alone. We are together. I am in love."

Ivy fussed with the hem of her dress, not making eye contact with Daveed. "That made you think of me?"

"Every word."

Ivy looked up. "I don't know what to say."

"Say what you feel."

"I'm really at a loss for words."

"I know you can do better than that."

"Well, you have me smiling on the inside."

"I take it that's a good thing."

"Come here," she said, beckoning him with her finger.

Daveed scooted closer to her on the blanket. She placed her hand on the back of his head and lured him closer. She planted butterfly kisses from his cheek to his mouth. Ivy whispered in between kisses, "It's a great thing."

Daveed wrapped his arms around Ivy's waist and drew her onto his lap. "This is real for me. I just want to know that you feel the same."

She captured Daveed's face between her hands and kissed his forehead, the tip of his nose, his lips. "You know how I feel about you."

"These past couple of months with you have been . . . unexpected." He tilted his head to the side as she kissed his neck. "You make me feel things, think things . . ."

Ivy placed a finger against his lips, shushing him. "Kiss me."

Daveed feverishly pressed his lips to Ivy's, tangling his fingers in her hair. Her soft lips were intoxicating, her tongue enticing him to go deeper. He wanted to become drunk on her essence. In a swift motion, he rolled them over on the blanket. He lay on top of her body with Ivy peering up into his eyes. Her expression— the intensity in her eyes—made his heart skip a beat. Again, he kissed her with a passion he could not contain. Daveed began a slow grind, his manhood growing in the process. Ivy shifted beneath him, giving Daveed access to settle between her legs. The thin fabric of her dress and his loose-fitting pants did little to serve as a barrier to their most intimate parts. He rubbed himself against her, coaxing a tender moan from Ivy.

Her hips moved in unison with his. The feel of his erection pressed against her made Ivy tingle all over. They moved as if they were engaged in a slow dance, their bodies rocking in time to an unheard melody. He kissed her exposed cleavage, moving his face back and forth across the soft, supple mounds. Daveed continued down the length of her body at a slow, measured pace. He laid his face on her stomach, while gently sliding her dress upward. He rose to his knees between her legs. He stared at the imprint of her lips covered by her small black panties. Daveed touched her flower with the tip of his fingers. Ivy's breathing became shallow. He leaned down and kissed it through her panties. Daveed looked up to see if Ivy was with him. She was biting her bottom lip and gazing at him.

He gingerly grabbed her panties from both sides and slid them down her legs. Daveed studied what was before him. A beautifully manicured blossom with a dainty, close-cut strip. He wanted to see all of her. He reached down and pulled Ivy's dress over her head. She wasn't wearing a bra. She was naked, natural, and stunning. Daveed wanted to kiss her from head to toe. He let his hands lead the way and his lips followed as he caressed her shoulders, breasts, and stomach. He licked his way down to her sweetness, flicking his tongue across her clit. She gasped. Daveed wanted more. He swirled his tongue inside of her, tasting her honey. He probed deeper and her hips started to move. He grabbed her thighs and tried to drink her down like champagne. The more Ivy moved, the more he held her steady, making her endure the pleasure his tongue was bringing her. Ivy's cooing and moans spurred him on. He sucked and nibbled, leaving no spot untouched. Daveed sat back on his heels, staring down at Ivy in the throes of passion, her breath labored, hair slightly covering her face and chest flushed. He became painfully aware of the throbbing in his pants. He pulled his T-shirt over his head and tossed it aside.

Ivy watched him through slightly parted eyes. He stood up and stepped out of his lounge pants. His penis was at full attention. He laid down beside Ivy, moving her hair from her face. "Are you okay?"

She nodded. "Better than okay."

"I mean, are you okay with this?"

"We did say we were taking sex off the table."

"I don't want to have sex with you." He traced a finger between her breasts. "I want to make love to you, Ivy."

She smiled. "Stop talking."

He pulled her close, positioning his thigh between hers. Ivy instinctively draped her leg over Daveed's hip. His penis and her flower touched. They watched each other, silently connecting. Daveed kissed Ivy on the forehead. She kissed the tip of his nose. Their lips met as he eased inside her. He squeezed her tight, unhurriedly inching deeper. He felt her wetness cover him and moaned. She was so warm and inviting he didn't want to come out. Daveed began a slow and steady tempo, savoring the way her body hugged him. He didn't want Ivy to move. If she moved, he didn't know how long he'd be able to last. He held her leg over his hip and dipped deeper, picking up the pace. She clenched around him. He faltered, pulling out to the tip to recover. Ivy grabbed his ass and pushed him back inside. He let go of her leg and laid her on her back. She wrapped both legs around his waist. Daveed thrusted his hips, filling her up with every inch. Ivy rolled her hips beneath him, controlling the flow. He kissed her long and fervently, his senses taking over—the feel of her wetness around him, her tight contracting walls, her soft breasts against his chest, his erection growing harder with each thrust. He was overwhelmed by the feel of her. He pulled out, exploding with a resounding cry.

Ivy froze, her legs still wrapped around Daveed's waist.

He collapsed on top of her, his face buried in the crook of her neck. "I'm sorry," he muttered with bated breath. "It's been a while."

"You don't have to apologize."

"It's my job to make sure you're satisfied. You didn't even—"

"Stop. It was wonderful."

He tapped her thigh and she moved her legs from around his

waist. He lay propped beside her. "You're a beautiful woman, Ivy, *inside* and out. And, you know just what to say."

"I mean it."

He kissed her forehead. "Let's get cleaned up and enjoy the rest of our picnic."

TWENTY-THREE

*D*riving into the city on a Saturday night was never at the top of Brooke's list, but as she sat in the back of the room listening to Sebastian's speech, she knew it was for a good cause. Watching him engage the audience and speak to their challenges, as if he knew them personally, was enlightening. If everyone took the time to learn to be effective communicators and listeners, the world would be a much better place. She was impressed with the way he worked the room, answering questions, using anecdotes, and citing relevant societal examples.

She hadn't told him that she was coming. Brooke wanted to see Sebastian in his element. She figured that sitting in the back of a room with three hundred people, she would go unnoticed. He spotted her about an hour into the event. He winked at her and continued with the point he was making, not missing a beat. She thought about raising her hand to ask a question to put him on the spot, but thought how unprofessional and silly that would be. Instead, she decided to sit quietly and watch him at work. He was helping people with all sorts of issues, truly trying to get them to embrace the concept of being your better self.

A woman at the end of Brooke's row stood up and asked how it is possible to forgive someone, specifically an ex-husband, when he is still treating you poorly.

Sebastian nodded, acknowledging the woman's question. "I'm sure this is not the first time you've heard this. Forgiveness is for you, not for him. It's important you understand that. If you don't forgive, it will eat you up inside. Meanwhile, he'll be living his best life, not thinking twice about the changes you're going through. Now, what you really have to work on is how to interact with this person, if at all, so they don't have so much sway over you to impact your life in any way."

He asked a lot of follow-up questions, taking his time to figure out how to help the woman. She revealed that they didn't have any children together and it seemed she was struggling with letting go of a toxic situation. Sebastian instructed her to contact his office to set up a complimentary session. He told her if she was ready for a change, he would help her get there.

Brooke sat and listened, enthralled with the way Sebastian commanded the room, balancing motivation, compassion, and tough love. After taking his last question, he gave the audience a daily affirmation to say in the mirror. "Today is the day I meet my best self." He explained that every day, one should strive to be their best self. It's a personal challenge that never ends. Everyone can always be better and do better.

As the room cleared, there was a line of at least ten people waiting to talk to him. Brooke quietly waited as he took time to speak to each person. She watched him, thinking about how much you can learn about a person when they are in their natural environment. He was poised, well spoken, and as much as she didn't want to make it about looks, so damn handsome. He carried himself with authority. Not cocky or arrogant, but self-assured and confident. She noticed the look some of the women gave him during the event. It would have been naïve of her to think that women weren't sizing him up and wondering about the potential of being with a man like Sebastian. His smile alone could melt hearts; add in that voice and all bets were off. Brooke smiled in spite of herself. She had come to see Sebastian in action, not to lurk in the back daydreaming about how good-looking he was, especially in what appeared to be a custom suit. He wasn't wearing a tie and the top button on his shirt was undone. The vibes he was giving. She fanned herself with the program. She wondered if he had any idea how the smallest details could trigger a physical reaction in her.

Forty-five minutes later, he patted the last gentleman on the back and thanked him for coming. They walked toward the back of the room together. The man exited and Sebastian sat down in the chair beside Brooke.

He placed a hand on her knee. "What a pleasant surprise to see you in the audience."

"I hope you don't mind."

"Mind? Why would I mind?"

"Well, I invited myself and you are working."

"Seeing your face made my evening. You are welcome to any of my events."

"I'm glad I came. You were brilliant."

He chuckled. "Flattery will get you everywhere with me."

"I'm serious. You have a knack for helping people."

"It's my passion."

"I can tell."

"Okay, ma'am. What were your takeaways from the evening?"

"Wow, I'm a *ma'am* now?"

"Well, you did attend my professional event. So, as an audience member, I'm asking what you're taking away from the experience."

"Okay, sir, or is it doctor?"

"Either one is fine," he teased.

"My takeaway, doctor, is a big one."

"Oh, let's hear it."

Brooke cocked her head to the side and looked directly at Sebastian. "You make me want to let my guard down."

"Do I?"

A smile tugged at the corners of her lips. "Yes."

"So put that in the context of an actionable takeaway."

"I have officially let down my guard . . . with you."

Sebastian gently touched her chin, leaning in and placing a kiss on her lips. "I think that's the best takeaway of the night."

"You had a room filled with three hundred people. How can you be certain?"

"Because your takeaway just made my night a hundred times better."

Sebastian grabbed Brooke's hand and kissed it. "Thank you for coming."

"You're welcome."

"Can I entice you with a late dinner? I know a place not far from here with an amazing chef who will prepare anything you want."

"What's the name of the place?"

"My place."

"That sounds nice."

TWENTY-FOUR

*I*vy sipped on ice water while waiting for Dylan and Brooke to arrive. The sun was perched in a clear blue sky, a gentle breeze rustling the tablecloth. She couldn't wait to catch up with the girls. She hadn't spoken to them all week and was anxious to debrief. She looked down at her phone to check the time. They weren't late, yet. She had arrived a bit early and requested outdoor seating so they could bask in the sun. It was a popular brunch spot, and the coveted patio seating went quickly. Ivy looked up to see the hostess leading her friends over to the table. They were adorned in sunglasses, sundresses, and designer bags—summer style at its finest. They greeted one another with air kisses and compliments.

"I missed you ladies," Ivy said.

"You just saw me last week with your unexpected drop in," Brooke replied.

"Oh hush. That was only for a few minutes. I have been dying to catch up with you two."

"I know I've been missing in action," Dylan said. "Work has been kicking my butt."

Ivy rolled her eyes. "I hope you have more than just work going on. I want to hear how the Referral Program is going for you."

Dylan looked down sheepishly, then exaggeratedly fluttered her eyelids. "Barrett is one smooth dude. I have to be careful with him."

"Why careful?" Ivy asked. "Isn't the point of the program to be open?"

"Oh, I'm open. That's the problem," she said with a chuckle.

"So, it sounds like it's going well," Brooke chimed in.

"Extremely."

"Thank goodness! I didn't want to refer a dud. I know how picky you can be."

"*Brooke* is calling *me* picky," Dylan said, looking to Ivy for a co-sign. "The nerve!"

"We all have our preferences," Ivy replied. "Some more than others."

The friends laughed. They knew each other all too well. Dylan most definitely had the most criteria, but Brooke was the most discerning and would not settle for anything less than what she wanted from a man. Ivy was most likely to give a man a chance regardless of type.

"I like Barrett. He's mature and in touch with who he is. Brooke, you didn't mention his love of travel. He seems so worldly."

"I shared some things about him, but I think it's important for us to get to know these men through our own lenses. I don't want to tell you everything about him or how I see him. You have to get to know him in your own way. I'm just glad you like what he's showing you."

"Are there any sparks?" Ivy inquired.

"What do you think?"

"I don't know. That's why I'm asking."

Brooke and Ivy waited for Dylan to spill the tea.

"We definitely have chemistry."

"Do you know what he's working with?"

"Ivy, you know she isn't going to tell you all of that. And, honestly, I don't know if I want to know that much about my childhood friend."

"I'll say this, ladies. I know enough to know that if we get to that point, I won't be disappointed."

Ivy squealed. "Now that's what I'm talking about. How about you, Brooke? How are things going with my cousin?"

"You absolutely know I won't be telling you too much about your *cousin*."

"He isn't my cousin, so you can definitely tell me all the intimate details," Dylan said.

Brooke shook her head. "I don't know what to do with you two."

"I mean we're supposed to enjoy the program. Sharing the dirty little details is part of the fun," Ivy countered.

Dylan placed her elbows on the table and leaned forward. "Okay, let's hear your dirty little details."

The server approached the table. "Good morning, ladies. Are you ready to order?"

"Saved by the bell," Ivy said.

The server glanced around the table with a puzzled look. "Do you need more time?"

"Yes," Dylan replied.

"No," Ivy answered.

The server stood waiting for them to come to a consensus.

"We'll order now," Brooke offered.

They rushed through the menu and placed their orders.

"French toast, pancakes, and an egg scramble . . . got it." The server collected their menus and excused herself from the conversation she'd intruded on.

"Back to the question at hand, Ivy. What dirty details do you have to share?"

She hung her head in feigned shame. "I slept with Daveed."

Brooke's eyes were as wide as saucers. "Whaaaat?"

"Yes, I did. Close your mouth, Dylan."

Dylan slowly obliged. "Now, I wasn't expecting that."

"It sort of just happened."

"*When* did it happen?" Brooke asked.

"The day I dropped by your house."

"When was that?" Dylan asked eagerly.

"Last weekend," Ivy said, before taking a sip of water.

"Well, how was it?"

"Damn, Dylan."

"Don't act like you don't want to know, Brooke."

"Honestly, I'm not too sure. This is my next-door neighbor we're talking about. Do I really need to know that much about him?"

"I didn't realize the Referral Program was going to put constraints on our girl chat. You might need to cover your ears."

Ivy giggled. "I'll keep it clean."

"Please do," Brooke said.

"Daveed and I had actually agreed to take sex off the table. We wanted to get to know one another without complicating things with sex. And things were going fine. But last weekend, we were supposed to have a picnic and it was raining that day."

"I recall."

"When I got to his house, he had set up a picnic indoors. It was so sweet. He read me poetry and one thing led to another. We didn't plan it, but it felt right."

"So, how was it?" Dylan asked.

"Do we need the details, Dylan?" Brooke asked in return.

"I don't want to make Brooke uncomfortable, so I'll keep it PG. It was nice."

"Does this mean you have found your man?"

"I hope so. I feel like this is real and can be something really special."

"I'm a little scared of that. Things got a little hot and heavy between me and Barrett, but I pulled back. He's a great guy, but I want to get to know him more before taking that step."

"I can relate to that, Dylan. Sebastian is checking all the boxes. Even though I'm not going to keep my guard up and miss out on a potentially good thing, I still want to take my time with him."

"Oh, great. You two are making me feel like I should have waited."

"Don't be silly. We're grown women and we each have individual journeys. You did what was right for you. There's no judgment here."

"Thanks, Dylan. Brooke, I see it in your eyes. You're judging," Ivy said with a laugh.

"Maybe a little bit," Brooke replied, giving Ivy a playful push. "I'm kidding. We're too old to be worried about what others think. I trust your judgment."

The breakfast arrived and the girls continued with their light-hearted banter. They didn't harp on Ivy's revelation. They agreed to continue to be open and let the program take its course. Gone were the questions of whether the program would actually work. One thing had become clear. They were on the journey together, but their paths were their own.

TWENTY-FIVE

The day was a whirlwind from the moment Dylan arrived at the office. There were messages piled up and back-to-back meetings until noon. It had been a crazy week, but she refused to let the frenzy overtake her. She returned the calls in order of importance and put her staff on notice that she would be behind closed doors for the rest of the day. She only wanted to be interrupted if some sort of natural disaster was imminent.

There was a knock on her office door. She glanced at the clock on her desk. It was almost three in the afternoon. "Come in," she called out.

Her assistant, Callie, poked her head in. "Sorry to interrupt."

"This better be an emergency."

"You have a call and you have your do not disturb on."

"For good reason . . ."

"It's just that Barrett has been calling. He said he hoped you wouldn't mind the reprieve."

Dylan smiled. "Thanks, Callie. Put him through."

"You got it." Callie closed the door.

Dylan's desk phone rang. "Good afternoon."

"You aren't easy to catch up with," Barrett said.

"I know, I'm sorry."

"How are you?"

"Having the day from hell."

"I'm sorry to hear that. I won't keep you. I'm sending you something. I wanted to make sure you were there first because you need to sign for it."

"What is it?" she asked with a lilt to her voice.

"You'll see. I'll talk to you later."

He hung up before she had a chance to question him more. What could Barrett be sending to her office, she wondered. She smiled to herself and got back to work. As busy as Dylan was, she wouldn't trade business ownership for anything in the world. It was hard work but rewarding. She was proud of her accomplishments and poised to achieve so much more.

About an hour later, there was a knock on her door. "Come in."

Callie escorted a messenger inside. "He insisted you needed to sign for this personally."

"No problem." Dylan took the envelope from the messenger and signed his paperwork. "Thank you."

"I promise no more interruptions," Callie said, closing the door behind them as they exited.

Dylan opened the metal clasp on the manila envelope and peered inside. A smile spread across her face. She shook her head, picked up the phone, and immediately dialed Barrett.

He answered on the first ring. "I hope my delivery made your day a little better."

"Did you really send me a first-class ticket to Riviera Maya?"

"Will you be my travel companion this weekend?"

"This ticket is for tomorrow."

"Friday kicks off the weekend."

"Wow . . . um . . ."

"I would love for you to join me."

Dylan tried to gather her thoughts. She wasn't sure whether she could join Barrett on his jaunt to Mexico on such short notice. "I'd like to—"

"Come on. Take tomorrow off and fly with me to Riviera Maya. Let's get those pretty toes in the hot sand," he said.

Dylan laughed. "Okay."

"Okay?"

"Yes, I'll go with you to Riviera Maya."

"Just what I wanted to hear. I'll call you this evening."

Dylan hung up the phone and couldn't stop smiling. She wanted to go, and it didn't make sense to fight it. She had a lot to do and very little time. She asked Callie to schedule wax and nail appointments for her, then resumed what she was working on, feeling a lift in her mood.

She decided to call it a day after half an hour. She needed to get to her appointments and then home to pack.

∘ ∘ ∘

DYLAN FASTENED HER seat belt as Barrett placed her carry-on in the overhead compartment. He got situated in the seat next to Dylan and took her hand in his. "You are officially a member of my travel club."

"You did say you don't want to travel the world alone. I'm glad I could make your dreams come true."

Barrett threw his head back and laughed heartily. "You are definitely doing that."

"Seriously, thank you for inviting me."

"I want you to relax and enjoy this weekend."

Dylan leaned over and gave Barrett a kiss.

"One more." He puckered his lips.

She kissed him again, taking time to show her appreciation.

The flight attendant came over and interrupted. "Good morning. Can I offer you a beverage? Maybe some coffee or tea, a cocktail?"

"No, thank you. I have everything I need right now," Barrett replied. "Dylan, would you like something?"

"No, I'm fine."

The flight attendant nodded and continued through the rest of the first-class cabin.

Dylan looked at Barrett. His cream linen shirt and slacks were wrinkle free. The color contrasted beautifully with his pecan brown skin. His goatee was freshly trimmed. He was wearing an expensive-looking watch. Hands moisturized, nails manicured. Barrett was easy on the eyes and he smelled delicious.

"The way you look at me does something to me," he commented.

Dylan blushed. She hadn't realized he was watching her. "You caught me."

"What were you thinking?"

"I was thinking how handsome my travel companion is."

"Do you know what it does to a man to have a beautiful woman compliment him?"

"Tell me," she replied, slightly above a whisper.

He moved in close and placed a soft kiss on her lips. "It makes me feel like the world is mine."

"The ultimate ego boost."

"Ego plays a part, but it's deeper than that. When a Black woman compliments a Black man, it makes him feel invincible, like there's nothing he can't do."

"Did I tell you I think you're smart, too? It's not just your beauty, it's also your brain."

He chuckled. "I love your sense of humor." Barrett gazed at Dylan. "I'm looking forward to this weekend with you."

"What do you have in store for me?"

"I recall you said you wanted to lie on a beach doing nothing. I plan on wining and dining you, but I want you to unwind the way you want to."

"Are you always this attentive?"

"When it comes to you."

"So, you haven't treated all the ladies this way?"

Barrett shook his head. "All what ladies?"

"Come on. I'm sure plenty of women consider you a catch."

"That doesn't mean I share their sentiments. If there is one thing you don't have to question about me, it's my intentions. They're authentic and apparent. It takes a special kind of woman to catch my eye and get my attention. *You* have my attention."

Dylan tried to read Barrett's expression to see if she could detect any untruth in what he was saying. Everything inside of her was saying that he was being sincere. She relaxed back into her seat. Barrett had invited her for a nice weekend getaway, and she would do her best to enjoy every minute. In the rush of it all, Dylan hadn't called her girls to let them know she was going away. She thought about sending a text prior to takeoff, but she sort of liked the secrecy of it all. She decided she would tell them all about it once they returned.

After a smooth takeoff, Dylan rested her head on Barrett's shoulder and drifted off. She had been up late trying to figure out what ensembles to take on the trip. She ended up overpacking, but had an abundance of options suitable for a resort getaway. Her travel outfit was a dusty rose maxi dress with thong sandals. Comfort and style were the objective.

Barrett sipped on a mimosa and scanned through a magazine while Dylan dozed. He had gone out on a limb purchasing the additional ticket for her. He had hoped that she would accept his invite, but knew it could have gone either way. They were just getting to know one another. And, though things had been going well, he didn't want to do too much too soon. Barrett knew his own mind. He was a good judge of character and once he wanted something, he didn't allow anything to dissuade him. Aside from his own intuition, he trusted Brooke almost as much.

When Brooke had called to tell him about Dylan, Barrett had to admit he was surprised. They hadn't tried to set one another up since junior high school. As is common with teenage love, that didn't go well at all. They didn't vow not to do it again, but they hadn't since then. The way Brooke spoke about Dylan, Barrett knew he would be a fool not to meet her. He glanced down at the woman snoozing on him. She looked so peaceful, vulnerable. Something stirred within him. Barrett immediately felt protective. He kissed Dylan's forehead and a quiet sigh escaped her lips. He closed his eyes and leaned his face against the top of her head, relishing how comfortable it all felt.

o   o   o

THE DRIVER NAVIGATED the SUV through the gates of the resort. A sprawling landscape of green plants, exotic flowers, and palm trees swayed in the balmy breeze. The SUV glided to a smooth stop beneath the hotel's portico. The resort's staff descended upon the vehicle, opening the doors and taking luggage from the trunk. Dylan stepped from the car and into warm, tropical air. She did a slow spin, taking in the scenery. The resort sat atop a hill. She could see various buildings comprising the resort and the ocean in the distance.

She turned to Barrett. "What a view."

He smiled. "Let's get checked in."

Barrett took Dylan's hand and led her into the resort lobby. While he went to check in, she was greeted with a cool hand towel and iced fruit water. She walked the circular, open-air lobby. The resort grounds looked beautiful. People strolled the network of tree-lined walkways, footbridges, and paths. Music played in the distance. Barrett came up beside Dylan holding a small portfolio.

"Are we set?" she asked.

"We're good to go. Do you want to go to the room first or do you want to grab lunch?"

"I would love to slip into my swimsuit first. Maybe we can have lunch poolside?"

"Whatever your heart desires."

That earned Barrett a smile. He signaled to the bellman and informed him they would be going to the suite. The suite was a short distance from the main hotel requiring a quick ride in a golf cart. Dylan held on as the bellman zipped around the curves heading to their suite, then came to an abrupt stop in front of their building. He escorted them to the third and top floor.

Barrett handed Dylan a room key. "You're right next door to me."

Dylan opened her door and entered the suite—bright, airy, and spacious with the scent of fresh-cut flowers. The bellman carried in her luggage. She stood in the living room gazing out of the glass balcony door at the crystalline blue ocean. A rap on a door pulled her out of her reverie. Surprise registered on her face as the bellman went to open a door Dylan hadn't noticed before.

"Adjoining suites . . ." she said as Barrett entered her living room.

He handed the bellman a tip and waited for him to exit. "I hope that's okay."

"Of course, it's fine. This place is beautiful."

"I'm glad you like it. I'll let you freshen up. Let me know when you're ready for lunch."

"Give me twenty minutes and I'll be poolside ready."

Dylan quickly toured the rest of the suite, then ran into the bedroom to change. She slipped into a white bikini and added a blue sarong on top. She packed her beach bag with sunscreen, lip balm, sunglasses, and a book, then knocked on Barrett's door. He answered wearing a pair of swimming trunks and a T-shirt.

He took her in from head to toe. "Let's go, gorgeous."

They walked hand in hand down the pathway to the pool. Dylan had a moment of disbelief that she was actually in Riviera Maya. At the same time the day before, she was at her desk inundated with work. As the fluffy white clouds drifted across the blue skies and the sun beamed down on her face, she embraced the moment—the feel of the strong hand wrapped around hers, the smell of the ocean air, the sound of birds calling to one another, and the excitement of doing something completely on impulse.

As they approached the pool, two staffers rushed over with their arms full of beach towels to drape over the lounge chairs. Dylan pointed out an area partially in the sun, and not too close to the pool, to get situated. The staffers covered the chairs and made a pillow roll with one of the towels. Barrett wanted his umbrella up and Dylan wanted hers down. She took off her sarong and they got settled on their loungers.

Dylan pulled the sunscreen lotion from her bag and began applying it to her arms, stomach, and legs.

"Is it cliché for me to ask if you want me to do your back?"

Dylan laughed. "Not at all. I was just about to ask you." She handed Barrett the bottle and turned her back to him.

Barrett squeezed the sunscreen into his hands and began to massage the lotion onto her shoulders and down her back. Dylan's head lolled to the side.

"Good?" he asked.

"I was considering getting a massage while here, but I don't think I need to with your magic hands."

He ventured lower, smoothing lotion right above her bikini bottom. He firmly kneaded, his thumbs moving in a circular motion. "That's up to you." Barrett clapped his hands together. "All done."

Dylan looked over her shoulder at him. "Thanks." She reclined back on her lounger. Barrett's hands felt so good she hadn't wanted him to stop.

Barrett stretched out on his lounger, hands behind his head and legs crossed at the ankles. "I'll ask for some menus when the next server passes."

"I want a big frozen tropical drink."

"How about some food to go along with that?" He chuckled.

"Oh, definitely, but the drink is at the top of my list."

"Then I guess I better get someone over here." Barrett signaled to a server. He came over, took their drink orders, and gave them a couple of menus.

Dylan turned on her side, facing Barrett. "I can't thank you enough for this weekend."

"It's nothing."

"An all-expense paid trip is not *nothing.*"

"Dylan, I learned a long time ago that you invest in what's important to you. I work very hard. Relaxation and peace of mind are essential to me. I refuse to put a price on that. And, in case you haven't noticed, I enjoy spending time with you. I'm willing to do whatever it takes to make that happen."

It was apparent to Dylan that Barrett wasn't worried about spending money. She assumed they would be sharing a room. The fact that he was gentleman enough to make sure she was comfortable and was paying for two suites in a five-star resort was more affirmation that Barrett was a good guy and worth giving a chance.

"Well, I have noticed, and I enjoy spending time with you, too," she replied.

"Sounds like we're on the same page and that's just how I like it."

"You're used to getting what you want, aren't you?"

"If I say yes, is that a bad thing?"

"Not necessarily."

"I'll answer your question, but let me take the long way around the park."

"Please do."

The server came over with their drinks and placed them on the small tables beside their lounge chairs. They quickly scanned the menus and ordered lunch.

"I mentioned before that I'm an only child. I was raised in a middle-class home by both of my parents. Even though it was just me, my parents did not spoil me. In fact, they made me work for every single thing I got. I had chores, needed to get good grades, and still they were conservative with rewarding me for doing well. I was raised to understand from my parents that nothing in life is just given to you."

"Okay, so you aren't used to getting what you want?"

"Well, let me finish. That was just part of my story. I also had my maternal grandparents. They were very wealthy and very elitist. It was a classic case of daughter meets an *unsuitable* man from the wrong side of the tracks, falls in love with that man, gets disowned by her parents, marries that man, and has his child and the elitist parents accept the grandchild but never accept their daughter and her husband, no matter how successful he became."

"That had to be tough on your parents."

"I'm sure it was, but as a kid I didn't know the extent of the situation. My mother had a good heart. She never kept me from her parents. Every summer, I spent a few weeks with them at their estate in Maryland. During those few weeks, I was given any and everything I wanted. But, you better believe, as soon as I returned home to my parents they put me back on the straight and narrow. They wanted to make sure that I knew money isn't everything. My mother walked away from a life of privilege to be with my father. They made sure when I returned home from Maryland each summer that my values were intact and that love and family came first. My grandfather passed away when I was seventeen. In his will, he stipulated I was to inherit everything when I turned twenty-one. I haven't shared this with many people. However, I wanted to answer you honestly in hopes that you will understand who I am as a person. I don't want you to get the wrong impression about my values. I understand having the best of both worlds. I also understand, probably more than most, that getting what you want comes at a cost."

"I appreciate you sharing that, and I hope I didn't make you feel that I was judging."

"Not at all."

"I think it's beautiful that your parents found love and no one and no amount of money could keep them apart."

"My parents have something special. There was a time when all they had was each other. The way they are with one another is hard to describe. My mother often says they were made for each other. I believe it."

"A love like that can be hard to find. Definitely relationship goals . . ."

Barrett reached over and took hold of Dylan's hand. "What are your relationship goals?"

"Wow, you're putting me on the spot," she demurred.

"That's not my intention. I just want to know your thoughts."

Dylan sipped from her drink. "I can honestly say I have given this a lot of thought."

"You have my undivided attention."

"My parents have also served as a great example for me. I know what a healthy, loving relationship looks like. They set the bar for me. I can remember dating guys in high school and college that I knew I shouldn't have given the time of day. You know how you go with the flow even though it doesn't feel right?"

"I've been there a time or two."

"I chalk it up to youth, but even back then I knew what I wanted. As I matured, it became more about knowing what I deserved and not being willing to settle."

"What do you want?" Barrett peered at her intently.

"Something genuine, something real. I want a solid relationship on a firm foundation with an honest and caring man. I want to laugh and experience the joy of loving someone with reckless abandon. If we have disagreements, I want to communicate from a place of love, not anger. There must be passion, mutual respect, and a shared purpose for life's journeys."

Barrett smiled. "A shared purpose for life's journeys . . . I like that."

"Your turn."

"My relationship goals are simple."

"Let's hear them."

"I want a relationship with you. *You* are my relationship goals."

Dylan's pulse sped up. "There you go again being Mr. Smooth."

"Let me be clear because I don't want you to get the wrong impression. I'm not trying to charm you or be charismatic. I know what I want, and I mean every word I say. I have never been into superficial attributes. The woman I want to be in a relationship with is principled, relatable, and determined. She operates from a place of integrity. Her inner spirit shines from her eyes. She's humble, yet confident, and beautiful from the inside out. With that woman by my side, nothing is impossible. To that woman, I would give anything. For that woman, I would move mountains. I would spend every day making sure there was a smile in her heart. With that woman, I would raise a family and grow old. Relationship goals aren't something you *hope* to have in the future. Just like any other goal, they're something you put your time, energy, and effort into achieving. I want you to know where I stand. It serves no purpose for me to play it cool. That would only stymie my efforts." Barrett sat up and faced Dylan, placing his feet on the ground between their loungers. "And, as I said before, I know what I want."

Dylan wrapped her hand around his biceps and tugged him closer. Their lips touched. His energy swept over her like a wave of vertigo. She opened her eyes and stared at him, wondering if he felt the same thing she did. "You're doing something to me," she breathed.

"Nothing you haven't already done to me."

She felt it. He meant every word he said. She kissed him again, relishing the headiness of the moment.

Barrett rested his forehead against Dylan's. "You want to take a dip in the pool before our food arrives?"

"Yes, please. I need to cool off."

He stood up and extended his hand, helping Dylan off the lounge chair. As he led her to the pool, Barrett admired her flawless skin and the many curves on display in her strappy white bikini. He thought to himself this was how he wanted to travel from that moment on.

o o o

DYLAN AND BARRETT had stayed out all day and finally returned to their suites to get ready for dinner. Dylan was in the shower bathing and washing her hair. After a couple hours at the pool, they'd moved down to the beach. She'd soaked up the sun along with a few too many drinks. Barrett had wanted to lounge beneath an umbrella but she'd coaxed him into the ocean. They'd frolicked in the water together, Dylan wrapping her legs around his waist as he waded deeper than she would have gone alone. She reminisced on her chest pressed against his and how his strong hands felt on her back supporting her weight. Barrett made her feel cherished. With him she felt safe.

Dylan rinsed the suds from her hair and body. She stepped out of the shower and dried off, draping the towel around her nakedness. The air-conditioning was on full blast. She went to the living room to adjust the thermostat. The adjoining door to Barrett's suite was still open. As she passed by, she caught a glimpse of him in his living room with a towel wrapped around his waist, looking through his travel bag. He looked up and spotted her.

They stared at one another with curious expressions. Barrett slowly advanced toward the adjoining doors. Dylan felt the pull. Silently, she approached him. They stood toe-to-toe in the doorway, words unspoken, seconds passing. Barrett bit his bottom lip and took a step forward. Dylan took a step back. Barrett tilted his head. She nodded and a smile flitted across her lips. He took another step and she backed up a little further into her living room. He moved closer, simultaneously reaching out for her. His hand on her lower back, he lured her in. Her head tilted upward, eyes closed, in anticipation of his descent. Barrett's lips brushed Dylan's. A knock at the door interrupted them just as he was about to maneuver their bodies further into the room.

He groaned and extricated himself from Dylan's arms. "I can't imagine who that is." He kissed Dylan's forehead. "One moment." Barrett went back to his suite to answer the door.

A member of the resort staff handed him an envelope. "Good evening, sir. This belongs to you. It was left at the front desk during your check-in."

Barrett peeked in the envelope. It was his driver license. He hadn't noticed he didn't get it back earlier. "Thank you."

He closed the door, eager to return to Dylan. Unfortunately, she wasn't where he'd left her. "Where did you disappear to?" he called out.

"I'm getting dressed," she replied from her bedroom. "Everything okay?"

"It was," he mumbled. Louder he said, "Yes, the front desk sent someone to return my license."

"They have really attentive staff here."

"With horrible timing."

Dylan sat on the edge of the bed, flushed, holding her hand to her racing heart. "That was close," she whispered.

TWENTY-SIX

*B*arrett and Dylan walked arm in arm across the resort grounds back to their suites. They had dinner and dessert at a steakhouse, one of the many resort restaurants. Barrett ordered a filet mignon and raved about it through the entire dinner. Dylan wasn't in the mood for anything quite so heavy and ordered a grilled shrimp salad. He teased her about ordering seafood at a steakhouse, likening it to ordering hot tea at a milkshake shop. They were already planning the next night's dinner at either the French or Italian restaurant.

"I know we've had a long day, but it's still sort of early. Do you want to go to one of the clubs?" he asked.

"I don't think I have the energy for that tonight."

"How about a pajama party?"

"A what?"

"A pajama party in my room. We can put on our pajamas, just relax, and watch movies."

"That actually sounds pretty good."

"Great. A pajama party it is."

They arrived at their building and took the elevator up to their floor. Dylan unlocked the door to her suite. "I'll see you in a few."

"One more thing," he said. "Pajamas are optional."

They entered their suites laughing. Dylan went into her bedroom reflecting on how much of a good time she was having with Barrett. She appreciated that he shared personal details about his family and even his wealth. It gave her some clarity on his approach to life and priorities. Dylan did wonder if Brooke was aware of his financial situation. It wasn't Brooke's style to mention something like that, but he did say not many people knew.

Dylan slipped into a short, black silky nightgown, spritzed on a light fragrance, and put her hair up in a topknot. She threw the matching robe over her nightgown, put on a pair of flip-flops, and was ready for the pajama party. She listened for a brief moment at the adjoining door to Barrett's suite, took a deep breath, and then knocked.

Barrett opened the door with a broad smile on his face. He was wearing a pair of pajama bottoms and nothing else—shirtless and glistening. "Don't you look cozy," he said, guiding her into the living room.

"So do you."

Dylan followed Barrett over to the couch. He sat on one end and she the other. He looked puzzled by the distance between them.

"What would you like to watch?" he asked. "Are you in the mood for action, horror, suspense, romance?"

"Let's watch something scary."

"You're going to have to move closer if we watch a horror movie." He patted the cushion beside him.

"Do you mean to tell me you're scared of horror?"

"If I say yes, will you sit next to me?"

Dylan chuckled. "I'll come closer but I'm going on record to say I don't believe you."

"I'm even going to let you pick the movie."

Dylan scrolled through the options and settled on an alien invasion flick.

There was a knock at the door and Dylan jumped. Barrett patted her leg. "Jumping already? We haven't started the movie yet. Are you sure you want to watch horror?"

"I wasn't scared. I just wasn't expecting anyone to be knocking on the door at this hour."

"I ordered some champagne."

Barrett went to the door and let the server in. He wheeled in a cart with a bottle of champagne, glasses, a covered bowl, and a platter. The server opened the bottle, careful to avoid overflow, and filled their glasses, placing every item on the table in front of the couch. He removed the cover from the bowl revealing freshly made popcorn. Lastly, he uncovered the platter. Plain and chocolate dipped strawberries and fresh whipped cream decorated the dish. Barrett escorted the server to the door and slipped him a tip. He closed the door and returned to the couch, making sure there was no space between him and Dylan. Barrett handed Dylan a glass.

"Cheers, beautiful."

"Cheers."

They sipped their champagne. Dylan placed her glass on the table and started the movie. As the opening credits rolled, Barrett put his arm around Dylan's shoulders.

"Comfortable?" he asked.

Dylan nodded. "Yes."

"Do you want a blanket? Not that I want to cover up your cute nightgown."

"No, I don't need a blanket."

"Do you want some popcorn?"

Dylan chuckled. "Are you going to talk through the whole movie?"

He kissed her temple. "No, I'm done."

Barrett finally directed his attention toward the movie playing on the television screen. The story started off slow but had finally piqued his interest. Dylan covered her eyes during a gory scene and he pulled her in closer. The intimate proximity, her short nightgown, and the scent of her perfume caused a stir. He planted a kiss on her forehead. She removed her hands from her eyes and looked at him.

Barrett placed a delicate kiss on her lips. "We have some unfinished business."

"I believe we do."

He caressed her neck and shoulders. "This time, we shouldn't have any interruptions."

Dylan loved the way his strong hands felt on her. She had seen him all afternoon at the pool and the beach without a shirt, but there was something about him being in just pajama bottoms that was tugging at her insides. Barrett's sex appeal was undeniable, damn near overwhelming.

He reached over and picked up a strawberry, swirled it in the whipped cream, and brought it up to Dylan's mouth. She took a bite and then he took one. Barrett kissed her, the taste of berries and cream on her tongue.

"Mmm, you taste better than the strawberry," he said. Barrett kissed her again.

Dylan cradled his face in her hands as they fell deeper into one another. She felt the electricity and the connection between them getting stronger. Everything was feeling right with Barrett and the soft lighting, champagne, and strawberries were leading somewhere. She was wearing her sexy nightgown and he was partially clad, the bedroom was a stone's throw away, and there was nothing to stop them from taking things to the next level. Dylan wondered if she was ready for the next step. She second-guessed whether it was a good idea to introduce sex at their current stage of the relationship. If it didn't work out, she thought how it could impact his relationship with Brooke or even hers, for that matter. That was definitely a major caveat to the Referral Program. Dylan should have been completely caught up in the moment, but instead she was in her own head.

Barrett drew back from their embrace. "I feel like I lost you there. Is something wrong?"

Dylan sighed, placing a comforting hand on Barrett's thigh. "No, everything is perfect."

"Then what just happened?" He looked perplexed.

"This"—she waved her hand at the champagne and strawberries—"us in our pajamas, is wonderful. I really don't know what happened. One moment your kiss is making me think all sorts of sinful thoughts. The next thing I know, I'm wondering if we're rushing things."

"You think we're moving too fast?"

"The funny thing is, that didn't enter my mind until this very moment."

"I hope you know I'm not some flighty guy who doesn't understand the magnitude of what's occurring between us."

Dylan touched his shoulder. "I absolutely don't think that."

"I'm into you and I'm into us."

"I know that." Dylan paused to gather her thoughts. "It's just that I started thinking about all this sexiness in front of me, that big ol' bed in the other room, one thing leading to another, and I guess I got a case of cold feet."

"I see."

"You knew what you were doing opening the door with all that chest showing and glowing."

Barrett laughed. "What about you? Your nightgown isn't exactly conservative."

"You did say it was a pajama *party*. I came dressed accordingly. I can put on something less revealing, if you prefer," she rebutted, with a mischievous smile.

"Believe me, I am not complaining."

"I didn't think so."

They laughed together.

"Dylan, I invited you on this trip because I wanted to spend some quality time with you. It wasn't my intention to make you feel rushed or as if I expected anything. I got you your own suite so you would be comfortable and not feel pressured in any way. I wanted to be respectful of you and our burgeoning relationship."

"You are so considerate, and never once did I think that you were trying to pressure me into anything. What's happening between us feels natural and special. I just don't want anything to jeopardize that."

"You think sex would?"

"Not necessarily, but tonight the thought crossed my mind."

"I don't know where tonight might have led but, when the time comes, I want you to be one hundred percent sure. Please know that we can wait until you have zero doubt."

Dylan pecked him on the lips. "Thank you."

"Let's rewind the movie. I got distracted but I promise to devote my full attention to the rest."

Dylan cuddled up close to him. "Well, maybe not your full attention."

TWENTY-SEVEN

*I*vy sipped from her coffee mug. It wasn't often she was able to sit on her balcony on a Saturday morning doing nothing other than taking in the sights and sounds of the city. She had slept a little later than usual and was in the mood to lounge around. She'd worked late every night during the past week and needed to decompress. Social work was far from easy and a few of her cases were downright complicated and emotionally draining. She had every intention of relaxing and spending time with Daveed.

She reached for her phone and dialed his number. It rang a few times before his voice mail picked up. Ivy left a message for him asking what they would be getting into for the day. She ended the call, weighing whether she should also send a text. They'd spent the majority of the day before texting back and forth. With her hectic caseload, she hadn't spoken with Daveed much during the week. She missed hearing his voice and speaking with him every night before falling asleep.

The phone rang in her hand. She looked at the number and smiled as she answered. "Good morning to you."

"Hey, sorry I missed your call. I was in the shower."

"No worries. I'm just sitting on the balcony thinking about us."

"Oh really?"

"I want to see you today."

159

"Unfortunately, I can't."

"Why not?" she asked, pouting.

"I got called in to work today. Someone tried to hack into the system."

"I know you're a cyber expert, but no one else from your team can handle it?"

"It's all hands on deck."

"Maybe you can come by after work."

"I'm not sure, Ivy. Depending on how serious it is, I might have to work all weekend."

"I sure hope not. I want to see you."

"We'll see. I have to get to the office."

She sighed. "All right, well, call me later."

Ivy hung up the phone feeling unsettled. She replayed their exchange in her head. She was aware their relationship was relatively new, but up until the past week they had been inseparable. In that moment, she felt a little disconnected from Daveed. She was trying not to read into his abruptness. Or, perhaps it was dismissiveness, she pondered. Ivy told herself that he had a work emergency on his hands and not to take it personally.

Ivy kept returning to the thought that something didn't feel right and that feeling was making her extremely uncomfortable. She drank her vanilla coffee as if the contents of the cup would provide comfort and soothe her in some way, but her worries kept bubbling up to the surface. She attempted to tamp down the one thing she had convinced herself wasn't an issue. That she had made the right choice and it wouldn't come back to bite her in the ass. That she hadn't moved too soon with Daveed. That sex wouldn't complicate their process of getting to know one another. That two mature adults could engage in a physical relationship and continue to grow in a positive and constructive manner. She stared at her coffee as if the answers were at the bottom of the cup.

Ivy figured if she and Daveed weren't going to spend the day together, she would not stay home thinking about him all day. She decided to get dressed and go volunteer at the Phase College program. There was no question that would be a positive and constructive use of her time.

TWENTY-EIGHT

Perched in the bay window in Sebastian's kitchen, Brooke watched him at work while he prepared dinner. He insisted she enjoy her wine and let him do the cooking. The kitchen was filled with the aroma of spices and herbs melding together in a way that enticed the senses. Sebastian told her that he was preparing lobster gnocchi, roasted asparagus, and a frisée and arugula salad. Brooke hadn't realized just how much Sebastian loved to cook. The first time he made her dinner it was late and she didn't want him to do too much. She asked him to prepare something quick and light. He broiled steaks and served them with romaine wedges. It was quick and easy, but the steak was seasoned and cooked to perfection. She figured a lot of men could pull off a steak and didn't appreciate that he really had an affinity for cooking. But, as they ate dinner that night, he told her that he wanted to make her a real meal and detailed some of his specialties. She was intrigued and looking forward to trying some of his culinary offerings.

As Brooke sat observing Sebastian in action, she could tell he knew his way around a kitchen. She was starving, having skipped lunch earlier in the day. Working on her second glass of wine, Brooke knew she had better eat something soon before the alcohol had its way with her.

"It really smells delicious in here," she said.

"As soon as the asparagus is done, we can eat."

"Can I at least set the table?"

"It's already set in the dining room."

Brooke assumed they would be eating in the kitchen. Apparently, it was a different kind of evening. Sebastian tossed the salad with vinaigrette. He pulled a sheet pan from the oven and sprinkled the asparagus with fresh-ground pepper and a drizzle of lemon juice. He plated the lobster gnocchi and asparagus and picked up the two plates.

"Brooke, can you grab the salad bowl?"

"Of course." She went over to the island, got the salad, and followed him into the dining room. Lit candles in the center of the table illuminated the room. Sebastian placed their meals on the charger plates on the dining room table. He plated the salad and the wine was poured. The only thing left to do was to sit and enjoy the meal he'd prepared. They sat across from each other rather than at the head seats.

"This looks amazing," Brooke said, admiring the food on her plate.

"I hope you enjoy it."

Brooke tasted everything. "This is delicious. I wasn't sure what to expect from a man who wants his woman to do the cooking."

Sebastian laughed. "I told you I cook, too, and I don't expect the woman I'm with to cook all the time."

"I'm kidding. I am impressed, though."

"I might not grow my own food like some people, but I do know where to buy fresh ingredients."

"Well done, doctor."

"Do I get any points for serving dinner by candlelight?"

"Sure, how many do you want?"

"As many as I can get."

"We'll see how the rest of the night goes first." Brooke delighted in their teasing. Since the day they met, they'd engaged in witty repartee.

"Since I made dinner, does that mean you'll be taking out the garbage?" He could barely keep the smile off his face.

"I don't want to take my own out!"

"I told you, as long as I'm around, my woman will never have to worry about that."

"Do you consider me your woman?"

"I'm not seeing anyone else."

"If we were out and ran into one of your friends, how would you introduce me?"

"I would say this is Brooke . . . my girlfriend."

"Did you tell this to your cousin?"

"Ivy knows how I feel about you."

"Is that a yes?"

"Yes, I told Ivy, my mother, and the mailman."

Brooke burst into a fit of giggles. "Not the mailman."

"He was the first person I told."

"Will you be serious," she said, trying to control her own laughter.

"Okay, let's get serious."

"Thank you."

"I would be proud to call you my girlfriend to anyone who asks. Hell, I'll tell anyone who hasn't asked. Are you okay with that?"

Brooke reminded herself that she'd taken down her walls. "Yes, I'm fine with that."

"Now tell me, if I need to officially ask you to be my girl, I will."

"We're not in high school."

"I don't care. If I need to be official, I will. In fact, that's exactly what I'm going to do."

Brooke felt herself about to laugh again but refrained. "Seb—"

"Shhh," he said, cutting her off. "Brooke, as we sit here by candlelight, just the two of us . . . alone . . . together . . . together but alone . . . will you be my girlfriend?"

She threw her head back and laughed. "I *can't* with you. Yes, I'll be your girlfriend."

Sebastian got up and came around to Brooke's side of the table. He kissed her cheek then pecked her on the lips. "Sealed with a kiss."

"You are so silly."

"Silly but serious." He went back to his seat and resumed eating.

Brooke shook her head. Sebastian made her smile. He made her laugh. He made her feel excited about being in a new relationship. "I think you're good for me."

He looked up from his plate. "I know I am. I'm just glad to hear you say that."

"You have a disarming way with people."

"I'm great with parents, too. So, whenever you're ready to take me home . . ."

"Oh, I'm pretty sure my parents would love you. However, I wouldn't subject you to them anytime soon."

"Why is that?"

"They wouldn't care that we just started dating. They would interrogate you on when we're getting married and having children as soon as you walk through the door."

"Is that all? I know how to handle those conversations."

"Oh no. My parents are next level."

"I would just assure them that I would be an amazing husband and phenomenal father to our kids."

Brooke's lips twisted. "And that's why you won't be meeting them anytime soon."

"You don't think I'd be an incredible husband to you?"

She was thankful for the candlelight to conceal the fact that she was blushing. "I haven't considered it."

"You haven't thought about whether I'm husband material?"

"Not necessarily."

"Why not? The day we met I was weighing what type of person you were and whether there was marriage potential."

"You were?"

"Come on, be honest. That's what men *and* women do. At this stage in our lives, when we know we're looking for something more than casual dating, you start from a baseline of where can this lead."

"That's interesting."

"Brooke, I'm always going to be upfront and open with you. It's who I am. I know you aren't as comfortable with that level of openness—yet—but in time I know you'll get there."

"Am I dining with the doctor or my . . ." She faltered.

"You're dining with your *boyfriend*. You can call me your boyfriend."

"I know."

"I get it—it's new. But you should know, I'm looking for something serious. I don't want you to think I'm talking today or tomorrow, but marriage and family are a priority for me."

Brooke avoided his eyes, looking down at her plate. "No, I understand."

"I just hope you see the same potential in me that I see in you."

"I don't want to give you the wrong impression, so let me be clear." She met his gaze, allowing him to feel the weight of her words. "I'm ready to see where this goes with you and me."

"There's one more thing you should know," he said.

"What's that?"

"I've been celibate for the last year."

"By choice?"

"Of course by choice. I made a conscious decision that I would abstain from sex."

"For how long?"

"Initially, I decided I was done with having casual sex. Unless I was dating someone seriously or in a meaningful relationship, sex wasn't an option."

"Can I ask what brought you to that decision?"

"I wanted more for myself, out of my interactions with others and from my relationships. I was seeking more clarity about my life, my future, and my mission."

"And abstaining from sex was the answer?"

"It was a part of a broader journey to self-awareness. As the months passed, I decided to make abstaining more permanent. How do you feel about that?"

"I don't know. Sex is important."

"I don't disagree with you. It's important for a couple to be able to connect on a higher level."

"Exactly."

"But there's no stipulation stating that connection has to take place before marriage."

"I don't know about that. We're responsible adults. I'm on birth control. We both know our status. I think it's important to take everything for a test drive."

"If you're with the right person, sex will only enhance what you've cultivated and shared with one another."

"So, you mean to tell me you don't want to take all of *this* for a test drive?"

"I'm fully aware celibacy is not popular, especially for two mature, attractive adults. And, I'm not saying it will be easy. What I am saying is over the years I've indulged just like anyone else, been responsible and obviously taken the necessary tests. Since making the decision to be celibate, I try to view sex and relationships through a different lens. I realize my decision may not align with your wants and needs and I thought you should know—so you can decide if this will or won't work for you. Just let me say I hope this isn't your deal-breaker because I know our story is just beginning."

Brooke sat quietly for a moment. "Why didn't you mention this sooner?"

"Because, honestly, I've been wavering. You made me feel like maybe abstaining had run its course. I see something in you that tells me this, what's happening between us, is real."

Again, she was thankful for the dim lighting. "Then why tell me now?"

"Tonight, you officially declared that you're my woman. We're no longer in the casual zone. I wanted you to know where I am on my personal journey. Right now, I'm still celibate no matter how difficult that may be when it comes to us."

"It's not a dealbreaker, but I can't tell you that I'm on the same page. I need to process all of this."

"I can respect that. How about some dessert to lighten the mood? Maybe a little pound cake with fresh strawberries, whipped cream, and a chocolate drizzle?"

"That sounds perfectly sinful."

"Coming right up."

o   o   o

CUDDLED ON THE sofa with her legs thrown over Sebastian's lap, Brooke rested her head in the crook of his neck as they watched a movie on television. He gently stroked her thigh. She kissed him on the neck. His hand stopped moving. She pressed her lips against the same spot, lingering, waiting for a reaction. He looked down at her. Brooke touched her hand to his face and guided it toward her lips. She kissed him deeply, her kiss conveying all she couldn't verbalize earlier. She wanted to be his woman and for him to be her man.

She touched her hand to his chest, feeling his muscular pecs. She trailed her fingers down to his abs and explored the definition. His kiss intensified. Her hand wandered down further, stopping near his zipper. Brooke slid her palm across the front of his pants, slowly caressing his manhood. He put his hand on top of hers. She cupped between his legs. Sebastian tenderly wrapped his hand around Brooke's, halting her probe.

Brooke pulled away from their kiss. "You don't want me to touch you?"

"I could tell you wanted to see what I had going on. I figured you got your answer."

"I definitely felt some things. *Seeing* would be something completely different. Now, if you want to show me, that works, too."

Sebastian kissed the tip of her nose and pulled her back into the crook of his neck. He resumed stroking her thigh and watching the movie.

Brooke peered up at him—wanting more and getting her first taste of abstaining.

TWENTY-NINE

$\mathcal{B}$ rooke lay in the middle of her bed staring up at the ceiling. She left Sebastian's house hopeful and confused. They were officially an item. She had a boyfriend. It had been a long time since she had called someone her man. Brooke only wished he had shared that he was celibate sooner. She didn't know if it would have made a difference, but she felt like she was already invested in him and the program, and not necessarily willing to walk away. Sebastian was a good man. She knew that for certain. For that reason alone, sex wasn't a dealbreaker. At least that was how she felt in the moment. How she would feel about it down the road, only time would tell.

Her phone rang. Brooke wondered who could be calling at such a late hour. She fumbled as she reached for it. "Seb?"

"I couldn't stop thinking about you."

"That's sweet," she said, barely above a whisper.

"I can still smell your perfume on me. Open the door . . ."

"What?"

"I'm outside."

"Outside of my house?" Brooke said in disbelief.

"I'm standing on your doorstep."

Brooke rushed downstairs in her T-shirt and panties, still holding her phone to her ear. "I can't believe—"

"Just open the door," Sebastian said, and ended the call.

Brooke turned off her alarm and unlocked the door.

Sebastian stood on the front steps with his head bowed. "I tried to sleep but my mind kept leading me to you."

"Come in."

Sebastian stepped inside, his body brushing against Brooke's as he passed. She closed the door and felt his heat directly behind her. She turned around into his waiting arms and held on tight as their lips feverishly connected. Brooke's knees buckled and she leaned back against the door. Sebastian's body melted into hers. She clutched the back of his head. Hot kisses wandered from her mouth, to her neck, down to her shoulder and back again. Overtaken by desire, Brooke tried to catch her breath in between kisses. She pulled away from his embrace. Brooke grabbed Sebastian's hand and led him through the darkened house, upstairs and into her bedroom.

They stood face-to-face in the center of the room, moonlight shining through the blinds illuminating their forms. Brooke slowly began unbuttoning Sebastian's shirt. He watched her silently, the rise and fall of his chest perceptible. She pushed his shirt from his shoulders and down his arms, tossing it to the side. Her hands unbuckled his belt. She glanced up at him. He was observing her every move. Unhurriedly, Brooke unfastened his pants and let them drop to his ankles. Sebastian stepped out of his shoes and pants simultaneously.

Moon rays beamed on him like a spotlight. Bare chested, donning only boxer briefs, Sebastian drew Brooke against his body. He reached down, grabbing the hem of her T-shirt and pulled it up and over her head. He let the shirt fall from his hands. Her breasts grazed his chest. Sebastian deftly swept Brooke up in his arms and carried her over to the bed. Placing one knee on the bed, he laid her down and covered her body with his own. Sebastian gazed into Brooke's eyes. "You're irresistible," he breathed.

Sebastian kissed Brooke with urgency, letting her feel the craving she left him with. He wrapped his arm tightly around her waist and

began to gyrate against her. Brooke responded in kind, feeling everything she had been trying to assess earlier.

She pulled away from his kiss. "Are you sure about this?"

"Don't I feel sure?" he said, grinding on her. His voice was husky
and filled with lust.

Brooke moaned. "Yes."

"Let me show you how sure I am." Sebastian wedged himself between her legs and positioned his hard penis directly on her clitoris.
He slid back and forth in long strokes, his erection growing. Sebastian buried his face between her breasts, kissing one then the other.
He filled his mouth with her supple breast, flitting his tongue across
the areola then sucking on the nipple until it hardened.

Brooke began pushing his briefs over his ass, attempting to take
them off. He grabbed her hands one at a time and held them over
her head. When she tried to move them, he pressed them firmly into
the mattress, letting her know to keep them there. Sebastian's tongue
traveled down her body. He inserted it in her navel and licked and
nibbled her abs along the way. He placed a single, prolonged kiss on
her silky panty–covered kitty. He kissed and licked from her hip bone
to her thighs, her knees, calves, and the arches of her feet.

She snatched her foot from his grasp. "That tickles."

"Is there something else I can tickle for you?"

Brooke moved her arms from above her head and removed her
panties.

Sebastian crawled up on the bed beside her. She tugged at the
waistband of his briefs. "Take these off and lay down right here."

Sebastian didn't hesitate. He slipped out of his underwear as
Brooke got on her knees. He laid on his back, his erection pointing
skyward. Brooke trailed her fingertips over his defined abs and ventured lower. Gently, she wrapped her hand around his eight inches—
acclimating herself with its girth and weight. She leaned down and
kissed the tip. His penis jerked. She did it again, covering it with her

full lips. Sebastian made a noise that sounded like a cross between a moan and a whine. She ran her tongue around the edge of his tip. He grabbed a fistful of the sheet in his hand. Sebastian's reaction excited Brooke. She sucked him into her mouth. Sebastian cried out and instinctively grabbed the back of her neck. She moved his hand and placed it by his side, pressing it into the mattress, as he had done to her moments before.

Brooke sucked and licked his penis, her hands firmly working the length of him. The more he moaned, the more aroused she became. His labored breaths matched her own. Brooke stopped sucking on him but continued to stroke him. She looked up at Sebastian and licked her lips. Holding his erection in her hand, she straddled him and eased down on his hardness. Her juices covered his shaft. Brooke moved up and down, her senses registering exactly how Sebastian felt inside her.

He gripped her hips, moving in sync with her and burrowing further inside. Sebastian knew he wouldn't be able to resist Brooke for long. The euphoria he was experiencing from the sight, sound, and feel of her body erased any reservations he might have had. She was so soft and warm and snug around him.

Sebastian sat up and scooted to the edge of the bed. "Wrap your legs around me," he said, holding her close with one arm.

She obliged and he stood up. Sebastian held Brooke beneath her ass and continued to thrust inside. Incoherent words slipped from her lips, high pitched and pleading. His grunts were almost as loud as her reverberating cries.

Sebastian gently lowered Brooke to her feet, slipping out of her in the process. He turned her around and guided her back to the bed, the front of his body pressed against the back of hers. They climbed up together, Brooke on her hands and knees and Sebastian on his knees behind her. He leaned forward and kissed down her spine. He could feel her trembling. He hugged her from behind.

"I want you," she whispered. "Give it to me."

A deep growl emanated from his chest. Sebastian grasped his penis and rubbed the tip in her wetness. He slid inside, spreading her walls as he entered. Sebastian gripped Brooke's hips and glided in and out of her kitty. Brooke pushed back and popped on him with each thrust. The harder she popped, the stronger he pumped. He held her steady and gave it to her long, deep, and hard.

Brooke felt her leg shaking. "You're going to make me cum."

"I want you to cum for me." Sebastian thrust faster and harder. "Cum for me, baby."

Brooke floated higher with the intensity of each thrust. Sebastian was taking her to the point of no return. His stroke was powerful. Brooke reached her peak and rained all over him. "Oh my God," she exclaimed.

Her wetness flooded him. Sebastian felt the pressure building, each deep dive bringing him closer. He was on the brink. Brooke twisted her hips and that was it. He released with a force so strong it left him shuddering. He lay down on his side, pulling Brooke down with him so they were spooning. Sebastian's heaving chest rubbed against her back.

"That was one hell of a test drive." He kissed her shoulder. "The kind that will have you making a commitment on the spot."

"It was incredible."

"Better than incredible."

"What does this mean for your celibacy?"

"It means that when it comes to you and me, there's no such thing as celibacy."

THIRTY

*B*rooke found herself at the gym on Sunday morning. Sebastian left her house around ten and thirty minutes later, she was running on the treadmill. She was full of energy and planning to do at least five miles. She didn't have any clients and could spend her time on her own fitness. Brooke's night with Sebastian had her floating on cloud nine. Never would she have imagined that her evening would have ended the way it did.

Brooke had come home from Sebastian's place frustrated and questioning how being in a relationship with a celibate man would even work. If he was celibate, then so was she by default. Brooke found it interesting that it never came up in any of their previous conversations, including the one where they discussed dealbreakers. She was aware that conversation took place during one of their first dates, but isn't that the time you would bring something like that up? It would seem that information should be shared in the beginning in order to give someone the opportunity to decide if they were willing to accept that type of lifestyle. Brooke smiled to herself. She was ecstatic that issue was now water under the bridge. She never expected Sebastian to show up at her door and certainly didn't anticipate that his celibacy would be ending that same night.

There was something about the way he looked standing on her doorstep. There was a hunger and a vulnerability to Sebastian that made her want him more. Brooke felt a twinge down below at the thought of what had transpired between them. She replayed taking

175

off his clothes piece by piece, visualized his naked body standing in her bedroom. She could feel his weight on top of her, his well-defined musculature, the smoothness of his skin. Brooke tingled thinking about how he felt inside . . . of her mouth . . . of her kitty . . . It was so damn good, she thought. Their bodies melded together. She could still feel his length and girth filling her up. The notion that she could have been denied that taste of heaven was near blasphemous. Brooke wanted him again and again and as soon as possible. Maybe she should take a page out of his playbook and show up on his doorstep, she thought. Brooke decided she wouldn't be doing that. Just because they'd had sex, didn't mean she wanted it to become all-consuming. She still wanted them to continue to cultivate their friendship and romance. Lust could not be the driving factor in their relationship.

Sebastian had shown her that he was a mature man and capable of expressing his feelings, wants, and needs. He made her feel secure that they wanted the same things. She was still working on prioritizing romance, but being around him made it easier to emulate his behaviors. Sebastian made her feel like she was safe to be herself and to be vulnerable sometimes. She couldn't remember the last time a man had made her feel quite that way.

Brooke wrapped up her workout and headed back toward her office. Michael called out as she passed his door. She popped her head in.

"Come in and sit down for a minute. I haven't seen you all week," he said.

"I know," she said, walking into his office. "We missed each other by minutes on Tuesday and Thursday."

"I left an analysis of the impact our marketing is having on membership on your desk."

"Thanks, I'll take a look. The gym is buzzing today for a Sunday morning."

"It absolutely is. The new pole dancing class we added is drawing a unique crowd."

"Unique?" Brooke laughed. "You know that's not what you really want to say."

Michael laughed. "I'm trying to be politically correct."

"We are way past P.C."

"Okay, fine. That pole dancing class has brought in some flexible members."

"We've always had flexible members."

"No, this is different."

"I think the only difference is they're showcasing talents you're not accustomed to seeing in our gym."

"Delightful talents."

Brooke chuckled. "You are officially banned from going anywhere near that class."

"You know me better than that. I don't go anywhere near the studio when that class is in session. I see them coming in or at the juice bar after."

"And how many of them have you hit on?"

"Not a one."

"Uh-huh."

"I'm serious. I'm talking smack with you, but I keep it all the way professional. Although, I am single . . ."

"And?"

"And, if by chance one of the lovely ladies initiates a conversation with me, I might have to entertain her."

"So now you're the great entertainer?" Brooke threw her head back and laughed.

Michael narrowed his eyes at her. "You're in a good mood this morning."

"I'm always in a good mood."

"We both know that's not remotely true. What's going on with you? Something is different."

"Well, if you must know, I'm seeing someone and so far, things are going really good."

"What?" Michael exaggeratedly feigned surprise. "You gave someone the time of day?"

"Yes, I did."

"I know things must be good because you would have debated me on how most men don't deserve the time of day."

"I might have. I just don't happen to have the negative energy to spar with you today."

"Whoa, okay. No sparring today? I better go over to the pole dancing class to find a woman right now so I can be all rainbows and sunshine like you." Michael started laughing before he could even finish his sentence.

"Maybe you should. I know you bask in your single life and the follies that come along with it, but at some point—"

"Nope, I reject that."

"I didn't even finish what I was about to say."

"That's okay. I have heard it all before. I happen to enjoy being an eligible bachelor."

"Are you sure 'bachelor' is the best term?"

"What would you call it?"

"'Player' crossed my mind."

"Ouch."

"Come on, Michael. Since I've known you, you are always dating someone new."

"That's what single people do. Now, I know your single differs from my single, but for a successful man like myself, it's the norm."

"It can also be a problem."

"For whom? I don't have any issues with the lifestyle I'm living."

"How about all of the ladies you date?"

"You make it sound like I have a million women."

"Well, how many do you have?"

Michael's brow furrowed. "Aren't you inquisitive today."

"That's what I thought. A lot."

"I do not have a lot of women. I date a few women."

"So, you're currently dating three women?"

"Yes, there are three."

"Player . . ." Brooke sang.

"I'm not a player. I'm a single man who dates. I'm respectful and honest. There isn't a woman out there who can say that we haven't discussed our situation."

"I'm curious. What is that conversation like?"

"It's simple really. If I'm not honest from the beginning, it would only backfire on me. I would have to move in ways that would make my life a living hell. Why would I want that? I don't want to lie to anyone or have to account for my time with made-up excuses when I'm not available. Those things would be counterproductive to being single and living a single life. I tell the truth."

"Just how truthful are you being?"

"I see you're not letting me off the hook."

"Nope."

Michael leaned back in his chair. "When I meet a woman and we're having our initial conversation, sizing each other up, I ask her if she is single. I know that when I ask her that question, she will in turn ask me the same. When she does, I'm *extremely* honest. I tell her that I'm single and dating. I specifically say that although relationships are great, I am personally not looking for one. Sharing that bit of information typically opens up a broader discussion about my dating life. I'm transparent. I'll say how many women I'm dating. It serves no purpose to hide or conceal that information. At the end of the day, either they're interested or they're not. Believe me, there are plenty of women with whom I've had great conversations, but at the end of the discussion we go our separate ways. I understand a lot of women are looking for *the one*. I just let them know from the beginning that I'm not it."

"I assume they're dating other men?"

"Sometimes they are and sometimes they aren't."

"You're okay with it when they are?"

"Absolutely. I can't dictate what they do. If we're in a casual situation, we have to keep it casual."

"Do they ask about the other women you're seeing?"

"No, it's not anything we flaunt in each other's faces. Mature dating is honest dating. I won't pretend that feelings don't get involved, at times. It would be ridiculous to act like that doesn't happen. But, for me, once that starts to occur, I know it's time for me to extricate myself from the situation."

"Wait a minute. You're telling me if you start to have deeper feelings for someone, you abandon the relationship—I mean, situation?"

"I know you can't relate but it boils down to one thing. I'm not looking for a serious relationship. I enjoy being single. That's my lifestyle."

"I guess I understand. I just didn't realize that catching feelings meant you just walk away."

"Now why do you have to say it like that?" Michael laughed. "I don't just walk away. We're not teens, Brooke. We have adult conversations about where we stand with one another. I know you think dating means I'm a player, but I'm not. I'm not out there mistreating anyone. There are people who want a relationship and there are others who don't. I'm not conning anyone. I'm not convincing anyone to change their wants and needs. The women I date are on the same page as me."

"I can understand that."

"There are a lot of men out there playing women. I know some of them. However, that's not me. I don't have the disposition or the energy for it. I also don't think all single men should be painted with the same paintbrush."

"How do you mean?"

"Think about it. You called me a player because I date more than one woman. I think 'player' is a nice way of calling a man a dog. I'm not dogging anyone or playing anyone. I'm single, I date, and I'm honest about it."

"Clearly, I opened a can of worms. Okay, I take back what I said. You're not a player."

"Don't try to pacify me."

Brooke chuckled. "I'm not. You're right. I shouldn't lump you in with men who are out there dating indiscriminately and lying about it. You have decency and I should have known better because you're the best business partner a girl could ever ask for."

"Okay, now you're blowing smoke. Don't you have work to do? Get out of my office."

"I've been thrown out of better places."

"I bet you have."

They shared a lighthearted laugh.

"Fine." Brooke stood up to leave. "I'm going to look at the analysis you left on my desk. In the meantime, you just stay away from that pole dancing class."

"Hey, Cameo said it best about living the single life."

"At some point, you'll have a change of heart. It happens to the best of us."

THIRTY-ONE

Jvy was stretched across her bed with the television on mute. She had come in from work and taken a shower and she was feeling restless. She drank a cup of chamomile tea and forced herself to go into the bedroom to relax. She picked up her phone and dialed Dylan on speaker.

"Hey, Dyl."

"I don't know why that always makes me laugh."

"Probably because I would call you Dill Pickles in college."

"Probably. What's going on?"

"I was just calling. I didn't hear from you all weekend."

"Well . . . I have a good reason for that."

"Do you now?" Ivy said, her curiosity stirring.

"I actually went away for the weekend."

"Where? You didn't mention going anywhere."

"I didn't plan on going anywhere. It was sort of a last-minute trip." Dylan paused. "With Barrett."

Ivy sat up on the bed. "What!"

"He called me on Thursday and invited me for a weekend get-away to Riviera Maya."

"You went to Mexico with Barrett?" Ivy couldn't keep the surprise out of her voice.

"I sure did."

"I'm shocked."

"You know, Ivy, we're supposed to be doing something different.

I stepped out of my comfort zone and I followed my heart. I wanted to go with him—so I accepted."

"That's big for you."

"I know, right?"

"Well, how was the trip?"

"The trip, Barrett, everything was amazing."

"Okay, I'm going to need all the details. So, start from the top."

"How about I give you the highlights?"

"Whatever. Just start talking."

"I mentioned to him some time ago that I wanted to relax on a beach somewhere and he made it happen. From the moment he picked me up to the moment we got back home, Barrett was so attentive to my every want and need. It was unbelievable. I get goose bumps thinking about the way he looks at me, how he holds my hand . . . He's such a gentleman. We had the best conversations lounging in the sun. He was open and shared things about his life that were deeply personal."

"And?" Dylan couldn't see her, but Ivy motioned with her hand to speed it up.

"And what?"

"Get to the good part."

"I'm sharing the good parts."

"You know exactly what I mean. The spicy parts."

"Like I said, Barrett is a gentleman. It was so sweet. He got us separate suites."

"Separate?"

"Yes, but they adjoined. Could you let me tell my story my way, please?"

"Go ahead."

"Sheesh, thank you. We spent most of our time on the beach or poolside with a copious number of drinks."

"That's the way to do it when you go away."

"He wined and dined me for three days straight. I may need to do a detox for the next two weeks." Dylan chuckled. "I had the best time with him. We talked about everything. He asked what I want in a relation-ship. I figured if he was asking, then I would tell him exactly what it is I am looking for—and he didn't flinch. Our experiences growing up with loving parents influenced us in similar ways. We have similar ideals."

"Did you talk about marriage?"

"Not directly. We talked about our relationship goals and what we want from someone we *could* be with or *could* raise a family with. Al-though, he did tell me directly that he wants a relationship with me."

"That's big, Dylan."

"When he said it, I got butterflies. Having such a candid con-versation, no pretense, no reason to be anything but truthful, was so refreshing. We had serious conversations, trivial ones, and everything in between. It was an unexpected getaway and just what I needed. I completely disconnected. I didn't call or text anyone, avoided social media, and I didn't even check in at the office."

"You didn't even call me to say you were going. Did you tell Brooke?"

"I didn't tell a soul. It was just me and Barrett. I'm so attracted to that man. It's not just physical. He's assertive and sensitive and gener-ous. He makes me laugh."

"He turns you on . . ."

"Yes, he turns me on. He is damn sexy."

"You had sex on the beach . . ."

"We did not have sex on the beach. Girl, be quiet!"

Ivy giggled. "I was just helping to move the story along."

"Anyway, we're super attracted to each other and we had some really nice moments. A lot of kissing and touching and cuddling."

"But no sex?"

"No sex."

"Really? You're having a beautiful, romantic weekend with a sexy man and you don't sleep with him?"

"Honestly, Ivy, I was close. I mean, I wanted to for sure."

"So, what stopped you?"

Dylan looked down, then shrugged. "I couldn't get out of my own head. I was wondering if it was the right time. Was it too soon? I also was thinking about the program. We promised to take care with one another's referrals. That was in the back of my mind, too. I thought it might be best to keep it as uncomplicated as possible for now."

"That's probably a good idea," Ivy said, followed by an audible sigh.

"Then why the sigh?"

"Oh, that wasn't for you. That was for me."

"What's wrong?"

"Maybe I should have done like you and kept things uncomplicated between me and Daveed. We slept together and now he seems to be acting differently."

"In what way?"

"For starters, we used to communicate all the time. We'd talk on the phone, get together sometimes after work, and we have spent pretty much every weekend together since we met. But since we had sex, our communication has fallen off drastically."

"Have you talked with him about that?"

"We've been out of sync for the past few weeks. It's been kind of hard trying to connect."

"There you go. It's probably just your work obligations getting in the way."

"That's not how it feels to me."

"You're probably feeling a bit sensitive since you took things to the next level. You know how we are. We start to second-guess and overthink everything. Sometimes we interpret things incorrectly when we're feeling emotional. Give it a little time."

"I guess I can do that."

THIRTY-TWO

*I*vy was armed with a floppy hat, basket, and a pair of small garden scissors. Brooke was on her knees digging onions from the ground. Ivy watched her technique. She was intrigued by Brooke's green thumb. It seemed she could plant just about anything and it would flourish and grow. Brooke was passionate about her garden and growing natural, organic food.

"Are you just going to stand there staring at me? Get down here and help."

"You are so bossy."

"I warned you that if you were coming over this afternoon, I would make you help in the garden."

"Yes, you did. But I thought you were kidding."

"You should know me better than that."

Ivy slowly approached. "The thing is . . . I don't really want to get my hands that dirty. Do you have any gloves that I can wear?"

"Girl, you are pitiful. It's just dirt."

"I just got a manicure yesterday."

Brooke fixed Ivy with a blank stare. "Okay. You can do something else."

"Oh, thank God."

"You still need to come down here."

Ivy was thankful she wore an old pair of jeans. She reluctantly got down on her knees next to Brooke. "What do you need me to do?"

Brooke pointed at the row of vegetables to her left. "You see all those cucumbers that are at the bottom of the plants?"

"The low hanging ones?"

"Yes. They're ready to be harvested. They can't stay on the vines any longer. You should be able to twist them right off but, if it's easier, use the scissors I gave you."

"I can do that . . . without messing up my nails."

Brooke shook her head and resumed harvesting onions. "When we're done, I can make us lunch."

"That sounds good. I had a cup of coffee for breakfast."

"You know you have to give your body real fuel to get through the morning."

"Don't go all health guru on me."

"It's what I do. Maybe I'll make you an energy-packed smoothie instead."

"I'd rather have a real lunch," Ivy said with a laugh.

"Smoothie first, then lunch."

Ivy was about to respond when a voice called out from the fence.

"Hey, neighbor. What are you picking today?"

Brooke stood up. "Hey, Daveed. Just some onions, cucumbers, basil, and eggplant. How's it going?"

"I can't complain."

Ivy stayed in a crouching position among the cucumbers with her back turned. Her heartbeat sped up.

"I have a lot of eggplant. Do you want some?"

"You know you don't have to ask."

"I figured but I thought I would double-check."

"I have a new sparkling wine for you to try."

"Red or white?"

"White."

"You might have missed your calling. If you ever consider a career change you should look into becoming a sommelier."

Daveed laughed. "I don't know about that. You, on the other hand, could definitely be a—"

Ivy stood up and turned toward the fence. Daveed fell silent. Brooke looked from Ivy to Daveed.

"Look who's here helping me in the garden," Brooke said, breaking the silence.

"Hey, Ivy." Daveed looked down at the ground. "Brooke, I'll get you that wine later." He abruptly stepped away from the fence and walked back toward his house.

Ivy's eyes stayed on him the entire time. He went inside and she looked at Brooke.

"What the hell was that about?" Brooke asked.

"I wish I knew."

"What the heck does that mean?"

"I don't know." Ivy bent down and started to busy herself with the cucumbers.

"Uh-uh. Leave those alone and talk to me. What happened with you two? The last time you were over here you were gushing about how much you like him. You told me and Dylan at brunch that you slept with him. What's changed?"

"Well, from the way you just saw him act, obviously he has. Things haven't been the same between us since we had sex."

"Did you guys have a fight?"

"Not at all. It's like he fell off. The week after, he wasn't texting as much . . . barely calling . . . The next couple of weeks, I thought it was because of my work schedule. I had a hectic schedule and wasn't able to stay in communication like usual and then the week after that he had to manage a new project at work. I figured we were a bit out of sync. But, you just saw that. I don't know what that was."

"I definitely saw that."

"He ran off like someone was chasing him."

"And you're here messing around in my garden like you don't have a care in the world. Were you going to tell me?"

"I was trying to figure out what was going on."

"This doesn't make any sense."

"Brooke, the day we were together, it was beautiful. He told me he wanted to make love to me. That's exactly what we did. We weren't screwing or just messing around. We made love. How we got from there to here with no good reason, I don't understand. If *you* don't think it makes sense, please know *I'm* dumbfounded."

"I think you need to go over there and talk to him. Go get some answers."

"I will not."

"You don't want to know what's going on?"

"I'd be lying if I said I didn't. But, with each passing day, I'm starting to care less and less."

"I don't believe that. That doesn't even sound like you."

"Maybe not but I am not going over there. He saw me standing right here in your garden and barely spoke to me. That hurt."

"I'm sorry."

"I don't know what kind of game he's playing, but I'm not playing along."

"This just doesn't sound like Daveed at all."

"Unfortunately, it is him."

"Are you sure you don't want to go talk to him? If you want a way to break the ice, I can give you his basket of vegetables to take over there. Maybe you guys could sit and discuss what's going on."

"No thanks, Brooke. If he wanted to talk, he had plenty of opportunities to do it over the past few weeks—and the biggest one was just staring him right in the face. As far as I'm concerned, there's nothing to discuss."

o   o   o

DYLAN ANSWERED THE phone on the first ring. It was after eleven and she was watching the Saturday night news.

"Did I wake you?" Ivy asked.

"Not at all. Everything okay?"

"I'm calling to let you know I'm ready for my next referral."

There was a brief silence on the line.

"Are you sure?"

"Yes, I'm sure. Isn't this what the Referral Program is all about?"

"Yes, but—"

"If it doesn't work out with one referral you must move on to the next one on your list. Those were your words, Dylan. You have my next referral and I'm moving on."

THIRTY-THREE

Sebastian exited the fitting room. He stepped in front of the mirror and tugged on the sleeves of his jacket. Brooke sat on a chair behind him, looking at his expression reflected in the mirror. It was a nicely cut suit and it fit him well. It wasn't too slim-fitting and it wasn't too loose or baggy. It was only the first one he'd tried on and the salesperson had set him up with at least six options. Sebastian had called her the day before to ask if she would be willing to go with him to find a new suit. He said he wanted her opinion and wouldn't take no for an answer.

"What do you think of this one?" he asked.

"It's nice. I like that it's not too tight. Lately, some of men's suits are cut too slim. The pants are so tight it looks like a thigh will bust out of the seams."

"I try to avoid that scenario at all costs." He winked at her in the mirror.

"Try the next one. I want to see how the dark blue suit looks on you."

"You're enjoying this, huh?" he said, on his way back into the fitting room.

Brooke dismissively waved her hand at Sebastian. Although, she couldn't deny he did look good in a suit. He had the perfect physique; broad shoulders, muscular but not too bulky biceps, toned abs, and long, strong legs. Brooke remembered the first time she saw Sebastian waiting outside for her for their first date at the paint and sip. She admired his body then, and now that she had seen him in all his naked glory, she admired it more. She chuckled to herself that she was crushing on him while she was supposed to be helping him find a suit.

He opened the fitting room door and walked out like he was ready to stroll down the runway.

"That looks *really* good on you."

He didn't bother to stop at the mirror. He went to stand directly in front of Brooke. "Is this the one? I'm not going to try on the others if you think this is the suit."

Brooke stood up. She tugged on the bottom of the jacket, testing how much room he had to move around in it. She buttoned it and turned him around to see the back. She walked around him so they were facing each other. "I think this suit says everything you need it to say."

"Smart, successful, and handsome?"

Brooke giggled. "All of the above."

"I want you to be my date. Will you go with me?"

"I thought it was an event for psychologists, like a conference or something."

"You obviously weren't listening to me last night."

"Well, you did call during my favorite show."

Sebastian frowned. "You really didn't hear what I told you last night."

"I heard some of it," Brooke said, in the most innocent tone she could muster. "I'm here shopping with you."

"You are lucky I think you're so damn cute. It's an awards dinner being hosted by the Black Men in Action Association."

Brooke wrapped her arms around Sebastian's waist. "I'm sorry, Seb. I should have been paying attention."

"What I didn't mention last night is that I'm being honored for my work in the Black community, particularly with the mental health of young Black men. I'm not a member of the association but I have participated in many of their panel discussions, consulted on and volunteered my time for a few of their programs. They have over thirty chapters around the country and boast a membership comprised of some of the most intelligent, successful, and wealthy African American men in America. The activism, philanthropy, and empowerment of this organization is changing our communities for the better."

"That's wonderful. You are really something, aren't you? I would be honored to be your date."

Sebastian kissed Brooke's forehead. "Thank you. We all have an obligation to our community. I try to do my part to make life better for others."

"When is the event?"

"It's next weekend."

Brooke looked up at him. "Next weekend? Could you give me any shorter notice?"

"I know. I've been meaning to ask you. It kept slipping my mind. Can you blame me? You're so distracting when we're together, I'm thinking about a million other things."

"Don't try to flatter me." She playfully nudged his arm. "You know women need more than a week to prepare for a special event. We have to have the right dress, the perfect shoes, purse, jewelry . . ."

"I guess it's a good thing you agreed to come with me today because, after we finish up here, we're going to find you that perfect dress that will match my suit. I already know that just having you on my arm will make me look good."

"I already agreed to go. You can do away with the flattery."

"You know I mean every word."

"I suppose you have left me with nothing else to complain about."

Sebastian posed in front of Brooke. "So, is this the suit?"

"That's your suit."

"If you like it, I love it. Let me change back into my clothes and we'll go to Neiman Marcus and get you something stunning."

Brooke sat back down to wait for Sebastian. She caught a glimpse of her reflection in the mirror. She turned her face from side to side thinking she looked different. Slowly she recognized the expression on her face. She hadn't seen contentment in quite some time, but she welcomed it back with a smile.

THIRTY-FOUR

Ivy pulled into the parking lot of The Aroma Bean Spot and waited in the car for a few minutes. She had made arrangements to meet Dylan's referral but was feeling a bit apprehensive. Her head kept telling her that she had agreed to the terms of the program, but her heart wasn't completely on board. Ivy was feeling defeated. She was convinced that Daveed was her man. She thought she was fortunate enough to have success with her first referral and wouldn't need to go to anyone else on her referral list. She never would have imagined that their romance would have fizzled out the way that it had.

She went into the program with an open mind and an open heart. She was aware of her past relationship issues and was determined to leave them behind. Ivy had done the work, was self-aware and ready for the blessings that were meant to be. Somehow, the wires got crossed along the way. No matter how many times she replayed what transpired between her and Daveed, she couldn't find any red flags. She asked herself if she had missed something. She wondered if maybe Daveed wasn't who he had portrayed himself to be, even though she didn't believe that he had been pretending. Ivy wanted to take a moment to reset, to regroup. Instead, she forced herself to make that call to Dylan to ask for her next referral. Resetting would have meant wallowing in the uncertainty, trying to come up with answers for the many questions she had. Ivy knew the answers didn't reside with her. No matter how much time she would have taken, the end result would have been the same. She needed to keep moving forward, no matter how difficult.

Ivy checked her face in the rearview mirror and willed herself to get out of the car. She headed into the coffee shop. She was still early, so she grabbed a table by the window. She flipped through their extensive menu of coffees, teas, and desserts while she waited. Daveed loved exotic teas. She shook her head and closed the menu. She could not let him seep into her thoughts again. Ivy knew she was kidding herself. Daveed would not be easy to shake. She could give herself a million pep talks. He had infiltrated her spirit. She had flipped and flopped over her feelings for him so many times over the past few weeks that she had lost track.

She stared out of the window and wondered if it would have been any easier to move on if she hadn't slept with him. They had connected on a spiritual level before having sex. A part of Ivy felt that the emotional connection was giving her the most difficulty in understanding the breakup. If you could even call it that. They hadn't really broken up. Daveed had pretty much ghosted her. Ivy had never been ghosted before. No one had ever left a relationship with her without any indication why. She finally understood why people had trouble moving on after being ghosted. There were so many unanswered questions, doubts, and regrets.

Ivy checked her watch and looked around the coffee shop for someone who fit the description she had been given. Then she felt a tap on the shoulder.

"Ivy?"

"Xavier?"

He extended his hand. "Yes, it's nice to meet you."

"You too."

"May I?" he said, motioning to the chair across from her.

"Of course, have a seat."

He was an attractive brother with one of the prettiest sets of teeth she had ever seen. Ivy attempted to put on her best face, at least something better than neutral.

Xavier was taking her in as he got settled at the table. His eyes wandered from her hair to her eyes and, almost imperceptibly, paused at her breasts before moving back up to her eyes. "Dylan told me you were a stunner."

Ivy wanted to groan. "I'll have to thank her later for such a glowing compliment."

Xavier laughed nervously. "I love Dylan and her family. They're good people. I've known them for about fifteen years now."

"Is that right?"

"Yes, indeed."

"You're their car salesman, right?"

"Well, after all these years, I look at them more as family."

Again, he laughed, and Ivy started to think it was more of a nervous tic.

"I see."

"I met Dylan's dad when I first started selling cars. He was my first customer. Over the years, I became his go-to guy. When I opened my first dealership, he referred his friends and family to me. In fact, Dylan purchased her first car from me—her brother, too. As I said, they're like family to me."

"That's a lot of firsts." Ivy couldn't think of anything else to say.

"So, what's good here? Any recommendations?"

"Basically, any of their coffees. It is their specialty."

"I gathered that from the name of the shop . . . The Aroma Bean Spot. What are you going to have?"

"I was thinking about The Motherland. It's an African coffee from Kenya sprinkled with Nigerian cocoa powder."

"That sounds good. I think I'll have the same."

"Okay." Ivy waved the server over to the table and they placed their orders.

"While we wait, why don't you tell me a little about yourself," Xavier said.

"What do you want to know?"

"Let's see. What do you do for a living?"

"I'm a social worker."

"What do you like most about your work?"

"Being able to influence the lives of children-in-need in a positive way."

"What's your favorite type of music?"

"Jazz."

"Do you enjoy live shows?"

"Who doesn't?"

"Have you ever been on a blind date before?"

Ivy hesitated. "It's not my favorite thing to do but, yes, I have."

"This is my first blind date. I was caught off guard when Dylan called to ask if I would be interested in meeting a friend of hers. I'm glad I didn't say no."

She gave him a wry smile.

He continued, "I have never been the sort of man to go out with someone I haven't met personally. In my line of work, I have to be a people person. I'll talk to anyone, anytime, anywhere. It's become like my special power. I have a way with putting people at ease and making them comfortable. So, blind dates were never a thing for me. If I see a beautiful woman, I have no problem approaching her and introducing myself. Obviously, I've been missing out on something. I'll have to let Dylan know she has opened my eyes to a whole new world."

Ivy told herself to say something, find some words to respond to what Xavier was saying. "That's something that you've never been on a blind date."

"Not in all my years."

"And, how many would that be?"

"I'm forty-three."

A nine-year difference. It showed. Ivy felt a flash of annoyance—at Xavier, at Dylan, but mostly at herself. "Oh, okay."

"I understand you went to college with Dylan."

"We sure did."

"She told me you're like sisters."

Ivy picked up her spoon, turned it between her fingers and put it back down. "We are."

"Ah, the coffee," he said, as the server approached the table with two steaming mugs on a tray.

Xavier and Ivy were quiet as they added cream and sugar to their beverages. In her head she kept telling herself to say something, engage him in conversation. Yet, she remained silent.

He sipped from his cup. "That's good."

"Glad you like it."

"So, Ivy, I'll state the obvious. You're a beautiful woman and, lucky for me, you're single. When was your last relationship?"

Ivy felt a pang in her chest. Of course, he would ask that particular question, she thought. She lifted her cup to her lips, trying to steel herself and conceal that she was fighting back tears. She took a couple of swallows of her coffee. "If you don't mind, I'd rather not discuss my past relationships."

Xavier observed her for a moment and then nodded. "In case you're wondering about me, my last relationship was two years ago. We were together for four years. I don't mind telling you that we broke up because her job moved her halfway around the world to run their new investment management office. At the time, I owned three car dealerships here and was in the process of opening a fourth. There was no way I would have been able to relocate. Neither of us thought a long-distance relationship was ideal. However, we're still

friends and want only the best for one another." He paused, waiting
for a reaction from Ivy. "What are your thoughts on exes remaining
friends and in contact with each other? Would you have a problem
with something like that?"

"Not really," she replied. She glanced at Xavier and diverted her
gaze toward the window.

Xavier looked down at his watch, slightly adjusted it and cleared
his throat. "It seems my time has gotten away from me. I have an appointment in about fifteen minutes and if I don't get moving now, I
will most definitely be late."

Ivy watched him as he stood up and pushed his chair to the table.
"I understand," she murmured.

"Ivy, it was a pleasure and I hope to hear from you again."

He departed swiftly and without even a look back, his cup of coffee relatively untouched. Ivy immediately thought of Dylan and an
overwhelming sense of embarrassment came over her. What would
Dylan think about how she behaved with her referral? What did
Xavier think of her? Even though she had been disengaged, he still
excused himself like a gentleman. Ivy was pretty confident he didn't
have an appointment, but he apparently didn't want to walk out on
her without giving a reason. Xavier had done a better job than Daveed on walking out. At least she knew why he was leaving.

THIRTY-FIVE

*D*ylan typed away on her laptop. Barrett sat across from her at the dining room table working on his tablet. The news was on the television in the living room, piping in the latest political drama. Dylan was doing her best multitasking—working on a profit analysis for a client and making dinner. She had invited Barrett over for Sunday dinner, yet they both had work to do for the upcoming week. They settled on a late afternoon of handling their business followed by a quiet dinner with no laptops or cell phones allowed.

"How much do you have left?" he asked, not looking up from his device.

"I'm wrapping up in a half hour. You?"

"Fifteen minutes and I'm done."

"We can eat as soon as I finish."

They continued their tasks with the only talking coming from the television. Dylan loved the fact that she could spend time focusing on her work while the man she was with was doing the same. There was no reason to have to neglect or push it off to the next day because he was just as committed to his career as she was. That hadn't always been the case. Dylan had dated a few men who didn't understand the number of obligations she had on her plate running her own business. She constantly had to explain why she couldn't go out or was unable to meet at a certain time. It was tough telling a man that he wasn't her priority, that her business was.

Barrett understood and respected her drive. And, though he

201

shared with her that he inherited significant wealth, Dylan recognized that Barrett had worked hard and was dedicated to being successful in his field.

"That's it for me." Barrett logged off his tablet. "I'll be in the living room." He got up and left Dylan at the table.

It was strange. She missed his presence. He had literally just walked out of the dining room, yet she yearned for him to be near. Dylan enjoyed his company. They hadn't been conversing or engaging in any way, but having him sitting across from her was comforting, more like comfortable. It felt right. Just as she knew things hadn't felt right with Carter, she was just as sure that they felt oh so right with Barrett.

Dylan completed her analysis and shut down her laptop. She sauntered into the living room and sat down next to Barrett. She kissed him on the cheek.

"What did I do to deserve that?"

"That was for being my accountability partner today. I needed to get some work done and I'm glad you were here supporting that effort."

He kissed her on the lips. "Then I should thank you for being mine, as well. I would much rather have given you all my attention, but we encouraged each other to remain focused. I'll admit, with you around, that's not easy."

"This is new for me."

"What is?"

"Being with someone who truly respects my professional grind."

"That's surprising."

"I think a lot of men can appreciate what I do, but respecting and supporting it is something different. With you, I don't feel like I have to downplay just how important my work is to me."

"I would never want you to do that. I want you to flourish and grow professionally. I know what it means for a Black woman to own and run her own business. It's not easy and it takes a lot of blood, sweat, and tears to pull that off. I would never do anything to hinder your trajectory."

"That means a lot to me."

"Anything for you."

"You really mean that, don't you?"

"Why wouldn't I mean it?"

Dylan thought about it. "I guess I'm not really questioning whether you mean what you say. I think I'm just astounded that you *truly* mean what you say, and I don't have to question it. I don't have to wonder whether you're being sincere."

"Have I ever given you a reason to doubt my sincerity?"

"Not once. I realize that more and more every day. You just happened to be here to witness today's realization."

"Dylan, you can trust me. You can believe what I say is true."

"I know you're a man of integrity."

"There would be nothing worse than me being deceitful with you. I'm not telling you things because they sound good. I honor and respect you. My words and actions will reflect that. If you ever think that they don't, I expect you to call me out on it."

"You don't have to worry about that," Dylan laughed.

"I don't doubt that for a minute." Barrett paused, looking Dylan in the eyes. "You're special to me. I want you to know that, maybe more importantly, I want you to feel that."

As if a magnet were drawing them together, they leaned in, their lips connecting. Dylan's insides stirred. She inched closer. Dylan couldn't deny Barrett's energy had an effect on her and she loved the way he made her feel.

She eased back from Barrett. "I'm going to burn our dinner if we don't stop."

"I don't mind."

"You'll mind when you have to eat it."

"That's true." He chuckled. "Speaking of dinner . . . Would you happen to know a beautiful woman, whose smile can light up a room, who happens to be free next Saturday?"

"I might know someone. It depends on who's asking."

"This handsome man sitting next to you is asking."

"Then I absolutely know someone, and she happens to be sitting next to you right now."

Barrett grabbed Dylan's hand. "I want you to come with me to a function next weekend. There will be dinner and dancing and me and you having a great time."

"How can I say no to that?"

"I was hoping you wouldn't."

"It sounds like an exciting evening. I'd love to join you."

THIRTY-SIX

Sebastian handed Brooke a glass of champagne. Music played softly in the background as conversations dominated the cocktail reception. The room was abuzz with men and women dressed in their finest. Many of the members of Black Men in Action had stopped to congratulate Sebastian on the award he would be receiving during the dinner ceremony.

The drinks were flowing and the servers worked the room circulating a variety of delectable hors d'oeuvres. The large ballroom was filling up as a stream of attendees were still arriving.

"This is quite an event," Brooke commented. "How many people are expected?"

"About six hundred."

"Everyone looks so dapper, especially you."

"*You* make me look good. I didn't think it was possible for you to look more gorgeous than you already do."

"We *do* look good together. We complement each other so well." Brooke posed in her shimmering silver gown for effect.

Sebastian planted a quick kiss on her shoulder. "Thank you for coming with me."

She touched a hand to his face. "You can thank me later."

He raised his eyebrows and smiled. "Don't tempt me with a good time. We can leave as soon as I receive my award."

"We'll do no such thing. We are going to mix and mingle with these six hundred people until we can mix and mingle no more."

205

Sebastian laughed. "I was only kidding. We'll go back to my place when the event is over."

Another man came up to Sebastian and greeted him with a forceful pat on the back. "Congratulations, young man. You deserve it."

"Thank you, sir."

"Who was that?" Brooke asked as he walked away.

"He's a former congressman and member of Black Men in Action."

"This seems like a prestigious organization. Are you planning to join?"

"I've been considering it. I want to be sure that I'm able to sufficiently give of my time."

"You do have a lot going on with your practice and motivational speeches. They would be lucky to have you."

"I'd be gaining something, as well. A sense of knowing that you're doing your part for the community is its own reward. Receiving the award tonight is a wonderful accolade, but the feeling I get from the work I do on a daily basis is just as wonderful."

"That's why you're so deserving. I'm looking forward to the ceremony. How are you feeling?"

"Blessed and excited."

"Did you write a speech?"

"No, but I thought about what I want to say."

"How could I forget I'm talking to the man who always knows what to say."

"Not always, just most of the time."

"Why don't you save those jokes for the stage."

"If you think I'm that funny . . ."

"I don't know if I do, but you seem to think you're a comedi—"

"What's wrong?" Sebastian turned around to see what caught Brooke's attention.

"Oh my goodness, Dylan, Barrett! What are you two doing here?" she asked, as they approached.

They looked equally as surprised to see her. Brooke hugged Dylan and then Barrett.

"What a pleasant surprise," Dylan said, her eyes widening when she looked at Brooke.

"I'm a member of the Black Men in Action," Barrett said. He looked over at Sebastian.

Brooke's mind raced. What were the chances of running into Dylan and Barrett?

"Oh, let me introduce you all. Sebastian, this is Dylan and Barrett. Two very good friends of mine." She hoped Barrett wouldn't mention that she set him up with Dylan. Knowing how chatty Sebastian is, he would definitely mention being in a similar situation where his cousin set him up with her friend, too. The next thing you know, Brooke and Dylan would be explaining how the guys were both a part of the Referral Program.

The guys shook hands first. "Nice to meet you, Barrett."

"Same here."

"Dylan." Sebastian paused, an unreadable expression briefly gracing his face. "Nice to meet you."

"You too," she said, shaking his hand.

Brooke watched their exchange wondering why Sebastian hesitated the way he did.

"What have you been up to, my friend?" Barrett asked Brooke.

"You know me. I'm juggling a lot these days. Between my nine to five and running the gym, I stay busy."

"That's why I'm surprised to see you out this evening," he replied.

"Well, Sebastian is being honored tonight."

"Oh, you're one of our honorees? Congratulations."

"Thank you, I appreciate it."

"I wasn't on the committee this year, so, I'm not in the loop tonight."

"Brooke, that dress is beautiful," Dylan said.

"Thank you. My handsome date picked it out."

"He obviously has great taste."

Sebastian looked at Dylan, his eyes squinting. "Dylan, you look familiar."

"Do I?"

"You do. I can't place your face, but you look really familiar. Perhaps you attended one of my seminars?"

"I haven't been to any seminars. So, it can't be that."

An announcement for guests to make their way into the main ballroom and take their seats at their assigned tables came through the speakers.

Relief washed over Brooke's and Dylan's faces. They hugged briefly, giving each other a conspiratorial squeeze, and ushered their dates into the main room and off to different tables.

THIRTY-SEVEN

Dylan and Barrett were situated at a table in the center of the ballroom. The waitstaff bustled through the room serving the salads. There was a sea of tables between theirs and where Brooke and Sebastian were seated. Dylan saw them heading to a table at the front of the ballroom, most likely because Sebastian was being honored. Dylan didn't care where she and Barrett sat, as long as they weren't near Brooke. That encounter was a little too close for comfort. It hadn't crossed any of their minds when creating the Referral Program that they might run into one another somewhere while with their dates. Dylan wasn't interested in explaining that she and her girls set up a program to introduce each other to eligible men until they found *the one*. Something would definitely get lost in translation.

"I can't believe Brooke is here," Barrett commented.

"I was thinking the same thing."

Barrett draped his arm over the back of Dylan's seat. "That Sebastian seemed like a nice guy."

"Yeah, he did."

"I noticed he couldn't keep his eyes off you."

Dylan scrunched her nose. "I didn't notice any of that."

"No, really. From the moment we walked up, he was staring at you."

"He said I looked familiar. I guess he was trying to figure out how he thought he knew me. He has to be confusing me with someone else because he doesn't look familiar to me at all."

"You're probably right. Though I wouldn't blame him for staring."

"With Brooke on his arm, he should have no reason to be looking at me."

"Now that's where I disagree with you. I'm the envy of every man in here. You look sensational in that black dress."

Dylan pursed her lips for a kiss. Barrett gave her a peck. They were interrupted by the emcee at the podium, tapping on the microphone to ensure it was on. He welcomed everyone and in unison the audience called out, "Good evening."

While the emcee was going through his introduction and talking about the history and progress of the organization, Dylan's mind wandered to her exchange with Sebastian. She racked her brain on whether they knew one another. Dylan came up empty. His face didn't look familiar at all. She was confident they had never met. She had always heard everyone has a twin in the world, someone who looked just like them. Sebastian must have met hers.

Aside from the anxiety of bumping into Brooke and her referral, it was nice to see the success of the program in action. Brooke and Sebastian looked good together. The universe worked in mysterious ways, she thought. Both of them ending up at the same event, with their men, was unbelievable. They didn't bump into each other when they were alone. Ultimately, Dylan was happy to get a glimpse of what the Referral Program looked like for her friend.

The audience began clapping. Dylan clapped right along although she didn't hear a word of what was said.

Barrett leaned over and whispered in her ear. "I can't wait to get you out on the dance floor tonight."

"I'm ready for anything."

THIRTY-EIGHT

$\mathcal{B}$ rooke kicked off her shoes in the car, thankful to be free from the four-inch heels. She knew better than to wear a new pair of shoes to a function where she would be standing and, even more so, dancing. She was prepared to walk barefoot from Sebastian's car to his front door.

"I refuse to put my feet back in these shoes tonight."

"Don't worry, you don't have to torture yourself. I'll carry you into the house."

"That's music to my ears."

"I'm also going to give you a foot massage and make you feel all better."

"As always, you know exactly what to say."

"I know what to do, too."

"Yeah, what's that?"

"I know how to take care of you. I'll show you how much I appreciate you attending the affair with me tonight when we get to the house."

"I can't wait."

"Having you on my arm made the night even more special."

"I'm happy I was able to experience your world with you."

"And what a small world it is. Imagine running into your friends at the event tonight."

"I couldn't believe it. I had no idea they would be there."

"It was nice meeting them."

"Have you met Dylan before?"

"She looked familiar."

"You were quite insistent."

"Was I?"

"Well, you said more than once how familiar she looked, and you were kind of staring. It was intense."

Sebastian chuckled. "It wasn't that serious. I was trying to place her."

"You asked her if she attended one of your seminars."

"That's what you do when you are trying to pinpoint how you might know someone. You ask questions."

"I know, but to assume she attended your seminars . . ."

"I didn't assume, I asked."

"You just seemed really insistent that you knew each other."

"I hope I didn't make your friend as uncomfortable as I obviously made you."

Brooke should've left it alone. This was supposed to be a good night. She was making something of nothing, pushing an issue that shouldn't have even been on her radar. "Now I've made you uncomfortable," she replied.

"We're just talking it out. Sometimes conversations like these get uncomfortable, but they're necessary to say what we feel. I won't put on my doctor's hat tonight, but there's a reason why this bothered you."

"You can diagnose me tomorrow. Tonight, all I want to do is unwind."

"That's exactly what we are going to do."

◦　◦　◦

BROOKE CURLED UP on the couch while Sebastian moved from room to room, switching on some lights and turning off others.

He turned soft music on and dimmed the lights in the living room. Brooke watched him as he took off his suit jacket and removed his tie. He undid the first few buttons on his white shirt and rolled up the sleeves, then sat down on the couch with Brooke.

Sebastian tapped his thighs. "Place your feet right here," he said.

Brooke quickly obliged, swinging her legs across his lap. Sebastian grasped one of her feet between his hands and started to gently knead.

"That feels good already."

"Lay back and relax."

Brooke reclined on the couch and watched him work magic with his hands. "You are wonderful. You motivate people, win awards, and give a mean foot massage."

"I'm a jack of all trades."

"You really were something tonight. Your speech was so poignant. If everyone who was in the room tonight does not make more of an effort to give back to their community, they weren't listening. I have even more of an appreciation for what you do."

Sebastian smiled. "That means a lot to me. I wanted to convey to the organization how much I appreciated the honor, but I also wanted to inspire them to share their knowledge and resources with those who can benefit from them the most. It's not always those who can afford to retain their services or even get an audience with them."

"Well, I was inspired. In fact, I'm going to create a youth fitness program. I don't know what it will look like yet, but I'm going to offer fun classes for kids to attend at their schools."

Sebastian gazed at Brooke. "You are amazing."

"No, you're the amazing one."

"I guess we're just an amazing couple."

"I'm aware that you didn't ask for my opinion, and I know you're already considering it, but I think you should join Black Men in Action. They could benefit greatly from a member like you."

"I value your opinion and I'm leaning toward it. It really is a matter of whether I can give one hundred percent. I won't join if I can't be all in as an active member. I'll continue to volunteer my time and expertise while I weigh my decision. However, that decision won't be made tonight . . . I'm sort of busy . . ."

"Okay, no more talk about the organization. I want all your attention on my foot massage."

Sebastian laughed. "That's what I'm trying to do."

"And you do it oh so well."

"I have the perfect elixir that will soothe not just your feet."

"I'm listening . . ."

"A nice hot bath. Candlelight. Cocktails. I can bathe and massage you all over."

"Mmm. A bath, candlelight, and cocktails?"

"Don't forget the full body massage."

"How could I turn that down?"

"I was hoping you wouldn't." Sebastian moved Brooke's feet from his lap and stood. "Give me a minute to set everything up."

Sebastian left the room to prepare. Brooke sat up and unconsciously hugged herself. She was comfortable in Sebastian's space and especially with him. A tingle ran down her spine as she anticipated his strong hands bathing her. *Every woman should be so lucky*, she thought. A man who dotes on his woman, without having to be asked, charmed her spirit.

"What are you smiling about?" Sebastian asked as he entered the room.

"I didn't realize I was smiling."

"Well, you were."

"I was thinking about my bath."

"*Our* bath," he corrected.

"Even better."

"The water is running. All I have to do is make our cocktails." He walked over to the liquor cabinet and opened it. "What would you like to drink?"

"Do you have any St-Germain?"

"I believe so." He moved a few bottles to the side looking for the liqueur.

"I think I'm in the mood for St-Germain and champagne."

Sebastian came to a standstill. "St-Germain and champagne . . ."

"Yes, if you have it."

"I have it." He slowly shook his head.

Sebastian resumed making Brooke's drink. He poured the liqueur in the glass and topped it off with the champagne. He came over to the couch and handed Brooke the glass. "I remember where I met your friend."

Surprise registered on Brooke's face. "Really, where?"

"It was about five years ago. My cousin had a New Year's Eve party."

"You met Dylan at Ivy's New Year's Eve party?"

"Apparently so." He hesitated. "You actually jarred my memory."

"How did I do that?"

"St-Germain and champagne . . ." He shook his head again. "That was the specialty drink Ivy was serving that night."

"Oh, okay. At least you remember where you two met."

"We actually had an unusual meeting," he said, slowly. "It was New Year's Eve and the drinks were flowing. Everyone was having a good time. I remember now that somehow Dylan and I ended up in the bathroom at the same time. One minute we were laughing and talking and the next we were kissing."

"*Now* you remember that?" Brooke asked incredulously. "How could you not remember before?"

"Brooke, it was five years ago on New Year's Eve. I was single and everyone was drinking a *helluva* lot. I'm not proud to say that I didn't even remember your friend's name."

"Is that all that happened?"

Sebastian looked down and then met her gaze. "We kissed and touched each other a little bit, through our clothes," he added quickly, "then she ran out of the bathroom."

Brooke got up, retrieved her shoes, and began to put them on.

"What are you doing?" he asked.

"What does it look like?" she responded, her eyes avoiding his.

"It looks like we need to talk."

"I don't think so. What I need is for you to take me home."

"Brooke—"

She held up her hand. "No, Sebastian. Just take me home."

"Okay. Let me turn off the water and we can go." Sebastian started heading out of the room but turned back toward Brooke. "Communication is important. I think you're making a mistake leaving like this."

"I'm fully aware of my mistakes and leaving right now is not one of them."

THIRTY-NINE

*B*rooke slammed the front door behind her and marched up to her bedroom. The last thing she heard was Sebastian calling her name as she bolted from his car. They rode in silence the entire trip from his house. She closed her eyes for part of the ride, feigning sleep. She had nothing to say, at least not to him.

Brooke could not understand how she ended up here again. She was flooded with emotions from the last time this happened to her. A few years back, while at happy hour with a few physical therapist friends from work, she was introduced to James. He knew a couple of the ladies and they struck up a conversation. He flirted with Brooke all night. She pulled one of her friends aside to ask what she knew about James. Fawn had all good things to say about him.

After that night, Brooke and James stayed in touch and, eventually, began dating. After a few months together, having regaled her coworkers with the progress of their relationship along the way, Fawn casually mentioned that James had not changed a bit since they dated. Brooke was floored. She did not believe in dating the ex of someone she knew. It was too close for comfort, with a potential to become messy.

She questioned James and Fawn why neither had mentioned their past relationship. At the time they were both with other people, basically cheating, and kept it under wraps. Brooke ended her relationship with James immediately. She always thought Fawn let it *slip* that she dated James because she wanted that ol' thing back.

The situation with James solidified for Brooke that she was not interested in dating a friend's ex. She couldn't believe Dylan was the one who said referrals couldn't be someone you had a *situation* with in the past. She and Seb definitely had a situation, and she didn't think to mention it.

Brooke grabbed her phone and feverishly searched her contacts. She dialed. The phone rang and rang. Ignoring the late hour, Brooke hung up and dialed again.

On the third ring there was an answer. "Hello?"

"Barrett, there's something you should know . . ."

FORTY

Dylan ordered another cup of green tea. She had been waiting twenty minutes alone at the table for Ivy and Brooke to show up for brunch. She sent them a group text when she arrived to let them know she had already been seated. Dylan wondered what could be keeping them. She hadn't heard from Brooke all week, not since running into one another at the Black Men in Action event. She had planned to call the day after but got caught up with putting out a client fire on a Sunday, no less.

Socially, it was a quiet week for Dylan. Barrett was out of the country on business and essentially off the grid. She texted him a few times and it would be hours before she received a response. That was unlike him, but she chalked it up to the difference in time zones and figured he must be inundated with the rigors of work. She missed hearing his voice.

"Hey, sorry I'm late," Ivy said, sitting down at the table.

"I didn't even see you come in."

"Yeah, I noticed. You were staring off into space."

"I was wondering what was taking you and Brooke so long to get here."

"I've been moving in slow motion today. I couldn't pull myself together."

"Is everything okay?"

Ivy waved dismissively. "I'll be fine."

"Have you heard from Brooke?"

"I texted her last night to let her know where we were having brunch and at what time, but she didn't reply. I didn't think anything of it. I just assumed she got the message and would be here."

"She's probably on her way."

"I guess." Ivy shrugged. "I can't keep wondering where people are or what happened to them."

Dylan examined her friend's face. "Really, are you okay?"

"I'm hanging in there."

"Come on. Tell me what's going on."

"Nothing. I'm fine."

"Ivy, I can see you're not yourself today."

She sighed and leaned back in her chair. "I really miss Daveed."

"Oh . . ."

"I thought we had something special blossoming. Dylan, there was such a connection between us. We were definitely on the same wavelength. I know he felt it as much as I did."

"Are you sure you didn't misread him?"

"You know how in tune I am with other people's energy. I have replayed every moment we spent together. The things he said and did—things *I* said and did. I thought we were in a good place. Obviously, I was wrong. The expression on his face the day he saw me in Brooke's garden . . . He barely made eye contact with me."

"I don't understand how he went from hot to cold in such a drastic way."

"As much as I don't want to admit it, I have to face the fact that I was wrong about him. He wasn't who I thought he was."

"Do you know if Brooke asked him what happened?"

"You know Brooke. She wouldn't get involved. Honestly, I wouldn't want her to be in the middle of anything. Like we said in the beginning, we all have to manage our existing relationships. What happened between me and Daveed should not affect Brooke's friendship with him."

Dylan nodded that she understood. She looked at her watch and decided they should order their meals. She called over the waitress and told her what they wanted to eat.

Dylan waited until the waitress was no longer in earshot before she resumed their conversation. "I was waiting for you to bring it up but, since you haven't, I will. How was your date with Xavier?"

"I was going to call you after our date, but I wasn't in a good space. I owe you and especially Xavier an apology."

"Oh no. What happened?"

"I probably shouldn't haven't gone on the date with him. I know the program stipulates that we're supposed to keep trying if things don't work out with a referral but, clearly, I was not ready. He was a nice guy and he made an effort. Unfortunately, I didn't. I wasn't very sociable."

"Were you rude to him?" Dylan asked with furrowed brows.

"Well . . ."

"Ivy, Xavier is a close family friend."

"Yes, I heard . . . and he's sold you all every car you own."

Dylan stared at Ivy. "Really?"

"I'm sorry. That wasn't necessary."

"No, it wasn't and if that was supposed to be an apology, you need to start over. In fact, save it. I'll call Xavier myself to smooth things over."

"You're mad at me."

"I'm annoyed, not mad. If you weren't ready, you shouldn't have gone out with him."

"I already said that."

"And I'm agreeing with you."

"My head wants to move on from Daveed. I guess my heart is holding me back."

"I understand. The heart wants what it wants. If you want Daveed, maybe you shouldn't give up on him."

"He gave up on me."

"But you don't know why. You at least owe it to yourself to find out what happened."

"I'll think about it." Ivy took a drink of her water. "I guess Brooke isn't coming."

"This is a first. She has never missed a monthly brunch since we started doing these."

"When was the last time you spoke with her?" Ivy asked.

"Last Saturday. I ran into her at an awards dinner. We were a little nervous because I was with Barrett and she was with Sebastian. We were hoping Barrett wouldn't mention that Brooke had set us up and in turn that Sebastian wouldn't mention you set them up. We didn't want to have to explain the Referral Program."

"What are the chances that you all would end up at the same event?"

"That's what I thought when I saw her. She introduced me and Barrett to Sebastian and we all chatted for a bit. It was interesting because Sebastian said he thought he knew me. I'm sure we'd never met before that night, but he said I looked familiar."

Ivy squinted. "I'm pretty sure you met him before."

"Where would I have met Sebastian?"

"At my New Year's Eve party."

"New Year's Eve?"

"Yes."

"That party you had five years ago?"

"That's the one. You met him there."

"I don't remember meeting any cousin of yours named Sebastian. He didn't look familiar to me at all."

"You met him."

"I only remember meeting one of your cousins that night. I think his name was . . . Doc or something like that. He had a full beard and long locs."

"That's him. The family calls him Doc sometimes. He has a PhD. We started calling him that to tease him when he was in school and it sort of stuck. He thinks it's pretentious and asked us not to call him that anymore."

"What?" Dylan said, barely above a whisper, the color draining from her face.

Ivy leaned forward in her seat. "What's the matter?"

"I remember that party. I had so many drinks that night."

"We all did."

"No, I was really drunk. I specifically remember that I had every intention of getting wasted. I had just broken up with Ace the day after Christmas. I didn't even want to come to the party, but you insisted. Remember?"

"I remember."

"I had drink after drink. I wanted to have a good time. I didn't want to think about Ace. But, when the ball dropped, I was doing everything I could to fight back tears. I thought I would be celebrating New Year's Eve with him. I slipped into the bathroom and closed the door, but didn't lock it. Moments later, Doc—I mean *Sebastian*—burst into the bathroom. He was singing and festive and completely engrossed with ringing in the new year. He didn't notice me at first. When he did, he asked if I had missed the ball drop and told me you're supposed to ring in the new year with a kiss. We made out in your bathroom for about five minutes."

Ivy sat across from Dylan with her mouth agape. "You never mentioned any of this to me."

"I was too embarrassed to tell you. I burst into tears over Ace while kissing him."

"I can't believe this. You had no idea that my cousin Sebastian and Doc were the same person?"

"How would I? Five years ago, you introduced him to me as Doc. How would I know his name was Sebastian?"

"And when you saw him last week you didn't recognize him at all?"

"Ivy, when I met the man, I was drunk," she repeated. "Apparently, five years ago he looked like a completely different person with a full beard and locs. I was drunk and reckless that night. I was hurting. I did something out of character. I literally started crying and ran out of the bathroom. Don't you remember that I left right after the ball drop?" she asked, her voice elevated.

"Vaguely. Why didn't you tell me?"

"I don't know. I mean . . . I said I was embarrassed. I was dealing with a lot. I just broke up with my man and I'm kissing your cousin in the bathroom days later . . . I blamed it on being intoxicated. I didn't even want to acknowledge it happened. I definitely didn't want to tell *you* that it happened. I pretty much put it out of my mind."

"Did anything else happen?"

Dylan frowned. "Like what?"

"*You know.*"

"Why would you even ask me that?"

"You said you were drunk."

"I wasn't *that* drunk."

"So, you didn't have sex?"

"Really, Ivy? No, we didn't have sex! I already told you I ran out of the bathroom after the kiss."

"All right, calm down. I was just making sure."

"I can't believe this."

"I don't believe it either. I told you I thought you had met Sebastian before."

"Girl, how the hell would I know Doc and Sebastian were the same person?"

"I know, I know."

"I didn't even remember his face when we met last week. I would have never made the connection. Damn, Ivy."

"We need to call Brooke."

"And tell her what exactly?"

"I'm not sure what to say but we need to tell her something."

"I wouldn't know where to begin."

"What if she already knows?"

Dylan shook her head in disbelief. She wondered if they needed to mention it to Brooke at all. Maybe it was something they didn't need to share. What good would it serve to tell Brooke that they shared a kiss five years ago? Dylan pondered whether she should ask Ivy to keep it to herself, but deep down she knew Ivy wouldn't do that and it wasn't right.

"Fine," Dylan replied. "Let's call her."

Ivy pulled her phone from her purse and dialed Brooke's number on speaker. The call went straight to voice mail. "Let me try again. She should hear this from us."

Again, the voice mail picked up.

"This is crazy," Dylan said.

"I wish you would have told me."

"Telling you that I kissed your cousin was the least of my worries back then. I was trying to figure out my future without Ace. I'm sure you can understand that."

"Yes, I can. But it feels like you were keeping secrets from me."

"You're not really trying to make this about you right now?"

"No, no I'm not."

"Good, because it's not the time for that."

"You're right," she quickly conceded.

The waitress approached the table with their breakfast. Dylan stopped her and asked if she could pack it up. "Sorry, Ivy, I have completely lost my appetite. I'm going to go home to get my head together."

"I understand. Take all the time you need."

FORTY-ONE

$\mathcal{B}$rooke's phone went straight to voice mail. Dylan had lost count how many times she called since getting home—five, maybe six, times. She left a message stating that they needed to talk. Brooke had never missed a monthly brunch. It wasn't like her not to call. She would have known that Dylan and Ivy would be concerned. As far as Dylan could remember, she had never called Brooke more than twice without receiving a call or text back.

Though she didn't know for sure, Dylan's gut instinct was telling her that Brooke knew. A crack had surfaced in the program. A wave of nausea overtook Dylan at the thought of it all. Referrals were not supposed to be someone any of them had had a past situation with—in any way. No ex-boyfriends, lovers, dates, nothing. As far as Dylan was concerned, technically, Sebastian didn't fit that criteria. They weren't ex–boyfriend and girlfriend, hadn't dated, and they hadn't had sex. Yes, they shared a kiss and maybe he rubbed her ass, but it was a *drunken* kiss. Dylan didn't even remember him, and he clearly didn't remember her. He said she looked *familiar*. That should say something. Nothing of significance had transpired between them.

Dylan hadn't wanted to attend the party that night, but Ivy had twisted her arm. She showed up and told Ivy to keep the drinks coming. It was the first time she had left her house in days. She had just broken up with Ace and wasn't in a good space.

Dylan sighed at the memory and how far she had come. Barrett was a great guy and, as far as she could tell, he wanted the same

things she did. Dylan picked up her phone and thought about calling Brooke again. She needed to talk to her . . . and Barrett. Somehow, it had escaped Dylan that she also needed to have another
conversation. She wanted to be the first person to tell him what was
going on.

FORTY-TWO

Dylan was at her desk getting ready to wrap up her day. She managed to drag herself through the afternoon, but it was a challenge keeping her mind on her work. Mondays were difficult enough, but after finding out about the Doc/Seb situation the day before, her day was ten times harder to get through. She grabbed her briefcase and started toward the door. Her phone vibrated with a text from Barrett asking her to meet him for a drink at a lounge in Midtown. She replied immediately that she would be there in twenty minutes. She went back to her desk, sat down, and refreshed her makeup. She spritzed on a bit of perfume and then headed out of the office to go meet Barrett.

The lounge was dimly lit and already filling up with the after-work crowd. Dylan scanned the room in search of Barrett. Just as she was about to call him to ask where he was, she spotted him seated at a table in the corner. She felt a smile tugging at the corner of her lips, despite herself. Dylan approached the table and Barrett stood to greet her. She leaned in for a hug and kiss. He responded with a chaste, stiff hug. They awkwardly pulled away from one another and sat down. Dylan took the seat in the chair across from him.

"I thought you said that you didn't know Brooke's date?"

"I didn't . . . I don't . . . not really," she stammered.

"Brooke told me you two used to be involved."

Dylan instantly got hot. Brooke couldn't find the time to speak to

228

her but had apparently reached out to Barrett with misinformation. "That's not true," she blurted, a little louder than intended.

Barrett looked around the room to see if anyone heard their exchange. "You're telling me Brooke lied?"

"No, I'm not saying that. I'm just saying that's not the case. I was never involved with Sebastian."

"But you do know him? Because I recall you told me that he had to be confusing you with someone else."

"I know that's what I said, and I meant it at the time. I didn't realize that we had indeed met before. I didn't recognize him because he looked completely different. He'd had a full beard and a head full of long locs. He did not look like the man we met at the event. That's the only reason why I told you he didn't look familiar, because he didn't."

"The one time you met him, when was that?"

Dylan took a deep breath. "I met him at a party on New Year's Eve five years ago. He was introduced to me as Doc, not Sebastian. I want you to know what kind of headspace I was in at the time we met and why I wouldn't have remembered him."

Barrett sat silently, not offering a response.

Dylan continued. "That night at the party, I had a lot to drink. I wasn't drinking because it was New Year's Eve and I was in a festive mood—I actually shouldn't have been there at all. Only days before, I went through a bad breakup with the man I thought I would marry. I literally thought he was going to propose to me at Christmas dinner with my entire family present. It didn't happen and I couldn't figure out what had gone wrong. I had strong indications that he had asked my father for my hand in marriage. I knew he had been talking to my mother about rings, but Christmas Day came and went and there was no proposal.

"The next morning, I found out why. He didn't want to get married; at least not to me. He was with someone else and, apparently, she supported him in ways I never had. So, we parted ways. One minute, I was in a relationship and the next, I was single. On New Year's Eve, I found myself at a party, still feeling blindsided, disappointed, angry, sad, near tears, and drunk. I went into the bathroom to pull myself together. Sebastian ended up in the bathroom at the same time. He kissed me to ring in the New Year. Yes, I kissed him back and, yes, we may have gotten a little handsy. Over our clothes, not underneath. We did not have sex. I ran from the bathroom in tears. It was uncharacteristic behavior for me—irresponsible and haphazard. I never saw him again. I was hurting and trying to make sense of what happened with my relationship. I pushed the New Year's Eve kiss out of my mind. In the scope of everything I was dealing with, it meant nothing. I didn't even tell my friends what happened. That's how insignificant it was to me and I'm sure to him. I'm being completely honest with you. I didn't know who Sebastian was at the event. We were never involved. We had a random, brief chance encounter. It was a long time ago. I would never try to deceive you or mislead you. I truly did not know who Sebastian was at the time."

Barrett stared at Dylan with his elbows on the table, hands tented. She wondered what was going through his mind. She hoped that she didn't share more than he needed to know. Dylan's main concern was that she assured him that he knew everything. If Brooke would have returned her call, she would have told her the same. Unfortunately, she went to Barrett and told him something that wasn't completely accurate.

"Thanks for being honest," he finally said.

"Where do we go from here?"

"I need some time to think about it. If there's one thing I've learned being a divorce lawyer, it's to determine whether or not you see a future together."

Dylan looked down. She felt transported back to her kitchen table five years ago. It sounded all too familiar. Yet again, her future happiness was on the line.

Dylan got up from the table to leave. "The past certainly does have a way of repeating itself."

FORTY-THREE

ylan hurried down the street to where her car was parked. It all made sense. Barrett had barely been in touch while he was out of the country because he knew about Sebastian. She understood that he and Brooke had been friends since they were kids, but Brooke didn't even think to ask her what had happened. Dylan didn't know exactly what Sebastian told Brooke, what she shared with Barrett, or what was going through her mind. Dylan unlocked her car, jumped in, and immediately dialed Brooke. Her hands were trembling. Brooke answered on the first ring.

"Brooke, we need to talk."

"There's nothing to discuss."

"Do you really believe that?"

"I believe you were with my man and neglected to tell me. As far as I'm concerned, the Referral Program is a wrap for me. I'm with a client and have nothing else to say to you." The call dropped.

Dylan was stunned. She could not believe Brooke hung up, unwilling to talk to her. She didn't say that she would call later when she was finished with her client. She said that she had nothing to say. Throughout all their years of friendship, they had never spoken to each other that way nor shunned each other. They were sisters. They had each other's backs. Sure, there were times when they had disagreements, but they didn't last. She couldn't remember a time when they'd gone without speaking because they were upset with one another. If they had a problem, they discussed it or moved on because

232

it wasn't worth rehashing. That's what sister-friends do. Ivy, Brooke, and Dylan had been sisters for too many years for anything to come between them. Dylan knew she was in uncharted territory and did not have the answers on how to get through to Brooke. She could be stubborn and once she convinced herself of something, there was no telling her any different. Dylan was near tears thinking how Brooke could believe she had intentionally neglected to tell her something. If only she had mentioned to Ivy what happened with Doc in the bathroom. It would have come to light that he and Sebastian were one and the same.

In that moment, Dylan wished she had left things alone and never created the Referral Program. They may have been single, but their friendship would have been intact.

FORTY-FOUR

*I*vy was thankful for the cool breeze blowing through her hair. The sun was strong and there wasn't much shade on the High Line. She spent many weekends at the elevated park, strolling its gardens or relaxing on a bench. She placed a hand over her brow to block the sun from her field of vision. She squinted and recognized the figure approaching.

"Hello, beautiful."

"Hi, Xavier. Have a seat."

He sat next to her on the bench. "I have to thank you, again, for reaching out to me. I was pleasantly surprised."

"I have to admit, I wasn't quite myself the first time we met. I wanted a do-over." Ivy chuckled. "I couldn't have you thinking I didn't have any manners."

"I didn't think Dylan would suggest I meet someone with no manners. I understand we all go through things. I figured you had something on your mind."

"Well, I appreciate your understanding. Do you want to walk the High Line?"

"Let's do that."

Ivy and Xavier abandoned the bench and began a leisurely walk through the park. Ivy surprised herself when she decided to call Xavier and invite him out. It weighed on Ivy that she had let her emotions over Daveed get the best of her. She had to remind herself what the program was all about and that she owed it to herself to keep moving forward. She did not want to be alone for the rest of her life.

"So, I have to ask, I heard Dylan refer to you as Xavi. Is that what most people call you?"

"Some folks do, but I get called everything from X to Xave to Xavi to XV to Professor X. It doesn't end."

"Which do you prefer?"

"X or Xavi is fine."

"Okay, X. The first time we met you asked me an awful lot of questions. Now, it's my turn."

He glanced over at her. "I'm here for it. Shoot."

"You mentioned you've been single for a couple of years. How often do you date?"

"You just jump right on in, huh?"

"With both feet."

Xavier laughed. "Direct and to the point. I like that. Let's see . . . how do I answer that question?"

"Truthfully."

"I can do that with no problem. My dating revolves a lot around my businesses."

"What does that mean? You're dating all the women that come to buy cars at your dealerships?"

"No, that's not what I mean. Although, I have met a few women that way. I spend an unreasonable amount of time on the management of my dealerships. It's something I have been trying to scale back but haven't quite managed to do. I haven't made much time for any serious dating. I tend to lean heavily on going on lunch dates."

"What you're basically telling me is you're squeezing dates into your workday." Ivy tried to stifle a laugh.

"When you say it like that it sounds pretty pitiful."

"Well . . ."

"On occasion, I have dates in the evening. The issue is I tend to work late on most nights."

"Did you keep those same hours when you were in a relationship?"

"That's an interesting question. I did not work the same number of hours then that I am now. After my relationship ended, I went into overdrive."

"When we were at The Aroma Bean Spot, you asked me about my last relationship."

"Yes, I did."

"The breakup was pretty fresh."

"I figured as much. People tend to wear recent breakups like a wet raincoat."

"Thank goodness it's a sunny day and I don't need my raincoat anymore."

"I won't ask you for any specific details, but I am curious just how recent we're talking about."

"About a month now."

"That means this is a rebound date."

"Aw, don't say that."

"I'm okay with it. I get to spend the afternoon with a lovely woman, how could I have a problem with that?"

"Let's get back to you."

"I'm still in the hot seat?"

"Yup. We have a slight age gap between us."

"Do we?" he quipped.

"About nine years. How young is too young for you to date?"

"I really am in the hot seat. I'll answer but I'm going to ask you the same question."

"I can answer first, if you like."

"No, it's my question and I'm enjoying our banter."

"Then stop stalling."

Xavier put his hands up in surrender. "I appreciate a mature woman and maturity isn't always determined by age."

"That sounds really nebulous."

"I wasn't finished. With that being said, I won't date anyone under the age of thirty."

"I wasn't expecting that."

"What did you think I was going to say?"

Ivy didn't want to offend him and had to be careful with her response. "I know plenty of mature twentysomethings. I thought you might say the same."

"I'm forty-three, Ivy. I don't want to be with anyone too young. At some point that age gap can rear its head and the differences become starkly apparent. What about you? No, wait, I want you to answer how much older would you date?"

"Firstly, I agree with you that a significant age gap could *potentially* cause issues. Second, when thinking about dating an older man, I'm always concerned whether we would be able to relate or will he behave like a father figure. Is he sexualizing me or not? Can we relate on cultural and social issues? Do we have similar points of reference on music or movies?"

"All valid concerns. So, how much older?"

"Ultimately, I don't think I would date anyone more than ten years older."

"Phew, I just made the cutoff."

They laughed together. Ivy took note of his pretty teeth again. Xavier had a warm and cheerful vibe and a good sense of humor to match. He looked damn good for a man in his early forties and appeared to take care of his body.

"How important is it that your family approve of whoever you're dating?" she asked.

"It's important but not a requirement. I'm not a young dude where I would be easily influenced by what my family thinks. However, you know how mothers are about their sons."

"Your mother included?"

"She is definitely an offender, but how many mothers really think any woman is good enough for their son?"

"Are you telling me you're a mama's boy?"

He pinched his fingers together. "Maybe a little bit. I'm her only son."

"Now that's interesting."

"It's not like she's doing my laundry or ironing my clothes."

"You don't have to convince me."

"The most she might do is make me Sunday dinner every now and then."

"That's sweet. I can't tease you for that."

"If she calls and tells me she's making dinner, I try not to miss it."

"Do you know how to cook?"

"I can do a little something. However, I'm pretty much banned from the kitchen for Sunday dinner. My sisters keep me out. They aren't too fond of my skills."

"How many do you have?"

"Three very opinionated, nosy, pushy little sisters. The youngest one is twenty-four. Now, they're the ones to watch out for. They seem to think that I need their seal of approval on who I choose to date. I've reminded them on more than one occasion that I'm their *older* brother and I'm a grown ass man."

Ivy didn't have any of those issues since she didn't have siblings. She could only imagine the amount of grief Xavier's three sisters would give his dates. They probably put many women through the wringer—eyeballing, questioning, judging, and shading them. She wondered if the youngest was the toughest of them all. She was probably spoiled, and her big brother probably contributed the most to the spoiling. Ivy giggled. She was concocting profiles on people she had never met.

"Did your sisters like your ex-girlfriend?"

"Two of them did."

"What about the other one?"

"She had it set in her mind that I was being used. She's the one that typically finds something wrong with every woman I date."

"I wonder why that is?"

"She's the second oldest. We're only two years apart. It was just me and her for a lot of years before my mother had my last two sisters. We've always been close. I was the older brother but, for some reason, she thought she was my protector. She still thinks that's her role. I don't want to scare you off, so, I'm going to stop talking about my overbearing sisters."

"Families love me . . . mommas, daddies, brothers and sisters, too."

"I bet they do. My sisters would probably love you, too."

Ivy thought about her own sisters, Dylan and Brooke. She wasn't sure what was going on with them. She hadn't spoken to either since the situation with Sebastian surfaced. Ivy couldn't believe Brooke was a no-show to their monthly brunch. Brooke intentionally ignored her text messages and calls. Never, in the history of their friendship, had any of them behaved in that manner. Ivy was in disbelief that they were even in that predicament.

Xavier slowed his gait in front of a cluster of benches. "Do you want to sit for a moment?"

"Is it too hot out for you?"

"Not at all. I just wanted to sit and talk for a while."

Ivy nodded. "We walked about a mile. I guess I'll give you a break."

"I would have never imagined you had a sense of humor after our first encounter."

"I know, that's completely my fault. And I owe you an apology."

"No, you don't. You've already explained."

"I'm sorry for being less than sociable when we met and—"

"Please, stop. I accept your apology. It's unnecessary but I appreciate it. Now can we move on to something else?"

"Gladly."

"When I was on my way here, I was on the phone with my friend, actually my ex, and mentioned I was meeting you this afternoon. She asked what you were like, and I told her I wasn't sure. I'm looking forward to telling her how much I enjoyed spending time with you today."

"How often do you two communicate?"

"All the time. We're good friends."

"That doesn't cause issues with the women you date?"

"I haven't dated anyone seriously since we broke up. I know not everyone is a fan of keeping in touch with exes, so I like to gauge where people stand on the issue. I don't know if you remember, but I asked you when we first met."

"What did I say?"

"You said you don't have a problem with exes being friends."

"I said that?"

"To be specific, you said not really."

"Interesting."

"I don't know how to interpret that response. Care to elaborate?"

"Well, my initial response might not be quite accurate."

"Okay . . ."

"I think we all want to end relationships on good terms, but being friends is something different. If I'm with someone, I don't necessarily want him chatting up his ex-girlfriend on a regular. I probably wouldn't take issue with an occasional conversation, but all the time would most definitely be concerning."

"Even if you had assurances that they're only friends?"

"They may be friends now, but they shared intimate and per-

sonal moments in the past. There are emotions and memories teth-
ered to that relationship and no guarantee that those emotions would
never be rekindled. I personally would prefer that whoever I'm with
wouldn't want or need to continue a close friendship with someone
they were previously linked to romantically."

"I would hope my situation wouldn't cause much concern. My
ex doesn't even live in the country. I know most women are worried
about cheating, but she's halfway across the world. That wouldn't be
an issue or an option."

"There is emotional cheating. It's not always physical."

"That's true. However, is it cheating if you know about the friendship?"

"It's cheating if you are satisfying intimate emotional needs and
desires from someone other than your current partner."

"Now it's my turn to respond with *interesting*."

"It's obvious you have a special relationship with your ex that you
likely won't ever let go. I just wonder if the reason you communicate
with her the way you do is because you aren't in a relationship with
someone else."

Xavier's head cocked to the side. "I'll have to think about that.
It's possible I've kept her in a certain box typically reserved for the
person you're in a relationship with."

"Is she seeing anyone new?"

"She says no."

"You don't believe her?"

"Sometimes I do, other times I don't."

"If you feel like she would have to keep you in the dark regarding
her dating status, that speaks volumes. If you two were only friends,
with no emotions involved, there would be no need for her to be
untruthful with you."

"You're right. I can't argue with that logic."

"How would you feel if she told you she was seeing someone?"

"I'd be happy for her."

"How would you feel if she didn't have as much time for your conversations?"

Xavier hesitated. "Truthfully, I don't think I'd like it."

"There you have it. That's why I wouldn't want my man talking to his ex. That emotional connection."

Xavier sat quietly for a moment. It appeared he was processing what Ivy had said. She leaned back against the bench and watched the people passing by, relishing the scent of flowers wafting through the air. She figured Xavier was still in a relationship with his ex and he didn't even realize it. He was emotionally bound to her. They had broken up because she was moving, yet they were holding on to each other. He wasn't emotionally available and needed to sort that out.

"You've given me some food for thought," he said. "How about we go get some real food?"

"Oh, not today. There's something I need to do." Ivy touched her hand to his leg. "Maybe next time."

"As long as there is a next time."

They stood and Xavier opened his arms. Ivy stepped closer and they hugged. "I had a nice time, Xavier. Thanks for meeting me."

"Any time."

Ivy walked off in one direction and Xavier, the other. It would've been nice to have a meal with him, but there was something more important Ivy needed to do.

FORTY-FIVE

The doorbell rang three times in rapid succession. Brooke looked up from her tablet and listened, as if she wasn't sure it was her doorbell. She jumped up from her sofa when it rang two more times. She straightened her T-shirt and smoothed her bob as she headed to the front door. She wasn't expecting anyone, so she approached quietly and peered through the peephole.

Brooke groaned and opened the door. "Ivy, what are you doing here?"

"Seriously, Brooke? Let me in."

Brooke unlocked the storm door and held it open. Ivy walked past her into the foyer.

"Come into the living room." Brooke led Ivy through the house. She returned to her spot on the couch. "What are you doing here?"

Ivy sat at the opposite end of the sofa. "I'm checking on you."

"I don't need to be checked on."

"Obviously, you do. You haven't answered a single text or voice message I've left you."

"I would think you would know that means I'm not in the mood to talk."

"So, you're just gonna ignore me?"

Brooke looked down at her hands. "I figured you would get the point and stop texting and calling."

Ivy glared at Brooke. "That's how you treat someone you don't care about. You don't treat your sister like that."

"Now that's funny. You came over here to reprimand *me*?"

"That's not what I'm doing. When have we ever gone without speaking for over a week? When have you ever not returned my call? What would make you think that I wouldn't keep trying to reach you? I wanted to make sure you're okay."

"You mean you're here to do damage control."

"Will you stop countering everything I'm saying? I told you why I'm here. I want to know why you aren't taking my calls."

"I know you like to pretend you are, but you're not that naïve."

"I'm going to pretend I didn't hear that and repeat my question. Why haven't you answered my calls?"

"Let's start with the obvious. I didn't want to talk to you. I'm pissed off and don't want to be bothered."

"And, instead of talking about it, you just shut me out?"

"Considering you're one of the reasons I'm so pissed . . . yeah."

"Well, I came all the way over here to find out what's going on. So, what are you pissed at me about?"

"What do you think, Ivy? You and Dylan talked me into being a part of that ridiculous Referral Program and, like a fool, I went against everything my instincts were telling me. You had the nerve to introduce me to Sebastian, knowing he had been with Dylan. What happened to not referring a man that one of us had been with previously? Did you just throw that rule out the window when it came to my referrals?"

"Do you hear yourself? You know that can't be true."

"I know that you totally disregarded the rules. I know that you set me up with a man Dylan was with."

"You need to calm down."

"No. You wanted to know what was going on with me and now you know. How would you feel if I hooked you up with a man your friend had been with?"

"Is that what Sebastian told you? That he was *with* Dylan? Because when I spoke to my cousin, he told me nothing really happened between them. He told me the same thing that Dylan told me."

"And you didn't know any of this happened before you referred your cousin to me?"

"Of course not. I didn't find out anything until Dylan mentioned she ran into you and Sebastian at an event."

"He said she looked familiar. I had a sinking feeling something wasn't right. Dylan could have told me that night what happened between them."

"Brooke, I understand this is upsetting, but you need to understand, Dylan did not remember Sebastian."

"How often do you meet someone named Sebastian? I would remember meeting a man named Sebastian."

"You need to listen to what I'm telling you. When I introduced Dylan to Sebastian, I introduced him by his nickname, Doc. I don't even remember how I introduced her—Dyl, Dill Pickles, Bestie— but, obviously, neither one remembered the other. I can show you a picture of Sebastian back then and you might not even recognize him. He had a face full of hair, locs down his back, and they were both drinking—a lot! It was New Year's Eve. You know Dylan can barely hold her liquor. She was drinking heavily that night. Think about it. She had just broken up with Ace and you know how low she was feeling. So, two strangers kissed when the ball dropped on New Year's Eve *five years ago*. They never saw each other again, haven't spoken to one another since, they don't *know* each other, and that brief encounter meant absolutely nothing. She didn't even tell me about it. That should tell you something. Are you really going to let that ruin your friendship with Dylan and your chance at happiness with Sebastian?"

Brooke sighed. "How would I continue anything with Sebastian knowing he's been with my friend?"

"First, you have to stop saying they've 'been together.' They kissed."

"Sebastian said they touched each other, too."

"A kiss with some innocent touching? An ass grab? Yes, something happened between them, but it was really nothing. Under the circumstances, it's insignificant. I know you're upset, but I didn't know they kissed. Dylan didn't know my cousin Doc and Sebastian were the same person, and Sebastian didn't remember Dylan's name and barely recognized her. I know both of them inside and out. You know Dylan would never intentionally deceive you or hurt you. And, I know my cousin—as do you, now. Sebastian is a stand-up guy. Is this worth throwing away the most happiness you've had in a long time?"

"I don't know, Ivy."

"Okay, well, I wanted to come see you to make sure you were all right. I'm glad we had a chance to talk." Ivy stood up. "I'm going now, but I'll leave you with one final thought. You need to think long and hard about what you're willing to sacrifice."

Brooke walked Ivy out and gave her a hug before she left. As soon as she closed the door, regret for the way she'd treated her took hold. She loved Ivy like a sister. No matter how upset she was, Brooke knew it was important to express that to her friend. She plopped back down on the couch and reflected on what Ivy had told her. What was she willing to sacrifice?

FORTY-SIX

Jvy meandered down the walkway toward her car. When she'd decided to check on Brooke, she wasn't sure what to expect. Showing up uninvited was a risk, but one she was willing to take. They had too many years invested in their friendship and Ivy was not going to shy away from the conflict they currently found themselves in.

She rummaged through her purse trying to retrieve her car keys. When she looked up, she spied Daveed getting out of his car.

"Ivy," he called out, with a wave.

She stared at him as she quickened her pace.

"Wait," he called out again, hurrying over to her.

She reached her car at the same time Daveed did.

"Hey, how are you?" he asked, standing in front of her.

Ivy glowered at him.

"I don't blame you for not wanting to speak to me."

She detected a slight tremble in his voice.

"I probably wouldn't speak to me either," he continued.

"You ghosted me."

"I owe you an explanation."

Ivy rolled her eyes. "I don't have time for this," she said, reaching for the door handle.

Daveed placed his hand on top of Ivy's, preventing her from opening the door. "Please, could you give me five minutes?" He waited for a response. "Can you come inside?"

"No. Right here is fine." She snatched her hand from beneath his. "Start talking."

Daveed audibly exhaled. "Please, Ivy, come inside so we can talk."

"Five minutes," she reluctantly agreed.

They walked to his house in silence. Daveed led her inside and to the family room. Ivy's stomach wrenched. The last time they were in that room together, a lot had happened.

"Have a seat." He motioned to the couch. "Can I get you something to drink?"

"No, I'm not here for that."

"I get it."

"So, talk."

Daveed sat in the club chair across from Ivy. "I was hoping I would run into you."

"You mean like the day you saw me in Brooke's garden? You didn't have much to say."

"I'm sorry about that. I was feeling self-conscious, ashamed, embarrassed . . ."

"*You* felt embarrassed? Imagine how I felt being snubbed in front of my friend."

He paused, gathering his thoughts. "You don't understand."

"No, I don't."

"I'm a flawed man, far from perfect. Sometimes I'm my own worst enemy. I found something so special with you and I destroyed it."

"Yeah, you did. What I want to know is why."

"There's a number of reasons but, mostly, my insecurity got the best of me."

"Insecurity?" she said, her voice rife with disbelief.

"The last time we were together, you and I spent an intense afternoon with each other. I told you I wanted to make love to you and what we shared was special to me."

Ivy looked away, not wanting to gaze in his eyes.

"After you left," he proceeded, "I was feeling all types of emotion—contentment, exhilaration, gratification . . . I wanted to have you back by my side. I couldn't stop thinking about you, thinking about us. I began to replay, and then *pick apart*, every moment of that afternoon. As you know, I'm an analytical guy. I thought about how I only wanted to make you happy that day. Our picnic in the park was ruined by the rain, but I wanted to arrange something special for you. I poured out my heart and read you a poem that struck a chord with me. It resonated on many levels, especially the ending when I said I was in love with you. When I thought about it later, I realized I didn't get the same kind of response from you. I even told you how real what we shared was for me. I asked if you felt the same and you said that I knew how you felt about me. What I felt was that I was falling in love all alone."

Ivy replayed that day in her mind. It was perfection. From the moment she walked through the door, Daveed had draped her in splendor. Ivy couldn't deny that he put his feelings on the table—she had not. She left him out on a cliff by himself. *Old habits die hard*, Ivy thought. And though she had to own her actions, Ivy had let Brooke's recommendation permeate her thoughts right before she came over that day. Brooke had told her to be cool when she was gushing about just how much she liked Daveed. Somewhere in the back of her mind it stuck and caused Ivy to temper her response to him.

"I told you that I've struggled with being transparent in relationships in the past," she said.

"I said I was in love with you." Daveed let that hang in the air. "When you didn't respond in kind, I figured you were treating our situation more casually and we weren't on the same page. I thought maybe you didn't feel the same for me." Daveed stopped talking and got up. "I need a drink. Are you sure you don't want anything?"

"I'll have one, too."

He nodded and exited the room. Ivy took a few deep breaths. She fanned herself with her hand, suddenly feeling warm.

Daveed returned and handed her a glass. "It's a vodka soda made with peach seltzer, the way you like." He went to sit back in his chair.

"Thank you." Ivy sipped from her glass.

"This isn't easy to say." Daveed took a healthy swig of his drink. "After you left, I began to question everything. Naturally, I wondered if you thought the sex was terrible. I knew I didn't last very long and that you didn't have an orgasm. We had waited all that time and I couldn't even pleasure you. So, I'm thinking, I told this woman that I'm in love with her, she doesn't say it back, and then I make love to her and come up short. My pride was hurt, my feelings were hurt, and the more I thought about it, the more I brooded about it. I hadn't been in that headspace for a long time and once I went there, I couldn't get out. I got stuck fretting over being in love and being embarrassed. I was feeling insecure and that's why I started to with-draw in the days after. I wanted to save us from an uncomfortable confrontation where you would have to explain why you just didn't have the same feelings for me. I couldn't bear to hear that and, like a fool, I avoided you."

Ivy shook her head. "That Saturday afternoon was beautiful. Your thoughtfulness touched me deeply. When you read the poem to me, I wanted to hear it again and again. You bared your soul and reached out to me, and I neglected to reach back. I didn't realize that until now. I thought I was showing you through my actions that I was right there with you—hand in hand. In retrospect, maybe we rushed things. We said we'd take sex off the table and we disregarded that. Had we known each other better, perhaps I would have been able to express myself in that moment. If you knew me better, maybe you would have known I was slipping into my old habit of not being transparent. I'm a work in progress. I never meant for you to feel that we weren't on the same page."

"So, I wasn't alone with the way I was feeling?"

"Absolutely not." Ivy smiled. "Daveed, I should have said how I was feeling instead of playing it cool. Only moments before I arrived that day, I was telling Brooke just how much I felt for you. She even implied that I felt more for you than I was letting on. She was right. You and I connected from day one. I felt the same way about you that you felt about me. I'm sorry that I didn't say it and you didn't know it."

"My insecurity and ego took over."

"I meant what I said that afternoon. When we made love, I thought it was beautiful. You pleased me in every way. I was looking forward to our next time."

"Ivy, I apologize with everything I am. I was wrong to treat you the way that I did. I don't always get the social and relationship stuff right. Can you ever forgive me?"

"I don't always get it right either. I'm still working on how to share my feelings more."

"Do you accept my apology?"

"Yes, I accept your apology."

Daveed tentatively approached Ivy on the sofa. He took her hand and pulled her up and wrapped his arms around her. He held her tightly and whispered in her ear. "I'm so sorry."

"I know," she replied.

After a long minute, they pulled apart. Daveed sat down next to Ivy. "Can we start over?"

"Only if we start over from the beginning."

Daveed beamed. "We can do that."

"Okay. I'm Ivy." She extended her hand to shake Daveed's.

He held on to it. "That's a beautiful name. It suits you. I'm Daveed."

"Thank you. A pleasure to meet you, Daveed."

"Ivy, I would like to get to know you better."

"Well, let's see. I'm a social worker. I love a good book. I volunteer my time helping high school students get into college. I have my own place in the city. I enjoy picnics in the park, particularly with someone special. I'm carefree and love to laugh. I've had issues in the past with not being as open and transparent as I should be, but I'm working on it. I'm learning how to share my feelings more." Ivy observed Daveed. "Can you see yourself with someone like that?"

"When it's someone I find funny, smart, sexy . . . and I've already fallen in love with, yes."

"That's good to hear, because I think you're intelligent, thoughtful, an amazing lover . . . and I can see myself with you, too."

Daveed placed a single, lingering kiss on her cheek. "I am in love with you."

"*We* are in love with each other."

They gazed into each other's eyes and Ivy felt the spark reigniting. Daveed leaned in for a kiss, fanning her flame.

FORTY-SEVEN

*B*rooke was secluded in her office at the gym occupying herself with employee schedules. She was relieved Michael wasn't in when she arrived. He liked to chat, and she wasn't in the mood to entertain him. She didn't plan to stay long. Brooke wanted to get home to take a hot shower and unwind. She worked a full day at the rehabilitation center providing physical therapy, and the gym's employee schedule was the only thing keeping her from relaxation.

A rap on her office window drew her eyes away from the computer monitor. She waved, signaling it was okay to enter.

The door opened. "Barrett, what are you doing here?"

"Well, hello to you, too."

"Oh, please. I know you aren't expecting a formal greeting. Come on in and sit down."

"I was hoping you would be here tonight."

"Yup. I'm just wrapping up a couple of things."

"The place looks like it's doing well."

"We're growing and evolving. It's a good investment."

"Your entrepreneurial spirit has taken over. I'm proud of you."

"Do you remember the summer before fifth grade when your mother let us have a bake sale in your driveway?"

Barrett started laughing before she finished her sentence. "And we sat behind the table *sampling* all the baked goods until every muffin, cookie, and slice of cake was gone . . ."

"I got so sick that night," Brooke recalled.

"My mother was pissed and grounded me for the last two weeks of summer vacation. The only thing I was allowed to do was walk my neighbor's dog to earn enough money to pay my mother back for all the treats she had bought for our sale."

"We did some crazy stuff. How about the time when we went to the creek with the older kids when our parents told us not to go any farther than our two streets? We rode our bikes nearly two miles and yours got stolen by some kid we had never seen before, but all the older kids knew."

"You had to let me ride on the back of your bike all the way home. My father whupped my butt," Barrett reminisced.

"You deserved it for not listening," she joked.

"You were there right along with me."

"True, but my bike didn't get stolen."

"I heard the same lecture for weeks about money not growing on trees and how they were not going to buy me a new bike."

"You didn't get one either."

"Not for two years."

Brooke laughed. "I don't know why we always got ourselves into hot water."

"Probably because you would come up with these harebrained schemes and I would follow along looking for adventure."

"I think that's called revisionist history. You were the one sucking me into your crazy antics."

"Whoever was responsible, we had some great times."

"I can't refute that," Brooke said.

"We've been through a lot. Minded each other's business, especially you, encouraged and lifted each other up. I'll never forget when I called to tell you I was getting divorced. First, you cursed me out for barely staying in touch and *then* you asked if I was all right. You told me I had no business getting married in the first place." Barrett guffawed.

"I sure did. Just like you told me not to waste my time with that pilot I dated for almost a year."

"There was something seriously wrong with that guy."

"I figured it out eventually. You, on the other hand, didn't realize that girl you dated from Texas was twenty years older than she said and a grandmother," Brooke reminded him.

"She was a little peculiar, but she looked damn good."

"I don't know about that."

"Through it all, we've always been honest with each other."

"We have to be when dealing with crazy people," Brooke said.

"Apparently, that's not Sebastian and Dylan."

"What?"

"They aren't crazy people, Brooke."

"I didn't say they were."

"You introduced me to a wonderful woman and Sebastian seemed like a really nice guy."

"Okay?"

"Neither of us could have anticipated the situation we would find ourselves in. I think we were all thrown for a loop. The question is what do we do about it? Do we walk away, or do we figure out a way to stay?"

"Wouldn't it be awkward? The woman you were dating and the man I was seeing shared an intimate moment."

"Aren't there levels to intimacy? They kissed. A conversation could qualify as a more intimate moment depending upon who you're talking to and what you're talking about."

Brooke thought about just how awkward it could be. Over the years, she always proclaimed that she would never date or be with a man if one of her friends or someone she knew had been with him.

Dylan was one of her best friends. Sebastian was the best man, by far, that she had been with in a long time. She didn't want any of her girlfriends to know what it was like to be with her man. She didn't want to sit around comparing notes on how he kissed or held her. She didn't want Dylan to have that kind of knowledge. "Are you saying that you don't mind that they made out?"

"It's not a matter of whether I mind. From what I understand, there was a lot of alcohol involved and it was a long time ago. I'm not necessarily comfortable holding someone accountable for a New Year's Eve kiss when they were single and I didn't even know them at the time."

"What if it were more than just a kiss?"

"Was it? I know when you first called me, you made it seem as if they had been together."

"No, I don't think it went that far. I mean, I know it didn't. Sebastian said it was kissing and touching over their clothes. Honestly, I was so upset that night. I heard kissing and I was done. I wanted you to know because I was the one who set you up with Dylan. I probably should have calmed down before I called."

"No one saw anyone naked. I've done worse than that on some of my travels around the world, with women I never saw again."

Brooke raised her eyebrows. "Come again?"

"That was a long time ago and that stays between us."

Brooke zipped her lips.

"All I'm saying," Barrett continued, "is things would only be awkward if *we* made it awkward or *they* made it awkward. It sounds like it's something they had long forgotten and probably want to forget again."

"And you won't feel like Sebastian knows Dylan intimately?"

"What does Sebastian know about Dylan or she about him? We saw them at the event together. They didn't look like two people who *knew* each other intimately."

"They looked like they were trying to figure it out."

"Who doesn't do that when they think they recognize someone from somewhere. I think that proves my case even more. If that kiss was so eventful and earth shattering, you don't think they would recognize one another immediately?"

"I guess . . ."

"I know you, Brooke, and if something doesn't fit within your perfect ideal, then you reject it. This is not going to fit. Sometimes you have to consider all the angles and weigh all the possibilities and deal with only the facts."

"Don't go all lawyerly on me."

"I deal with facts, Brooke. And the fact is, those two don't even know each other. Extenuating circumstances brought them together and it was a fleeting moment in the scope of their lives. Nothing more. We need to reconsider."

o   o   o

FINALLY HOME, BROOKE opted for a long, hot bath. It was good she had a chance to talk with Barrett about the situation. He was a trusted friend with a big heart and a good head on his shoulders. Brooke couldn't deny he had made some valid points. The entire drive home she couldn't stop thinking about her last conversation with Dylan. Brooke had been unfairly harsh with her. Even if she thought Dylan had been intimate with Sebastian, their years of friendship should have at least warranted a conversation. Brooke's anger had gotten the best of her. Dylan had never been anything but loyal and honest, a true sister. Regret washed over Brooke like a tidal wave. She expected a lot from her friends, but she needed to expect more from herself in the way she reacted to situations and dealing with the ensuing emotions.

Brooke toweled off and slipped on her robe. She went into the bedroom and grabbed her phone. She crawled on the bed, leaning against the headboard, and dialed her friend. Dylan's face filled the screen.

Brooke could feel her eyes filling with tears. "I'm sorry, Dylan."

Dylan wiped the corner of her eye. "Me too. I missed you."

"You and Ivy are my sisters. I know you two would never do anything to hurt me."

"I feel awful about how things happened. If I knew—"

Brooke held her hand up. "Stop. I know that and I understand. My emotions got the best of me."

"Just let me say this. Nothing serious happened between us. It was a chance encounter a long time ago. I was drunk and lashing out for being dumped by Ace. I wish I had mentioned it to Ivy."

"We're good, my sister."

"In the future, just come talk to me."

"I promise."

"I love you, Brooke."

"Love you, too."

o   o   o

BROOKE WONDERED HOW to move forward with Sebastian. She hadn't spoken to him since the event, having ignored all his calls. She hadn't answered any text messages or reached out herself. Brooke thought about the affirmation Sebastian shared with his audience during motivational speeches. Though she wasn't in front of a mirror, she whispered aloud, "Today is the day I meet my best self." She had not been her best self for weeks.

Brooke knew she had to be better and do better.

FORTY-EIGHT

*C*allie stuck her head into Dylan's office to ask if she needed anything before she left for the evening. Dylan was wrapping up a call and nodded, holding out a folder for Callie. She mouthed, "File this please."

She came in, took the folder, and jetted out of the office. Dylan planned to leave soon after her. It was already after six and a few of the staff were heading out. She allowed her employees flexibility with their hours. They either started at eight, nine, or ten in the morning and left for the day at either four, five, or six in the evening. Dylan learned long ago that people perform better when they have a healthy work-life balance. Everyone had to get their work done, but she wanted to afford them the option of coming in and leaving during the hour block that worked best for their lifestyles. Dylan typically worked from eight to six or later. There was no getting around it.

As she hung up and made her way to the elevator, she was already making a mental note of what she needed to do the following day. Dylan admonished herself for not disconnecting from the workday. She started humming a tune to clear her mind of the tasks that were trying to creep in.

As she stepped outside, Dylan inhaled the warm air, the sun still shining bright. Standing on the sidewalk, watching people pass by, she was inclined to take a nice, slow stroll to the train station. Distracted by her thoughts, Dylan didn't notice someone was approaching until Barrett was standing directly in front of her.

She touched her hand to her chest. "You startled me."

"In this sea of people?"

"They were bustling by. I didn't notice you until you suddenly appeared."

Barrett pointed to the curb. "I was right there leaning on my car, watching you from the moment you exited the building."

"I did not see you at all."

"You seemed consumed by your thoughts." Barrett smiled. "You look beautiful."

"Thank you."

"I have something for you."

Dylan eyed him suspiciously as he led her over to his car. Barrett opened the back door and retrieved a single red rose. He handed her the flower.

She looked down at the rose and back up at Barrett, waiting.

He cleared his throat. "My approach was off last week. I questioned you in an accusatory manner. I should have asked you about Sebastian with an open mind. I didn't and you shared something very personal with me because I was interrogating you. The details about your past breakup belong solely to you. I realized I put you in a precarious position where you had no choice but to divulge them to me. I was wrong and I'm sorry."

"I realize you and Brooke have been friends since childhood. She told you something and you would've had no reason to doubt what she said."

"That's no excuse." A truck horn blared repeatedly behind them. "Can we sit in my car for a moment, away from the noise?" They slipped inside the car and Joe, always behind the wheel, closed the partition. "That's better. I can hear myself think," Barrett declared. "I was saying, my friendship with Brooke does not excuse me from assuming what I was told was accurate. You and I had our own relationship, our own conversations, interactions, and level of trust. I should have asked you about what may or may not have happened, and I didn't. I left the country on business still confused and unclear on the situation, and I didn't make it a priority to get clarification until I returned. That wasn't fair to you or us."

"I agree it wasn't fair to me," Dylan said with a smirk. "I wasn't sure if there was still an *us*."

"Dylan, in the grand scheme of things, I don't care about a kiss from five years ago. It's not important to me. What is important is that you're my relationship goals. I'm not willing to let you slip through my fingers because of this nonsense. I can acknowledge I may have gotten a big fat C on our first real test. I didn't communicate properly, at all. But, if you would be willing to give me another chance, I promise to try to make all As from here on out. What do you say? Are you willing to give us another chance, maybe see the world with me?"

"Why don't we start with dinner and see where that takes us?"

o o o

DYLAN AND BARRETT sat side by side at his dining room table. The lights of New York City served as a backdrop, shining through the expanse of windows. He cut a piece of shrimp piccata and brought his fork to her mouth. "What do you think?"

"Mmm," she moaned as the flavors rolled around her palate.

"Try the sautéed spinach."

She obliged. "I'm impressed."

"I told you we didn't need to go out to eat tonight."

Dylan took a drink from her wineglass. "I should have known your mother raised you right."

"I can throw down in the kitchen when I want to but, trust me, it's not often. Tonight, I wanted you all to myself, not in a room full of people in a crowded restaurant."

Dylan looked over with a sideways glance. "Well, you have me."

"Say that again."

"You have me."

"I don't want that to change."

"If you treat me right, it won't."

"I'm ready to move mountains for you." Barrett caressed Dylan's cheek.

She placed her hand over his and held it against her face. "I believe you."

"Seeing is believing and I promise I'm going to show you."

They finished dinner, cleaned the kitchen, and were heading to the living room to chill with a bottle of wine. Dylan opened the button on her peplum suit jacket. "Do you have something comfortable I can put on? Maybe an oversized T-shirt? It's been a long day and I want to get out of this suit."

Barrett grasped Dylan by the hand. "Come into the bedroom. We'll find you something." He led her down the hallway to his room. Dylan slid her feet through the lush white shag area rug surrounding his California king bed as he went over to the dresser. While he rummaged through the drawers, she took off her jacket and laid it on the cushioned bench at the end of the bed. Dylan unzipped her skirt and stepped out of it, placing it with her jacket.

"How's this?" Barrett turned around with a large Brooklyn Nets tank top in hand. "It should be—okay," he said, barely getting the words out when he saw Dylan standing in her sheer lace camisole and panties. He walked over to Dylan and held the tank top out to her, staring in her eyes.

"Thank you." She reached for the shirt and let it slip from her fingers to the floor.

Barrett pushed a lock of Dylan's hair behind her ear. He slid his hand to the back of her neck, up through her hair, and cradled her head as he descended for a kiss. Their lips met and a rush of sensations flowed through them.

Dylan wrapped her arms around Barrett, her hands exploring his back muscles. She pulled away from his kiss. "Why am I the only one undressed?"

She sauntered over to the bed and lay across it, watching Barrett as he unbuttoned his shirt. Dylan desired him. All of him. The hardness of his body juxtaposed by his tenderness. She wanted to feel his naked skin on hers.

Barrett stripped down to his briefs and began to walk toward the bed. Dylan wagged her finger. "Don't forget those," she said, pointing to his underwear.

Slowly he pulled his briefs down, over his ass, down his thighs, and to the floor. He was nicely hung and was growing by the second. Barrett didn't move from where he stood. He let Dylan study every inch of his body. "Do you like what you see?" he asked.

She licked her lips. "Very much."

"I want to see all of you."

Dylan didn't hesitate. Sensually, she rose to her knees in the middle of his bed. She pulled her camisole over her head, revealing full C-cup breasts. She squeezed them together while she watched Barrett. She could see the rise and fall of his chest. "Do you want to touch yourself?" she teased.

He shook his head. "When you take off your pretty little panties, I want you to touch me."

"I want you to take them off." Dylan summoned him with her finger. "Come here."

Barrett climbed beside her on the bed and coaxed Dylan onto her back. He looked down the length of her body as if trying to memorize every inch, shape, and curve. He reached over and gently eased her panties off. He touched a hand to her bare flower, feeling its smooth skin. "I'm going to kiss you all over."

Barrett began a deliberate descent, starting from Dylan's expectant lips, down to her graceful neck, her beautifully brown nipples, smooth stomach, her heavenly garden, and all the way to her perfectly manicured curling toes. Barrett tortured Dylan with persistent caresses from his lips and tongue, working her into a state of sweet agitation.

Dylan spread her legs wide and pleaded with Barrett to stoke the fire. She wrapped one hand around his penis and grabbed his ass with the other. "I want you inside of me," she cooed as she lured him closer, stroking his tip against her dewdrop-covered flower. Barrett surrendered, enticed by the sweetness.

He covered Dylan's body with his, fitting them together like puzzle pieces—chest to chest, his pecs touching her pillowy breasts, close enough to feel rippling stomach muscles with each and every move, his masculinity deep within her femininity, the base of his shaft creating blissful friction on her pulsating clit, legs intertwined, nothing coming between them, hearts connected. Puzzle complete.

FORTY-NINE

S ebastian strolled back and forth onstage, delivering his message to a packed auditorium. He had a way of making people realize they had the answers and the power to make changes in their lives. Brooke sat in the back listening, feeling as if the message was meant for her. She knew Sebastian wasn't aware she was there, but every time he said something applicable to her own life, she wondered if he had spotted her in the audience.

The Q&A portion of the program was nearing, and Brooke grew more anxious. People were lining up at microphone stands in the aisles. There was one set up at the end of her row, but no one waiting at it. Sebastian called for the first question and fielded one from someone up front. After taking question after question, Sebastian announced they only had time for a couple more. Brooke felt something drawing her out of her seat. She stood and stepped up to the mic at the end of her aisle.

Sebastian pointed in her direction. "I think we have a question from the lady in the back."

Brooke looked around the room to make sure he was referring to her. "Um, yes," she started apprehensively. "I have a question."

"Yes, go ahead," he replied.

"I've been trying to be my best self for years. I even help others on a daily basis with their efforts. However, recently, I fell severely short on my own efforts. I told someone I care for deeply that I wanted him to be compassionate and able to forgive, but when it was time for me to put that into practice, I didn't show him compassion or forgiveness. Instead, I ran away. When dealing with such a glaring misstep, how can I make amends with not only myself, but especially him?"

Sebastian smiled at Brooke. "That's an excellent question. You're already halfway to a solution. You have acknowledged the misstep, you are exhibiting an openness and willingness to make change for yourself, and you are seeking a resolution to your conflict with this person you care for deeply. The only thing left for you to do is to forgive yourself first and every day say that *today is the day I meet my best self*. You have to say it, mean it, and put it into practice in all aspects of your life. Especially your relationships. Do you want to try it now?"

Brooke nodded.

"Repeat after me. Today . . ."

"Today . . ." she echoed.

"Is the day I meet my best self."

"Is the day I meet my best self."

"Okay, you're almost there," he said. "The last thing you should do is tell this person that you care for deeply that when conflict arises, compassion and forgiveness will always be a part of the solution."

"When conflict arises," Brooke began sheepishly, "compassion and forgiveness will always be a part of *our* solution."

"No running away . . ." he said solemnly.

"No running away."

"That was wonderful, thank you." Sebastian's grin lit up the auditorium. "Audience, please give that brave lady a hand. I think we just witnessed a breakthrough."

The audience clapped, looking from Sebastian to Brooke, trying to determine what exactly they were experiencing. Brooke couldn't hold back a smile as she headed back to her seat.

∘ ∘ ∘

AS THE ROOM cleared, Brooke made her way up front to the stage. She waited off to the side as Sebastian finished giving out nuggets of advice to the last few folks.

He came over to where she was standing and leaned against the stage. "I know that wasn't easy for you and I appreciate it."

"Today I met my best self and she's fabulous," Brooke said, with a chuckle.

"I thought that the day I met you and I still think it now."

"Sebastian, I could have handled that situation better. I didn't like what I heard, but I didn't make an attempt to understand the circumstances. I immediately threw the wall back up."

"And I thought we had done such a great job tearing it down."

"We did and I'm working on making sure I don't keep building it back up."

"I'm here to help however I can—with or without my doctor hat."

"How about with your boyfriend hat?"

"Thankfully, I always have that handy for you," he said, imitating putting on a hat.

"Thank you for being exactly what I said I want and need."

Sebastian stepped closer and swept Brooke up in his arms. "What I want and need is a kiss from the woman who cares for me deeply."

Brooke couldn't hold back her smile. "I can put that into practice on a daily basis."

She kissed Sebastian with an abundance of passion that left no doubt about just how deeply she cared for him.

FIFTY

*A*utumn was in full swing and the foliage had changed to hues of red, orange, yellow, and brown. Ivy and Brooke chatted as they sipped on cappuccinos at a sidewalk café. The amber sun that accompanies fall shined its rays down on the table without providing much warmth. The friends were bundled in their wool coats to protect against the seasonal chill in the air.

Ivy spotted Dylan coming up the sidewalk decked out in a camel-colored swing coat and matching gloves. "Here she is now strutting like she's on a runway in Paris."

"Hey, ladies," Dylan called out as she approached the café. She walked through the wrought iron gate that cordoned off the café from the sidewalk and came over to the table. Dylan gave each of her friends a hearty hug. "How are you, gals?"

"I was just telling Brooke it's been too long since we have gotten together for brunch."

"I thought so, too, but I swore off of initiating any more routine gatherings or programs."

"Don't be like that," Brooke said. "We bust your chops, but those gatherings, and even the program, came from a good place."

"It just seemed like it was time to give the monthly brunches a break. Besides, you two seem pretty preoccupied these days."

"Oh, just us two?" Brooke retorted. "I can barely catch you these days either. Thank goodness for a FaceTime here and there."

"Isn't that what we wanted when we started the Referral Program?" Ivy asked.

They looked at each other waiting for someone to respond.

"Ultimately, yes," Brooke said. "We agreed that we needed to do something different in order to find that someone to spend the rest of our lives with. I know I got off to a rough start with Vincent, and we all know what happened with Dylan and *Doc*—"

"Oh, shut up," Dylan said, laughing.

"But, as much as I may have been kicking and screaming in the beginning, I can't deny that you were right, Dylan."

"I was right?" Dylan's eyes were as wide as saucers. "Can you repeat that?"

"No, but I want you to know I appreciate that you always try to keep us connected and want only the best for all of us. I know I apologized months ago about how I behaved over *the kiss*, but I want to really apologize again for behaving the way I did toward both of you, my sisters. I know better and I'm going to do better. So, if you come up with a new crackpot idea for us, I'm all in because I know it's coming from a good place."

"Aw, I love you guys," Ivy sang. "In my opinion, the program did exactly what it was supposed to do. We went in assuming there wouldn't be any bumps and bruises. But nothing in life is perfect— no person, relationship, job, or anything else. I can admit I was devastated when things went awry with Daveed, but I persevered. Even when I wanted to quit the program, I called Xavier back after a disastrous first date, that I caused, and went out with him a second time. I was glad I did. I proved to myself that I can move on if and when I need to do so. I actually think I helped Xavier realize some things about his own situation."

"Overall, we took care with the referrals that didn't work out and were mindful that we have relationships with these people. I'm just thankful we didn't have to get to the bottom of our lists," Dylan added.

"I might not be saying such good things about the program if we had," Brooke joked.

"So, is the program officially finished?" Ivy asked. "Or would you go back to your list, if you had to?"

Brooke shook her head. "As far as I'm concerned, Sebastian is the one for me. I'm going to do everything in my power to make sure our relationship continues to grow. I'm not going back to that list."

"Daveed and I are in a great place. He's the whole package. And the sex is out of this world," Ivy said with a happy sigh.

"That's T.M.I.," Brooke said, frowning.

"It's not too much information, it's the truth," Ivy rebutted. "But, heaven forbid, if it doesn't work, I would go back to the program. What about you, Dylan?"

"Well, ladies, the Referral Program is *officially* finished for me." Dylan snatched off the glove from her left hand and squealed, "I'm engaged!"

Ivy and Brooke screamed in unison.

"Oh, my goodness, when did you get engaged?" Brooke shouted, grabbing her hand to inspect the ring.

"Last week when we were in Peru."

"I can't believe you didn't tell us," Ivy chimed in. "Let me see."

"I wanted to wait until I could show you in person. It was so hard not saying anything."

"It's beautiful!"

"Do your parents know?"

"Of course! I thought they would think it's too soon, but they love Barrett. You know my mother is already trying to plan the wedding."

"In their eyes, it's been a long time coming. And you know when you've found *the one*."

"Brooke, I am so happy that you introduced me to Barrett. I cannot think of the words to say to thank you enough."

"Dylan, your happiness is thank-you enough. You're proof that the program works and was a success."

"No, *we're* proof. We took control of our love lives and it worked. *Our* trust and love for one another is the real reason for its success. *That*, my sisters, is the true success of the Referral Program."

Dylan, Brooke, and Ivy raised their glasses in a toast. "To love."

Brooke grabbed Dylan's hand and beamed at her ring. Ivy took out her phone, capturing snapshots of the moment.

Dylan looked at her friends and thought *this is true love*.

ACKNOWLEDGMENTS

*L*ove. Needing love. Searching for love. Rejecting love. Not giving up on love. Finding love. Embracing love. Losing love. Being open to love . . . again and again.

Love. It's not perfect. Through its imperfections, it inspires the stories that I tell. It allows me to see the possibilities of what love could or should be for the characters in my books. Thank you for spending a bit of time with Dylan, Ivy, and Brooke. I hope you saw a bit of yourself in them and enjoyed their journey to love.

My family and friends—the loves of my life—I thank you. As seasons change, there's one constant. Our love endures. I'm truly thankful for each of you.

Sara Camilli, I've said it many times before, thank you for helping me keep sight of the finish line. I appreciate you!

Melanie Iglesias, thank you for your perspective and insight! Thanks to the Atria team who helped make the production process a seamless one.

Thanks to everyone for your support. I have more stories to tell and I look forward to you joining me for the next one!

ABOUT THE AUTHOR

Shamara Ray is a graduate of Syracuse University. She is the author of *Recipe for Love*, *Close Quarters*, *You Might Just Get Burned*, *Rituals for Love*, and *Cater to You*. Ray has a penchant for the culinary arts and enjoys entertaining friends and family in her North Carolina home. Learn more at her website, ShamaraRay.com.